IN THE END

An Ivy Nash Thriller

Book 6

By
John W. Mefford

IN THE END
Copyright © 2017 by John W. Mefford
All rights reserved.

Second Edition

Sugar Hill Publishing

ISBN: 978-1-943774-27-2

Interior book design by
Bob Houston eBook Formatting

To stay updated on John's latest releases, visit:
JohnWMefford.com/readers-group

One

To watch a person crumble before your eyes is a little like witnessing the demolition of an outdated stadium. You feel like you can stop it—you hope like hell you can stop it—if only you can somehow remove all the detonators before any irreversible damage occurs. But very quickly, as the first pillar buckles, you realize it's too late. And the exercise of stopping the destruction suddenly becomes pointless.

As a helpless bystander, you feel a hammering thud to your body with each detonation, all the while knowing that the building—a metaphor for the woman sitting on the other side of my desk—is enduring one targeted blast after another.

The cumulative effect, as I watched this grief-stricken mother, was as though an atomic bomb had released a mushroom cloud, massive and far-reaching in its destruction.

She closed her eyes for a long moment, and I wondered if a tortuous memory had just registered, leading to another invisible internal explosion. Like a neutron bomb. The kind that "kills people and spares buildings."

I never understood that premise on so many levels. But that's not my battle. I'm a private investigator by trade; someone who has a yearning—actually, a calling—to help kids, those who have little or no voice in society. Well, if you include social media, kids, unlike yesteryear, have countless opportunities to express themselves in all sorts of ways, to people they know and don't know. But rarely do adults listen, to hear the cries for help before damage occurs. And damage, as it were, can be manifested in ways most people can't imagine; nor do they want to imagine.

Through my years as a special investigator at Child Protective Services in San Antonio and even now as the owner of my little PI firm called ECHO, I have found a few adults who do care. Typically, these are the stalwarts who feel every little prick of pain their kids feel. They are the kind of parents who try with all their might to connect with their kids, even during those intense, troubling teenage years, a time when many would rather just give up and walk away. They are the heroes of society because they never give up—on hope or their kids. Consuela Romero was one of those parents.

She clutched about a dozen tissues against her nose, her arm quivering from applying pressure against her face, so full of red blotches. For about the twentieth time since she and her husband had entered my office, I wanted to reach out and take her in my arms, to let her know that everything would be okay.

But I knew it wouldn't be okay. It hadn't been in her past. And it wasn't now either. After all she'd endured, she was well beyond any type of consoling.

This unplanned meeting early on a chilly November morning with Consuela and Raul Romero had begun with Consuela conveying her concern over the disappearance of her daughter, Mia. Consuela showed me a picture of her daughter, and her smile could light up a room. Mia was an affable, cute seventeen-year-old, who was an honor student and the captain of her high school basketball team.

But less than five minutes into what had already been a mostly one-sided conversation, she happened to mention the name "Daniel," her son and eldest child. A tangent was born, and for good reason. I soon learned how Daniel had died just one year earlier, almost to the day. That was when Raul began to break down and excused himself to the restroom. He hadn't returned in the last twenty minutes.

"Daniel was always a bit of a rebel," she said through gasping sniffles.

I nodded and maintained eye contact. I would withhold my comments for now. I heard a raspy cough from the back room, letting me know that Raul was still upset. I wondered if he'd soon join us.

"He wasn't a bad kid. More curious than anything." Consuela, for the moment, had stopped crying, but the stress lines on her face had hardened into deep trenches. "But, dear Lord, he tried to push our buttons. He questioned us on every topic, from taking out the trash to politics to the price of a school lunch. At times he crossed the line, was argumentative. Raul…" She paused, glancing to the back. "Raul would get really upset when Daniel was disrespectful to us. It only made me sad, though. You know why?" She looked at me as if I were her psychologist. I wasn't unfamiliar with the role.

"Why?"

"Because I knew that he'd passed that innocent age. I'd forever lost my little boy, and it was impossible to get him back." She dropped her hand into her lap, taking in a heavy breath. "What kept me going was the hope…no, the belief that one day he would continue the evolutionary process until he came out on the other side of being a teenager and became a responsible young man. Even if he would never again lie on my lap and allow me to rub his head as he read a book, I'd be able to feel a sense of pride in seeing his maturity. Know what I mean?"

I've never given birth, so I couldn't claim to have felt a maternal attachment to a child. But I'd felt connections with dozens and dozens of kids in my life work. So, in many respects, I could imagine the feeling Consuela was relaying. "I sure do."

"Unfortunately, his attitude only got worse from there." She swallowed hard.

While I knew generally where the conversation was going, a feeling of dread crawled up the back of my neck. I wanted to alter the course of our discussion back to Mia—today's tragedy—but I sensed the path to Mia was blocked by the story of Daniel. I nodded to Consuela, hoping she could see my compassion for all of her heartache, while signaling to her it was okay to continue.

"Like most teenage boys, he lost his innocence in a major way. But that lost innocence…it grabbed him by the throat and dragged him into a dark place. I think he felt like he couldn't cope, even with Raul and me trying our best to talk to him, to surround him with a loving family and caring friends. It never seemed to work. I even took a second job to pay for a psychologist, but he never connected with her. He was too stubborn, too much of a manipulator to open up and just be a real person, to share his fears and his fallacies. And then—" She choked on a sob, unable to continue.

Raul walked back into the room, and he finished the statement in a low, shaky voice. "And then, after experimenting with heroin, he hanged himself in the school locker room."

Consuela burst into tears. Raul, thankfully, picked her up from the chair, and they embraced. I swallowed back some emotion, but I knew the difficult part was still ahead of us.

Two

Consuela and Raul Romero didn't let go of each other until the front door to ECHO opened. Metal scraped concrete, and I flinched. I shouldn't have, because I'd heard the cringe-worthy sound a thousand times since we moved into the office space a few months earlier.

"Did I miss the funeral?"

The Romeros slowly peeled apart, each wiping tears off their faces. I just stared at my lone ECHO employee, Cristina. Young and a bit brash, she had a habit of saying whatever was on her mind, sometimes before thinking. Like now.

My jaw clenched. "Oh," she said, sliding her backpack off her shoulder and shuffling toward me. "I was just joking." She looked at me as she parked her backpack next to the desk, her brown eyes wide. She knew she'd crossed the line.

I apologized for her insensitivity, then made brief introductions. She was just seventeen, but Cristina recognized the error of her ways and quickly tried to recover. She looked each of the parents in the eye, apologized again, and shook their hands.

I was about to sit in my chair, when I noticed Consuela not releasing Cristina's hand. She was just staring at Cristina.

"I'm sure you understand what Cristina said was just a flippant teenager thing," I said, hoping to lighten the mood.

Cristina tried to pull her hand away, but Consuela's grip was firm. Cristina glanced at me as Raul touched his wife's shoulder.

"I'm fine. I'm not having a nervous breakdown or anything," Consuela said. "It's just that Cristina's eyes remind me of Mia's." She let go and took a step back, inspecting Cristina from head to toe. "Mia doesn't dress like that, though."

I chuckled inwardly, since Cristina's preferred fashion destination was the Goodwill store, even though I paid her a fair wage. Enough for clothes and shelter anyway.

"And Mia's hair is always styled," Consuela continued, "but they could be cousins."

Cristina rocked side to side, sticking her hands in the pockets of her tight jeans. I could tell she was feeling awkward. So was I, for both Cristina and Consuela. It just hit me that Cristina's school day was about to start. After dropping out for almost a year, she was now just a few months away from graduating. It was a miracle that I'd been able to convince her how much a high school diploma mattered to her future. Not that I was looking for credit. I just didn't want anything, including ECHO business, to serve as an excuse for her not making it to school. Even something as important as a missing teenager.

I was about to whisper in Cristina's ear when Raul glanced at me and tried to smile. He never quite got there. Then he helped his wife take a seat. The Romeros stared at me, as if they were waiting for me to veer the Q&A session back to its original intent. I'd have to quiz Cristina later about why she wasn't on her way to school.

"At the beginning of your visit, you said Mia had disappeared. Can you tell me more?" I clasped my hands on my desk.

Raul said, "Not a lot to tell you. She went to school, but never made it to basketball practice apparently. Never came home last night."

"Last night." I don't know why, but I'd expected this was some type of cold case, where their daughter had been missing for weeks, if not months, and that the police had not been able to find any clues as to where she might be or what might have happened. Those were the types of cases we were used to seeing. Parents who were downtrodden, at their wit's end. We were the last resort, not the first.

"Have you not been to the cops?" I leaned forward, my palms flat on my desk.

Raul and Consuela looked at each other, then returned their gazes to me. I saw something in their eyes, and it didn't sit right with me.

"It's not a trick question," Cristina murmured.

"Cristina. Inappropriate," I said, shaking my head at the comment, although I was thinking much the same.

Raul held up his hands. "That's okay. No offense taken."

"I can see why you asked that question, Ivy," Consuela said. "Anyone would." She put a hand to her chest. "We live a quiet life. We try to make very little waves."

I tilted my head. I had an idea where she might be going with all this, but I wasn't going to suggest it.

She glanced at her husband again, then back to me and Cristina. "I clean houses for a living. Raul is a janitor in an office building. We don't make much money; it's just enough to get by. But we are still appreciative to live in a land that gives us opportunity, especially for our children."

I wondered if she had more kids than just Daniel and Mia, but that could wait. "If you're asking if I'll cut you a price break, the answer is yes. But I really think you should go to the cops. If they can't help you, or they don't have much luck, then feel free to—"

"You don't get it. We can't go to the police."

"Why not?" Cristina said. "It's not like they'll charge you a fee."

Consuela pressed her lips shut, then Raul said, "We came here together, almost eighteen years ago. We are from Guatemala. Consuela was pregnant with Daniel. We couldn't keep living there. Too much poverty. Too much violence in our small town. The kids in our town rarely got their education, and if they did, then most ended up in crappy jobs. We wanted a better life. For us. For our family."

"You're afraid to go to the cops," I said, finally understanding their apprehension.

"You think they're going to send you back after all these years, with kids who were born here and everything?" Cristina's voice jumped a half-octave.

Raul shrugged, releasing a deep breath. "We can't take any chances. Not with Mia missing. No matter where we live, or are forced to live, we have to be together. We have to find Mia." He gasped, but brought a hand to his face to stifle it, at least for now. "Will you help us?" He took his wife's hand and squeezed it.

I'd been asked to take part in countless missing children cases, and almost every time the parents' grief made my heart ache. But the Romeros took that to another level.

"Consuela, Raul…I want to help you. I want Mia to be found, alive and well. But I just don't want to overpromise my capability. It's just me and Cristina, and she works part-time around her school work."

Out of the corner of my eye, I could see Cristina arch an eyebrow. She always liked to think of herself as being ten years older than she was.

"We will pay you, just like any client." Raul pulled a wad of cash out of his pocket. "Our money is just as legitimate as anyone else's."

"I understand. That's fine."

Consuela inched up in her chair. "Then what is it?"

"I'm not sure I understand your question."

She touched her arm. "Is it the color of our skin?"

Cristina raised her hand. "Uh, I'm half-Hispanic. So, I'm not sure what you're implying."

"We are..." She formed quotes with her fingers. "Illegal immigrants, okay? There, I said it. To some, we are not at the same level as other American-born citizens. We are wetbacks. Spics."

Now Raul moved to the edge of his chair, his nostrils flaring. "Greaser, berry picker, chile shitter..."

"I get it." I had to cut him off. I could see their pain, hear it in their tone of voice. It was made all the worse by hearing the inflammatory words that so many others had used on them. I had a flashback to my childhood, when I was called every derogatory name in the book because I was a foster kid, made fun of for the way I looked, for always being the new kid at school, and for being a loner. The horrors I experienced at many of my seventeen foster homes was something no kid should experience. But as I'd grown older, I knew I wasn't the only person who'd been made to feel subhuman.

The Romeros had entered the country illegally eighteen years ago. I'd heard people, politicians mainly, argue whether families like the Romeros should be sent back to their original country or allowed to stay. To a degree, both ends of that argument could be convincing. But there was only one thing that I'd never waver on—the Romeros were every bit as human as me, or the man in my life, Saul, or my cop friend, Stan, or my best friend, Zahera, or anyone else. And they deserved to be treated with respect. But I also knew there were always a few people who were paranoid about having families like the Romeros in our country, as if they were substandard, as if all of them were criminals sent here to destroy the fabric of our nation. Those people were nuts. And then there were some who were simply filled with hate. Those were the ones that I couldn't deal with on any level.

"Ivy." Consuela put her hand on my desk, her voice surprisingly calm. "We know your reputation, the lengths you have taken to find missing kids. Our Mia is just as special to us as those kids were to their families. If I could give you my left arm, I would. Anything for you to help us. We don't know where else to turn."

"I'm so sorry, I—"

"You still refuse us?" Raul began rattling off a line of Spanish to his wife that I'm sure wasn't flattering toward me.

"No, no, please don't get upset. I never meant for you to feel like you had to beg me. I will take the case."

"*We* will take the case," Cristina said, nudging my arm.

Consuela dipped her head as her husband rubbed her back. "Thank you," he said in a raspy whisper.

I looked over at Cristina, who was smiling. "Get us some waters, and then you can tell me why you're not at school."

Three

Cristina retrieved bottled waters for all of us. During our brief break, she told me that today was a teacher in-service day. No school for the students. I asked if she was still passing all of her classes. She reached a hand in my direction. "Do you need me to put my hand on a Bible?"

"This isn't a court of law, sassy ass."

"I don't know, sometimes it feels like you're judge and jury."

A wave of heat crept up my neck. "Seriously? You're going to say that?"

"Okay. Maybe I overdid it a little."

"A little?

"A lot. Sorry. You know me," she said with a cheesy grin.

Boy, did I.

Raul, who'd been on his phone the last five minutes in an animated conversation in Spanish, finally pocketed his phone. He had a dejected look on his face. "What did they say?" Consuela asked, a hand on his arm.

He shook his head. "They haven't seen her."

I cleared my throat. "Who are they?"

"I spoke to the father of her good friend, Elsa. He quizzed his daughter numerous times, and she has no clue where Mia might have gone. She last saw her in fifth-period chemistry class."

"Do we know if she was in sixth or seventh period?" Cristina asked.

"Seventh period is athletics, basketball for her. We got word from two of her teammates that she wasn't there. Not sure about sixth period."

"Which is?"

"AP history."

"You haven't called the school?" Cristina asked.

"It all just happened last night. And school is opening in the next few minutes, right?"

Cristina checked her phone. "Five minutes from now."

"So when we get to the bottom of the hour, you can call and ask if her sixth-period teacher marked her absent. But for the next couple of minutes, I need to ask you a few questions."

"Fire away," Raul said.

"Is Mia dating anyone right now?"

"Not right now. She did have a boyfriend, but they broke up in August, right after the school year started."

"Name?" I picked up a pen and put it to a sticky note.

"Brandon McCarthy. He's a good kid, though," Raul said.

"Why would you say that?"

"Honor student, just like Mia. Goes to church. A good Catholic boy," he said with a hint of a smile.

"You were fond of him?" I asked Raul, then I glanced at Consuela. She offered a single nod.

"He treated Mia with respect," Raul said. "He is a responsible young man, works at a garden center. Always positive. And he's not into drugs."

"How would you know that?" Cristina asked. She was blunt, but that was my next question.

"Well, I, uh…" Raul looked at his wife, then to Cristina.

"I don't mean to be rude, but I've known plenty of kids who gave the appearance they were perfect little citizens, but they were on coke, selling coke, or just involved with some shady characters."

Raul shook his head. "We know why you're asking. But you don't know Brandon like we do, like Mia does. She had nothing but good things to say about him."

"Do you know why they broke up? And who did the breaking up?" I asked.

"It was Mia, but it's not like he was overly possessive or anything crazy. She was…" Raul closed his eyes momentarily. "She *is* serious about her schoolwork and all of the extracurricular activities. She just didn't have time for Brandon. And if you ask me, she's not going to let some innocent high school crush disrupt her plans. She always has a plan, always looking ahead. Very confident and mature for her age."

"Which makes this disappearance even stranger," I said, wondering if I'd get an agreement.

"Without question," Raul said.

Consuela nodded. For a quick second, I thought I saw a flicker of hesitation. But about what? Raul's assertion that Mia's disappearance was is in no way connected to Brandon? Or was it something less sinister? Maybe she hadn't bonded with Brandon like Raul had.

"It's time to call the school," Cristina said.

I held off my second round of questions, hoping there would be nothing to investigate.

Four

His breathing was deep but even, a steady snuffling of air through his nose. He rolled his eyes toward the back of his head, found his place of tranquility, then recited the words that he'd spoken more than a thousand times.

"…forevermore," he stated, ending the first paragraph.

The chant had, at one time, filled his heart with a calming, peaceful love. Over time, though, he'd grown weary of the ritualistic mantra. And not for the typical reasons. Most who had listened to the words usually ignored their true intent, because that was just how people were—easily distracted, mentally lazy. They went through the motions because everyone else did. It was as though they were living life on an assembly line. His aversion to the chant was at a more fundamental level. He simply believed he'd evolved and, thus, unlike the sheep, sought a deeper meaning to his life and everything that was part of it.

So how did he cope? He looked beyond the surface-level explanations provided over the last two centuries. And what he'd found altered the significance of his existence. Through intense study and scrutiny, he found context and substance where he'd previously thought there was none.

It had all been about the interpretation, not just of this chant, but in every symbolic gesture created by mankind.

On he went, speaking of sacrament, and flesh, and blood, and body. Sure, there were other words, but those were the ones that now gripped his heart so tightly he had difficulty breathing. *Inhale, exhale.*

He finished the chant uttering the same last words, "…forevermore."

A feeling of accomplishment washed over his body. Self-control had been an absolute requirement to complete this activity—it was something he'd worked on a great deal in every phase of his life. At one point, he'd lost his way. The constant pressures from those who controlled his every movement had felt like a tumor growing inside, to the point of choking off his ability to take in oxygen. They had refused to listen to his concerns about society, about how they could combat the issue. In his mind, they had ignored the opportunity to evolve.

Evolution. Shouldn't that be of utmost importance to every living being? Flames from two candles flickered off the dusty stone walls, illuminating chisel marks that likely predated anyone currently living on earth.

Was there irony in that observation? Later, perhaps, he'd contemplate why he'd ended up in this room, on the grounds of this building. It had seemed like the obvious choice. But there had to be a deeper meaning. All actions in the world were, after all, connected—whether people wanted to believe it or not—a symbiotic relationship that linked all mankind to each other. Altering the course of mankind, though, was what took courage and tremendous foresight, something he would try to achieve without the support of the vultures.

Try? No, that wasn't the appropriate word, because it wasn't how his mind processed information any longer. Not when it dealt with issues of this significance. He would achieve his goal. He had to achieve his goal. Too much was riding on it to accept any other possible outcome.

Lowering his eyes, slim shadows danced across the two objects before him. They were still. They hadn't moved in the last two hours, in fact. Before then, it was another story. While their struggles had been noteworthy—he'd nearly separated his shoulder when he'd slipped on a pool of sweaty blood while trying to subdue one who'd had thoughts of escape—it was completely expected. What creature on this planet was ever prepared to die? And he felt almost certain that they both had known how they would die.

The two had been about the same size, but now the corpses matched even more, nearly identical. Their mouths were agape, their eyes partially open. Blood splattered various parts of their bodies.

He had ensured that they were given a fair chance to live—by divine or some other type of intervention. Once they were secured and could not escape, he had inserted the blade no less than four inches deep in six separate places, ending with the center of the chest. Fate could have intervened. His blade could have somehow missed the prominent arteries or organs. He'd read countless medical articles that chronicled stories of people with near-death experiences. Were they just lucky? Perhaps. He personally believed it wasn't their time to move on to the next plane, and so they lived. Unlike these two in front of him.

A damp chill caused his body to quake. Perhaps it was not the chill, but instead another burst of adrenaline. He inhaled and took in the mixture of smells around him. The heavy scent of copper hovered over a sour smell—most likely a result of leaky pipes. Wafts of vanilla floated by his face from the burning candles. The melted wax had hardened down the sides of the candlestick holders. The flames were nearly suffocated.

This had been a fruitful event, one he would not soon forget. But it was time to pack up his kit and move along.

He saw his clothes neatly folded off to the side—remaining stain-free had been another requirement he'd given himself. But what he hadn't expected was this primal feeling of freedom. To be with his subjects in this manner had taken this encounter to a level he couldn't have predicted.

And for that, he was very thankful.

He lifted to his feet, cleaned the knife, and returned it to its sheath. It was then that the man ran his fingers across the carved skin on his chest. The symbol and what it represented had, in his mind, like so many things in his life, gone through a metamorphosis. Whereas before it signified so many utterances of kindness and devotion and turning the other cheek, it now embodied one simple thing: hope.

Hope that the world would not implode. Hope that he would be the one who created a new understanding of how mankind could thrive.

Five

In the conference room, the Romeros were still on the phone with school officials. I considered this a positive development. My concern was that they were so fearful of stepping forward to reveal much of anything to any authoritative figure who worked for any level of government, we'd lose the opportunity to gain valuable information. But I had hope that teachers and school administrators cared far more about the safety of their students than anything else.

"They seem really stressed," Cristina said into my ear as we watched them from the front office. Raul raked his fingers through his hair for about the umpteenth time in the last hour. At times, Consuela was right at his side, an arm wrapped around his waist; at other times, she was pacing, less engaged. We all had ways to deal with stress and anxiety. I'd seen so many couples tear each other apart during times of stress; in contrast, the Romeros seemed to be holding up rather well, all things considered.

"At least they're not ripping into each other. I can see a bond there. They'll need that if they hope to get through this." Just then, Consuela looked over her shoulder and caught my eye. It seemed like she wanted to say something. I held her gaze for an extra moment, but the sounds of Raul's voice moved her attention back in his direction. He was now by our large window, which overlooked a fountain and a patch of grass.

"Think they're making any progress?" I asked as much to myself as to Cristina.

"Who knows?" Out of the corner of my eye, I could see the blur of her thumbs moving across her cell phone screen.

"Catching up on the teenage gossip of the morning?"

She actually pulled her eyes away from the screen. "Dude, I'm trying to get started on this investigation."

"Okay. By doing what?"

"Well, Consuela told us earlier that Mia goes to Lee High School. I go to Jefferson. They're rival schools."

"You're not saying that someone from your high school might have kidnapped Mia because of some silly high school rivalry, are you?"

She tilted her head and gave me a look.

"Okay, fine. What's your plan?"

"I don't really have one yet. I'm just reaching out to some of my peeps, asking if they know Mia, or even if they might have heard about any shit going down."

"Shit?"

"It's a general term for anything bad. Teenagers sometimes don't like to use formal words like *kidnapping*; and by using *shit*, it's kind of an open term, you know, in case she might have taken off on her own. Or even with someone else."

I don't think she knew I was joking about not getting her use of the term, but having Cristina on my ECHO team had been invaluable. She had a real hunger to pursue the truth, to expose those who were evil. That was what we had in common. And as much as I tried, I couldn't think like a teenager, not one in the modern era.

"Keep working your text toy, and let me know if you hear any noise about Mia.'

"Noise?"

She knew what I meant. I ignored her question since I just saw Raul end his call. I walked toward him and Consuela. "What did you learn?"

"They can't find anyone who's seen her." He put a hand to his chest and tried to clear his throat. I looked at Consuela.

"Raul, are you having another episode?" she asked.

"I'm fine. Don't worry about it."

She looked back at me. "He's got a heart condition. Stress is the worst thing for it."

"Do we need to call nine-one-one?"

"I said I'm fine, dammit." He pushed out two strained breaths, then dropped into one of our leather chairs that surrounded the large meeting table. "I'm sorry. I know you're only trying to be helpful. I just don't like to be treated like a child."

Consuela put a hand on his back. She rolled her eyes so that only I could see, which made me smile. They took care of each other.

"Can we get him some more water?" she asked.

Cristina volunteered to do that and soon returned with four more bottles, one for each of us, even though I'd barely touched my first.

"Thank you, Cristina." Consuela cracked the top and handed the bottle to Raul, who took a drink.

"I love being the water girl," Cristina whispered to me.

"At least you're not sitting in geometry class."

Raul seemed to get his breath. I took a swig of water myself before firing off some additional questions. "The sixth-period teacher, did he mark her as absent?"

"Mr. Tucker? He was out yesterday. But the sub, yes, she marked Mia absent."

Cristina and I traded a quick glance, then she went back to her phone. She was a master multitasker.

"Did they talk to other kids or teachers who might have seen her leave or maybe heard her talking about leaving school?"

"That's why I was on hold so long. They pulled ten, fifteen kids from class and talked to them. So far, no one knows anything."

Or no one is saying anything, I thought to myself. "Mia is rather popular, is she not?"

"That's not something she really tried to achieve. She wasn't into all the teenage games where kids are essentially in a *class* system," Consuela said.

"I'm just saying a lot of kids know her, right? She's a strong student, she plays basketball—"

"She's a member of the National Honor Society," Raul said with a hint of pride.

"My point is, she's not one of those kids who sits in the back and no one ever speaks to her. Why wouldn't someone know where she is?"

They both shrugged their shoulders.

"I need you to list every person Mia knows. First name and last name is preferable, but if you just have one or the other, then we'll go with that."

"I'll do it right now," Consuela said. Cristina got her a pen and paper.

"Okay," I said, noticing Consuela had already written a couple of names, "what about video tapes? Don't they have cameras on all the main exits of the school?"

"They treat us like prisoners, so I know they have it. I've seen the cameras myself."

We all looked at Cristina. Did she have to use the word *prisoners*? I shook my head and turned back to Raul.

"I asked about cameras. They said they had them, but it would take a while to review."

"But that shouldn't take long, right? I mean, we have an idea of when she left. She was in fifth period, but not sixth." I flipped over to Cristina. "What time frame are we looking at?"

"Uh…" She looked off, then back to her phone. I guess that held all the secrets. "Fifth period ends at one forty-five."

"Do you think I need to call back and give them this information?" Raul asked.

The school officials should know this. Were they dragging their feet? Had they not taken Raul seriously? I really had no way of knowing, since I hadn't been on the call. Now I was pissed at myself for not listening in. I'd just assumed that the school officials would understand the gravity of the situation. Maybe, without cops showing up at the school, they thought it might be another case of a parent/student argument, and the kid rebelling by walking out of school.

My mind went back to getting help from the police. I thought about Stan Radowski, a detective with the SAPD, and a dear friend. He'd overcome a great deal in the last few months, losing his arm to a psycho while trying to save me, then his son being kidnapped. We'd found Ethan unharmed, and the Radowski family was intact.

"I know you guys are very leery about having the police involved, but with your okay, I'd like to reach out to a detective friend of mine. We go back a ways—"

"You used to be married?" Raul asked.

Cristina snorted out a guffaw. I shifted my eyes to her for a quick second, then said to Raul, "Stan and his wife, Bev, are both good friends. And they have a son, Ethan. I believe Stan is someone we can confide in without him turning this into an official investigation."

"If you trust him, then I guess it's okay," Consuela said.

Raul closed his eyes for a moment, then nodded. "If you must, then so be it."

"Just to warn you a bit, he's likely going to push me to have you guys file a missing persons report. If not now, then by tomorrow...if she's not found before then."

Consuela bit down on her fist as new tears welled in her eyes. Raul reached over and touched her arm.

I gave them a moment and took another sip of water. "Consuela, Raul, time is very important right now. So, just another question or two."

"Anything," Consuela said.

"Have you been getting along with Mia recently?"

"Of course," Raul said. "Hard to remember a time when we had a cross word for Mia. I mean, she's a normal teen and has her moods, but she respects us. She knows that we love her."

I looked to Consuela for some type of validation of what Raul had said. She blinked a few times. I had to ask her straight out. "Would you agree?"

She spoke calmly. "I would agree with what Raul said."

I closed the doors to the meeting room and let them get to work on the friends list. My mind was swirling with possible theories. And one had me thinking the worst: that Mia might already be dead and there was some type of cover-up going on.

Six

I left Cristina with the Romeros at the office and started walking down the sidewalk. A chilly, swirling wind bit into my face. I buried my hands in my jeans pockets and hurried along, already regretting that I hadn't worn a jacket over my untucked button-down. I watched a few other pedestrians across the street scurrying between office buildings. No one in San Antonio was used to wind-chill temperatures in the forties. Not in early November.

I used to think that coats were for wimps. Having lived my entire life in South Central Texas, that was easy for me to say. Even as I felt a shiver up my spine, I still believed it—sort of. I would be loving a coat right now. How long would I be outside? Hopefully, no more than five minutes if I hurried. I was on my way to the local community center. I'd texted Stan, hoping to get some time with him to discuss Mia's disappearance. It turned out he had taken the morning off and was just four blocks away with his son and wife at the Mandy Amaya Community Center. A personal conversation would make all the difference in the world with Stan.

The ECHO office was on the south side of San Antonio's downtown, in an area that had long been neglected…well, until recently. The community center had really brightened up the area. On the block where our ECHO office was, three other businesses had recently rented space. I approached the end of the block and glanced inside the window of the business at the corner. No sign was up, but I saw two contractors rolling out carpet and the owner of said business with his sleeves rolled up, looking at a blueprint. I poked my head in and whistled at Saul, the kind of whistle that said, *What's up, sexy?*

A smile cracked his lips as he walked over and pulled me inside what would soon be the office of Saul Modesto, Attorney at Law.

"Still opposed to wearing a coat?" He dropped the blueprints and wrapped his fingers around both of my arms, then leaned in and hugged me.

"Then what would I use you for?"

"Oh, I can think of a few things."

"Shh, the guys over there will hear you."

He looked at me. "Did you know the blue in your shirt matches your eyes?"

"You know me. It's all about color coordination." I blinked my eyes a few times—Miss Prim and Proper—and he laughed.

Saul, who had been working as a legal aid at one of the city's most prestigious law firms when I first met him, was what most would call a serious boyfriend. Fortunately, he wasn't into labels. We just went with "significant other," if ever asked.

He grabbed me by the hips and drew me closer. He was about to lay one on me when I noticed one of the contractors looking in our direction. I pulled back to a respectable distance. "I just realized you're wearing a suit."

He twisted his lips.

"I thought you quit your job at Wilson, Mendoza, and Ross two weeks ago?"

He shook his head, not saying a word.

"Did you put in your notice a week ago?"

A slower shake of the head.

I didn't want to point out that he'd lied to me, but…he'd lied to me.

"You're thinking I lied to you, aren't you?"

"I wasn't going to say it exactly like that. It isn't like you were under oath." One of my eyebrows inched upward.

"I'm sorry. I just chickened out. Ross is going to be pissed. He's going to be even more pissed when he finds out I'm opening a firm of my own."

"Babe, what are you so afraid of?"

"Oh, that he'll pick up the phone and order a hit on me."

"Funny," I said, patting his chest.

"I know, it's ridiculous. Every time I'm about to walk into his office, I start visualizing his response. I see it playing out in two ways: he either throws a stapler at me and cusses me out, or he laughs at me."

"Hope for the first. Then you can sue him. He could be your first big legal victory." I made my voice sound like I was the host of a kids' TV program.

His response was less than enthusiastic.

"I didn't mean to demean what you do. I'm just trying to show that it shouldn't be that big of a deal. People quit their jobs all the time."

He nodded, then glanced over his shoulder at the guys putting down the carpet. "You're right. I just need to man up and do it. Gotta say, though, I'm a bit nervous."

"I get it. Sounds like me when I started ECHO. I had no idea what I was doing or, really, how to even run a business."

"I just don't want to let down my parents. They've supported me a lot, loaned me the money to start the firm. Momma thinks I'm on my way to being the next state attorney general."

His mother. Wow, she was a piece of work. Lots of history there. But we'd learned to coexist, even if I wasn't the girl she had in mind to be her son's significant other. So I understood the pressure he felt to succeed, even if it was unspoken.

"They loaned you some money; that doesn't mean they own you or your first born." I didn't think before I spoke. Having children was a topic we never really talked about. Why? I wasn't exactly sure. I loved kids and hoped to have a couple of my own someday. Saul had a big family with plenty of nephews and nieces running around. So I had no reason to believe he didn't want kids. The more I thought about it, the issue regarding kids had less to do with us individually and more to do with us together. To discuss kids would mean we were close to putting a label on our relationship. And to me, that was pressure.

"Hey, I need to get over to the community center. Just picked up a new case on a missing teen, and I need to talk to Stan."

"Didn't you have a case like this about a month ago? If I remember it correctly, the parents and the kid got in a big fight, the kid took off, and they finally found him in Los Angeles. Said he wanted to be an actor."

I'd forgotten about it, probably because we'd been so busy lately, and it had taken all of about two hours of my time before we found out what had gone down. The kid's best friend stepped forward and shared everything, including where to find his friend in LA. I could only hope for a similar outcome with Mia—friend steps forward, Mia is found safe and sound. I gave Saul the twenty-second recap, then put a hand on the door. "Gotta run."

"Oh, crap, I knew I needed to tell you something."

He hurried over to a chair and picked up his phone then rushed back over. "That PI we hired to try to find your birth parents contacted me."

My stomach instantly did a flip-flop. "What did she find out?"

"Well, for starters, she says she tried to reach you, but you didn't respond."

"Sorry if I missed it. Been busy. So...?"

He moved his thumb across the screen. "Says in her text that she's making good headway and has followed up on several leads."

I waited for more, then I realized I wasn't breathing. I inhaled and pushed out a breath. "And?"

"And the retainer you put down...she's burned through all of those hours."

"She needs more money before she'll tell me anything?"

One of the contractors looked in my direction. I'd spoken a little louder than I meant to.

"She didn't say that exactly. Just that she's making good progress and has more leads. I think this is good news, Ivy."

I'd given her three grand up front, which had cleaned out my savings account. We'd had a pretty good two-month run, but writing four-figure checks wasn't something I could do on a routine basis. "She has my credit card number. If she's getting close, then tell her to charge that."

Saul tapped his phone against his opposite hand and walked back over to me. "I could hold off on opening up my law office and then I could help you out."

"Hell no, mister. You're going to open this office within two weeks or you're cut off."

"Cut off?" He chuckled.

"Well, I'm not sure I could follow through on that threat," I said, leaning in for a quick smooch. "It's not a big deal. I'll figure something out. But nothing is going to stop you from leaving that firm and starting your own."

"I just want to be able to help. I know how much it means to you to find your parents, or at least find out what happened to them."

He was right, but I rarely went there. I'd end up in tears, and loads of self-doubt would come out of nowhere to consume me. Nope. I wasn't going to let that happen.

"If it's meant to be, it will happen."

He took me by my waist and breathed against my neck. Then he said, "One day soon, when we're alone, we'll have to break in my new office."

"Pop its cherry, so to speak?" I put a hand over my mouth to stifle a giggle.

"I could tell them to take an early lunch?"

I leaned back and arched an eyebrow. "Down, boy." I swung open the door. "Let me know today when you put in your notice, and then we'll talk."

A moment later, I was back out in the cold, wishing for a coat.

Seven

By the time I'd walked the remaining three blocks, my face was sufficiently numb—a weather anomaly in San Antonio if there ever was one. Once inside the community center, it was nice and toasty. And crowded. With kids out of school for the day, the place was brimming with action.

"Excuse me, Miss, may I help you?"

It was a girl, maybe college age, wearing the purple shirt that indicated she worked there. "Just looking for someone I know," I said, craning my neck to glance around. I suddenly felt her practically right up against me, and I pulled back. "I'm sorry?" That was my way of telling her she was invading my personal space.

"It's just that we have a strict policy that everyone needs to sign in and put on a wristband. It's our way of keeping it a safe space." She bobbled up and down. Everything about her seemed to be round—her head full of curls, her cheeks, even her face in general.

I didn't push back. I signed my name and held out my wrist while still searching for Stan.

"It's one of Dr. Amaya's most important policies. So, thank you for not making a big deal about it. Some people can be—"

"Real assholes?"

She giggled and shrugged her shoulders.

It had been a while since I'd visited the facility. I had a lot of horrific memories from this place, back while it was under construction with its previous owner, who also happened to be a psychotic killer. He'd gone to great lengths to lure me into his twisted funhouse. The experience nearly made me a mental vegetable. I almost died a half-dozen times. To make it even worse, that was when Stan had lost his arm and Cristina had been essentially skewered, almost losing her life to kidney failure.

Once we all had escaped with our lives and the killer had been sent off to prison, Dr. Amaya told me about his vision: to renovate the entire facility into more of a community center and to name it after his late daughter, Mandy. He'd actually asked me if I was okay with it, knowing the torture I'd been put through in the building. I figured it was a whole lot better to make something good out of the nightmare, although I knew I'd never forget what had happened to me.

I heard someone calling my name, and I turned to see Stan, or was it half of Stan? After ballooning to something north of three hundred pounds, he'd dedicated himself to changing his lifestyle, from his diet to working out. It had been a few weeks since I'd seen him.

"Did you lose another ten pounds?"

"Actually, since you saw me last, I've dropped thirteen pounds. But who's counting?" He had lost so much weight, even his voice sounded different.

I gave him a hug with a couple of slaps on the back. I could feel his prosthesis against my back. I made no mention of it because he didn't make a big deal of it. Sure, after his arm was severed by that lunatic, he went through his five stages of grief. But once he got past it and concentrated on his training, he was as focused as I'd ever seen him…and that included whenever he consumed a candy bar, which used to be about five or six times a day.

"And you're still on target for the Dallas Marathon in a month?"

"Yup. The goal is to qualify for Boston next April. So I'm working out like a crazy person. Just ask Bev. She's not thrilled when the alarm goes off at five a.m. and I get out of bed, have my bowl of fruit, then go on my morning jog. But she's happy with the results as much as I am. I finish up my day with a light jog in the evenings whenever I can."

"Going with two-a-days, huh? You're in beast mode."

"Gotta be if I hope to put in a good time next month. Finishing a marathon is one thing—something I never even dreamed about before you guys got my butt moving. But qualifying for Boston won't be easy."

"How many miles this morning?"

"Ten miles at a pace of nine minutes a mile."

"Not bad, old man."

"I'll do anything to beat Nick."

Nick was his cousin. They were born and raised in Brooklyn and shared many qualities, including their accents and the fact that they were both training to run in the Boston Marathon. They loved to razz each other, which I guessed gave them both incentive to outdo the other. Nick, though, had the head start. When I first met him back in the summer, he was already in good shape, a special agent with the FBI.

I saw Bev off in the distance working with their son, Ethan. He was autistic, but despite his issues with connecting with others, they were a close family. The center had a program that helped autistic kids and their parents connect on a different level by working together on creative projects.

"You mentioned a missing girl in your text," Stan said, waving his fake arm in front of my face until I turned my sights back to him. "How long has she been missing?"

I recited the basic facts of what I'd gathered from the Romeros, including the reason why they were reluctant to go to authorities.

"I don't care where they were born. You said she's been missing for less than twenty-four hours, though. Too soon to worry?"

"I realize she could have just gotten pissed and run off for a day, but so far nothing has turned up. Her parents called a few friends, and officials at her high school talked to a handful of fellow students. No one has any information. Mia would have had to walk out of school in the middle of the day. Someone must have seen it. Or at least someone must have known about it. She was too well-known."

"What do you think of the parents?"

"They're under a lot of stress, as you can imagine. I thought the dad was about to have a heart attack in my office."

Stan looked in the direction of Bev and Ethan, stroking his 1970s mustache, which meant he was thinking.

"So, I was wondering if you could do me a favor."

He turned my way, and I gave him a forced smile.

"This wouldn't be the first," he said.

"And let's be honest, it probably won't be the last. But you have to admit, I've tried to return a few to make it even."

"True. We are a pretty good team," he said. "Even though I'm forced to bend the rules on occasion. That's not what we're talking about here, right?" He raised an eyebrow.

"Not really. I just need you to put a little pressure on the school to review the school tapes as quickly as possible, that's all."

"If they don't want to do it, then it might take a warrant. But, frankly, if it takes a whole lot of pressure and I need to talk to the bigwigs at the school district office, then I'd look like an ass if we didn't have an open investigation. See my quandary here?"

He wanted the Romeros to file a missing persons report. "Stan, they're beyond nervous. If for some crazy reason they get deported and they don't have Mia with them, it will crush them. Actually, crush is probably putting it lightly. I'm not sure they'll want to live anymore. So, this is one of those life-or-death things on many levels, for Mia and her parents."

He released a grunt that sounded a little like the cry of a baby whale—I'd watched a documentary recently on how whales communicate.

"If you show up, flash your badge, remind them of the importance of maintaining a partnership with law enforcement, I'm sure they'll do anything you ask. If I do it, they'll tell me to take a number."

He checked his watch. Again, I was floored. He'd even lost "weight" in his wrist! It was like someone had pulled the plug on the balloon, and he'd returned to his normal size. I wondered now how he'd been able to hold up all that extra weight.

"I'm off until noon, but I suppose you need me to do this now."

"You're a mind reader, Stan, what can I—" Before I got out the last word, something slammed into my back, and I stumbled forward.

"Oh, sorry."

It was Cristina, standing there with her skateboard flipped over next to her.

"Don't you know how to control that thing?"

"I always forget about the slide factor on this industrial carpet."

Stan stepped away, pulled his phone out of his pocket, and took a call as the girl in the purple shirt from earlier hopped into our space. "Cristina, I must remind you that Dr. Amaya has said no one is allowed to ride their skateboards inside the facility. If you do this again, we might have to reconsider your all-access privileges."

Cristina did one of her infamous eye rolls, but said, "I get it. No worries."

My eyes shifted to Stan. By the look on his face, it didn't appear to be a friendly call.

The girl in the purple shirt bounced away, and I moved closer to Cristina. "What happened to the plan of you staying at the office with Raul and Consuela?"

"They bailed."

"What? Why?"

"They finished their list. It's about forty or fifty deep. Then they said they were meeting some cousins to start putting up flyers with Mia's picture on them."

"It's a good idea. A grassroots approach."

"Hoping they get lucky that someone saw something."

I felt a rock forming in my gut. "Dammit, it shouldn't take luck. She was in school and then she wasn't." I saw Stan still on his call, wiping a hand across his face. I addressed Cristina again. "I'm hoping that once Stan pays a visit to the school, and they review the tapes, we'll have a much clearer view of at least when she left, what exit she left from, and if anyone was with her."

"You think she just took off with a boy toy?"

"That would be a best-case scenario at this point," I said, knowing that type of behavior was in stark contrast to how Raul and Consuela described their daughter. But sometimes the heart wants what the heart wants, and parents may very well be the last to know, even in families who were tight-knit.

Stan stepped back toward us. "Lee High School. That's where Mia was last seen?"

"Yep. If you're ready to go, is it okay if I tag along?"

"I now have an official reason to be at the school." He blew out a breath, his beady eyes as wide as they could get.

The rock in my gut suddenly doubled in size. "What is it?"

"Two dead animals were found in the athletic building."

"Call animal control," Cristina said. "Why bug the real cops?"

"Because apparently it looks like the animals were killed in some sort of sacrificial ceremony."

"Say what?" Cristina asked before I could. "As in devil worshipping?"

"Who the hell knows at this point? Just a couple of uniforms on the scene right now. I'll know more once I get there. Kids with all of that social media stuff at their fingertips…well, this could blow up quickly, if it hasn't already."

Stan ran off to say his goodbyes to his family, as Cristina and I walked back to the front of the building, my mind still reeling about what had been found at the high school. Mia disappeared yesterday and now there was an animal sacrifice—all relating to Lee High school. More than likely the crime occurred overnight, which meant that the two events occurred fairly close together. But were they related?

A string of people began meandering out of a side room. I saw Dr. Amaya and a few other adults, but also a number of younger people, most under the age of twenty-one. The doctor nodded when he saw me and walked over. "So good to see you again, Ivy."

Every time I was around him now, he wore a smile. But that hadn't always been the case. Early on, when I first met him—well, it was actually more just being in his presence from across a room—his stare had creeped me out. While his eyes had this odd glare about them, rarely blinking, he really had a much warmer vibe than I'd first thought. I knew it had everything to do with opening the community center to honor his daughter, who had worked with special needs kids in Austin.

"The place is amazing, Doctor. Kids are happy. You've built something really special here."

"The MACC is the bomb," Cristina added.

"The MACC?"

"Do I need to spell it out for you?" she asked, the palm of her hand turned to the ceiling.

"Oh, you used the acronym. I get it. Must be a teen thing," I said, trying to conjure up a smile.

"Says the woman who started a company called ECHO."

Cristina just didn't know when to stop. Sometimes I thought she was regressing in terms of her sassiness. But since it wasn't directed at anyone else, especially a client, I let it go.

"You look bothered by something, Ivy. Everything all right?"

Dr. Amaya's observation had caught me off guard, my thoughts lost in a sea of endless theories. "Who me? Pfft. It's nothing." I shouldn't have been surprised. He was a former psychologist, so he was quite used to reading people.

"You sure I can't help?"

"Honestly, it's a new case we're working. I'm just anxious." I flipped around and saw Stan heading in our direction.

Cristina added, "You wouldn't believe this shit they found—"

I reached out and grabbed her arm. "It's nothing he needs to worry about, right?"

She winced. "Yeah, I suppose."

I turned up my glare at Cristina.

"It's nothing, Doctor, really," she said.

I took a breath. The doctor must have sensed my unease, and he switched topics as Stan approached.

"Leo doing okay?" he asked Cristina.

I interjected, looking at her. "You saw him recently?"

Her eyes bugged out, which seemed to indicate she thought I was being too motherly. Maybe I was, but Leo was a twenty-one-year-old Hollywood actor. How they'd met was a long story. He seemed like a decent guy, but Cristina was still in high school. I'd told her repeatedly not to fall for this guy. He could have—probably did have—a dozen other girls pawing over him back in la-la land.

"He came into town a couple of weeks back. A real quickie."

Stan put his hand on my back as I processed what she'd just said. "A quickie?"

"I didn't mean it like that." Her face turned flush.

Stan said, "Pressler and the crime scene guys are already there. You ready?"

"More than you know."

Eight

Looping to the back of the school in Stan's navy-blue unmarked police car, I spotted pole after pole with flyers affixed to them showing a picture of Mia and a phone number to call if anyone had information.

Raul and Consuela had assembled their band of helpers and started distributing flyers with lightning-quick speed. I was reminded, again, that taking a child away from a parent, at least for most parents, was akin to removing an appendage. They would do anything to bring her back.

The parking lot nearest the athletic field house was only half full. Thankfully, kids weren't around because of the in-service holiday. But I still spotted plenty of women and a sprinkling of men behind the outline of yellow tape. Stan and I got out, walked through the crowd and under the tape. I'd been to so many crime scenes at this point that no one asked anymore about a badge, knowing Stan had my back. Almost immediately I spotted Detective Brook Pressler, one of Stan's colleagues. She was impossible to miss. Her red mane of hair set against her pale face was striking. Adding to that, she was wearing a pair of leggings that accentuated her curves. She kind of reminded me of an Irish version of my best friend, Zahera, who was part Canadian, part

French, Muslim…and a knockout. More than one person had said she looked like an international model—the kind who didn't look like they were on a hunger strike.

I missed Zahera. She'd recently left for a vacation all by herself. She said she needed the time away to heal and reflect, to figure out what her life was all about. I got it, completely. Her father had been killed and her fiancé had turned out to be some type of international gun for hire. We'd traded a couple of text messages, but mostly I tried to leave her be. The fact that she was by herself told me she was serious about her time of reflection. I wasn't even sure where she had gone.

"Hey, Ivy." Brook slipped off a pair of rubber gloves and then used her shoulder to scratch her face.

I reached to shake her hand, and she pulled both arms up in a defensive position.

"No offense, but even with rubber gloves, I can barely get near myself. The dead animals are attracting all sorts of nasty critters in there."

I leaned in front of Stan and glanced into the field house. It was a lot deeper than I'd expected. Thankfully, it blocked the northern breeze, so I could stand there without my teeth chattering. I saw artificial grass on the floor, but what stood out most were the number of police spotlights positioned at the far end by the back wall. There were so many it looked like a movie set. A quick thought of Cristina and Leo entered my mind. I wished she could find a boy closer to her age to hang out with. She'd once called Leo the "Latin Zac Efron." I wasn't sure any seventeen-year-old boy could compete with that.

Loud voices drew my attention behind me. A man with a receding hairline and a light-blue suit that fit about forty pounds ago was in an animated conversation with a lady half his size.

Actually, a third was probably closer to the correct ratio. He was wagging his finger at her. "Is he the principal?" I asked Brook.

"How'd you guess?"

"Do I need to go down the checklist?"

"Good point. He's upset, for many reasons."

"He doesn't have to take it out on one of his teachers."

"That's not a teacher. She's the assistant superintendent, Meg Burton."

"She's letting him berate her like that?"

"Not for long. She's a ball-buster. She just came in from Austin. I've got family in that area. They brought her to San Antonio to serve as the second-in-command while the old geezer superintendent does his farewell tour. Before long, she'll be the top dog. Mr. Peterson better watch himself or she might just bite off his finger."

Not a second later, Meg barked at the larger Mr. Peterson, who quickly withdrew into a submissive position. I wasn't sure which sagged more, his face or his shoulders.

"I want to take a look at the crime scene," Stan said, "but before I do, I need to talk to Mr. Peterson about another matter for a quick moment while he's, uh…on the other end of the leash."

Brook gave a *what's-up* tilt of the head. I shrugged and followed behind Stan. As he introduced himself to Mr. Peterson, Meg answered her cell phone and stepped off to the side.

"Nice to meet you, Detective Radowski." The principal shifted his eyes to Meg for a quick second as he held out his hand. Stan, who had no qualms with being transparent about his condition, held up his prosthesis, then extended his left hand.

"Oh…oh my. I'm so sorry." Peterson slowly connected hands with Stan and completed the obligatory introduction. It was awkward at best.

"I need a favor," Stan said, getting right to it.

Peterson's eyes finally landed on me. His brow furrowed for a moment, as if he were wondering who I was, what I was doing there.

"You listening, Mr. Peterson?"

"Of course." He moved his eyes back to Stan. "It's just horrible what happened in there," he said, nudging his head toward the field house.

"It is, and we intend on finding out who did it. But before you do anything else, I need you to run back into the main building, log onto your computer system, and search through yesterday's video footage until you find a clip of Mia Romero leaving the school. And then I want you to save it and show it to me."

He nodded slowly, then glanced at me again. "Wait, haven't I seen you before?"

"Sorry, I graduated over ten years ago."

He tapped the side of his nearly bald head. "No, that's not it. Wait." He snapped his fingers. "I've seen your picture on the news or in the newspaper. Somewhere, I know."

"It's not important," Stan said. But the guy kept gawking at me.

"Up here, sir." Stan pointed at his own eyes.

"I heard about Mia not being in school yesterday. I don't know what to say. Kids miss school all the time."

"You or someone from your administration spoke to her father, Raul, this morning."

"Wasn't me," he said with a chuckle.

We weren't laughing.

"Anyway, they said they would look at the video footage, but Raul didn't feel very confident that he was being taken seriously."

Peterson huffed out a breath. "We're snowed under, to be frank with you." Again, his eyes were drawn to me. "What did you say your name was?"

"I didn't. I'm Ivy."

He stuck out his left hand, and then his right. He looked confused, but I kept my hands clasped in front of me.

Stan spoke up. "We all have jobs to do, Mr. Peterson. But when a kid goes missing, that becomes a top priority."

"How do you know she's not in a motel somewhere smoking pot?"

I looked at Stan, then back to the principal. My eyes were not friendly. "Do you know Mia personally?"

"Eh. She's not on the student council, so I guess not."

"We're not going to debate Mia's character," Stan interrupted. "Assume she is doing just that, for the point of this conversation. Are you going to do what I asked?"

"I guess so. You *do* have a badge." He looked down at Stan's waist where his badge was clipped. "Just to warn you, the system that captures the video feeds all over the school is antiquated. It's always blipping and going down for minutes at a time. The company that supports it just went bankrupt." He turned his head, then spoke louder. "Another great decision by our school board."

He was trying to get the attention of Meg, who was still on her phone, now pacing on the other side of the yellow tape. She either was pretending she hadn't heard him or had learned to drown out his voice.

"If you'll do that, then I can go into the field house and try to figure out who's behind this crazy animal sacrifice."

"Man to man…" He kept his eyes on Stan, leaning closer. "I'd give my left nut if you could find the heathens who did this before school starts tomorrow."

Stan looked like he'd just eaten rotten eggs. He was no more impressed with this guy's locker-room talk than I was. But, like a good little girl, I just stood to the side and kept my mouth shut.

Anything to quicken the process for him to find the video footage of Mia.

Peterson kept going. "Otherwise, it will be a circus tomorrow. Emotional kids, more emotional parents. The media will descend upon us like the vultures they are. I can already feel an ulcer coming on."

"We'll do our best, but I can't make promises."

We turned around and saw Brook holding up rubber gloves for each of us. "Are you ready to throw up your breakfast?"

Nine

Brook had not overdramatized the gory scene in the back of the field house. Two dead animals—a dog and a cat. I'd seen dead animals before, victims of being run over in a busy street. But my first response, other than putting a hand to my stomach, was bewilderment. In what state of mind could a person be to do something like this?

"Twisted fucker," were the words that Stan uttered.

I was in complete agreement.

Each had been sliced open like a zipper down the front. Lots of blood. Their eyes were all white. I tried to remind myself that they weren't humans. But it didn't help. I have a black cat named Zorro. During my most difficult periods as an adult, including a period when the dark abyss of anxiety and depression nearly strangled the life out of me, Zorro was always there, nudging me to get out of bed to feed him, purring as he nestled next to me on the couch. It was odd to think about now, but I'd found his quiet desire to continue living in a pseudo-normal state as a subtle reminder that I had a purpose. And that had kept my motivation somewhere above zero. Ultimately, Cristina had marched in and demanded I get my ass in gear and stop wallowing in self-pity.

Damn, that girl could be a thorn in my ass. But where would I be without her? She'd been vital in helping our little firm develop a solid reputation for doing whatever it took to help children in trouble. She'd sacrificed a lot and, on most days, acted with a maturity well beyond her teenage years. On many levels, she was the little sister I never had. Not that we shared every little intimate detail of our lives. But when it mattered most, she knew I had her back. And I felt the same way about her. Our alliance was unspoken, but no less legitimate or sincere.

"A makeshift altar," Brook said, pausing for a moment.

I'd been lost in my own thoughts—probably a way of dealing with the grisly scene before me—and I hadn't yet noticed the particle board being supported by blocks of wood on either end. The altar was about three feet off the ground.

"Sorry. I was just thinking about something. The altar…" I said as a lead-in for her to continue.

"We found melted wax in two different places."

"As in the wax from a candle?" I asked.

"That's the only way I've seen wax used," Brook said.

I hesitantly searched the board, trying to avoid looking at the dog and cat, and she pointed at one mound of wax. The color was close to translucent, with a slight pink tone. But most noteworthy was the size of the mound—it extended at least three inches off the surface.

"Must have been a big candle," I said.

"Whoever did this was in here a while. A number of hours I'd guess," Stan said as he looked toward the corner of the high ceiling. "Any cameras in this place?"

"We found one, by the back entrance," Brook said. "Verified it with the athletic coordinator. Apparently, he has access to the video footage for that one camera. He and another coach are in his office reviewing the video from the last twenty-four hours."

Stan turned to the front entrance, through which we'd just come, scratching his head with his prosthesis. "They have a camera in the back, but not at the front? Makes no sense."

"I asked the same question. Apparently, when they designed this place, they'd only intended to open those massive metal doors in the front when they had to use a forklift to bring in heavy items, like new weight-training equipment. But since it faces the school, it's left open most of the time for anyone in athletics to come and go. They use a chain and a padlock to lock it up when not in use.

"And was the chain or lock broken?" I asked.

"Nope."

"So, was it locked this morning when the coaches arrived?"

"They said it was," Brook said. "But honestly, they had doubt in their voices. I think it's one of those things where they're assuming procedures were followed, but they can't be one hundred percent certain. I didn't want to put them through a lie detector test. They were trying to be helpful, and eagerly ran off to scan the video footage."

"Is a cop in there with them?"

Brook raised a shapely eyebrow. "Yes, I've got a uniform in there with them. You think they might destroy evidence?"

"Everyone's a suspect until we rule them out, right?" I said.

"*We* rule them out?" Brook looked at Stan.

He just shrugged.

"You created this monster," Brook said to Stan, throwing a thumb at me. Then she gave me a smirk. "I mean that in the warmest way possible."

I knew she was joking, mostly. "I've been called a lot worse."

"The crime scene guys are dusting everything for fingerprints, so maybe they'll find something. But for now, I want to show you one more thing." She walked behind the board and pointed to the floor. "This."

I craned my neck but couldn't see, then looped around the setup with Stan on my heels, stopping next to Brook. Burned into the artificial grass was a symbol—a circle with what looked like the letter A in the middle.

"What do you think it is?" I asked.

"One of the uniforms knew exactly what it was the moment she saw the symbol. Apparently, she has a theology degree, and to get that degree, she had to study all types of religions, including Satanism. This symbol represents animal sacrifice."

"Devil worshippers," I said in a soft murmur, my eyes still riveted to the mark. Then, I realized I'd used a plural term, assuming there was more than one perpetrator. "So do you guys think this was done by a single person, or was it some type of group session?" I asked.

"It's just my instinct, but I'm going with more than one perp. So I revise my earlier assessment of who did this," he said. "But whether it's one or one hundred, I can't wait to get my hands on the twisted teenage fuckers who did this."

"So you go straight to kids doing this?" Brook asked.

Stan was staring off at something, not responding, so I did. "It's my first thought too. Not sure if they're necessarily from this high school either. Maybe a bunch of kids from a rival school did this; maybe someone from this school…just trying to create a huge stir, make everyone go bonkers. Some kids get off on that kind of stuff."

Was there any way that Mia Romero was one of those kids? Like Cristina had said, kids could put on a big show for their parents and actually be a very different type of person. Of course, I had no idea why I'd made that leap. Mia was a missing child. This was devil worshipping. Didn't mean one was related to the other. "Good point," Brook said, bringing me out of my thoughts.

"Could be one of the teachers just as easily; one of the staff who just lost it."

"Another good point. I'll make a note to ask Principal Peterson for the HR files for each teacher, administrator...every adult who's on this campus."

"What about *his* file?" I nodded in the direction of Peterson.

Brook nodded, while pulling out her phone and tapping away on the screen. "I'll go to that assistant superintendent for everything instead, keep Peterson out of it completely. This will take some work. Unless we find hair or blood evidence..." We both glanced at the dead animals, then back to each other. "The human kind. Or a fingerprint, or get lucky on the video footage. Our suspect pool is huge; the school population is close to two thousand. If we take into account a rival school, we could be looking at double that."

"Maybe these idiots left some sort of digital trail," I said, staring at the symbol in the turf. "Maybe posted something on social media, texted friends."

"Yes, it's possible," Stan said. "Just takes man hours."

I added, "Or woman hours."

Brook and I smirked, then she said, "I'll ask the captain for more men and women."

A phone rang. We looked to Stan, who broke from his trance and answered it. He turned his back for just a few seconds. All I heard was, "You've got to be fucking kidding me. Was there some kind of full moon last night?"

Then he flipped around. "I'm out of here. Ivy, you're coming with me."

"What's up?"

"Double homicide. Same type of sacrifice setup as here."

"People, not animals?

"Don't know all the details, but I do know this: they're both teenage girls."

An unnerving chill swept across my heart.

Ten

Against everything that Raul and Consuela had shared with me, I had considered the idea of Mia being involved in some "shit," as Cristina would say—including the satanic sacrifice of two animals. But now, as Stan extended his badge out of his window to the uniform in the parking lot at Mission Concepcion, guilt consumed me for even having had that thought.

The lot had about twenty vehicles in it, including a green tour bus. Stan parked the car, and I just sat there. Part of me didn't want to get out. I'd be forced to confirm my worst fears—that Mia, who by all accounts was sharp, motivated, and a leader, lay inside the historical church, dead.

"What are you waiting on?" Stan asked, one leg out the door.

"I'm in denial. If I don't go in, then I can't confirm Mia is dead."

"We don't know it's her."

I turned my head and gave Stan a hard look.

"Okay," he said, "I've been thinking about it on the way over here myself. I know it's a possibility."

"I have this sick feeling in my stomach, Stan. I'm afraid for Raul and Consuela. And I'm mortified that I'll have to be the one to tell them."

"I can tell them." His voice was more subdued now. He released a tired breath. "Part of me doesn't want to go in there either. I'm tired of seeing these crazy, sick homicides. And I hate like hell having to tell a family or friend about a loved one being murdered. But usually, later, when I'm a little less emotional, I ask myself: *if not me, then whom?*"

I stared out the front windshield.

"Maybe I was put in this place to do just that, to make sure I could do it in the best way possible. Although my best, I know, will still feel like their heart is being put through a shredder."

"I suppose." My eyes were drawn to the front of the old stone church—two arches on either side of a thin cross.

"After I tell them, and it's the worst thing imaginable, this little seed comes to life inside of me. That's my way of remembering who died, recalling my conversation with the family of the victim. I use that as motivation to find the killer."

I turned back to him, my expression softer. "I had no idea you felt all of that."

"I'm no robot, Ivy. I thought you knew that by now."

"I knew you were that way with Bev and Ethan. I just thought you put some distance between yourself and your work. I underestimated you, Stan. Again."

"I've been through a few things," he said with a chuckle. "But you've been put through hell a hundred times over. Your strength to move past everything, to want to make a better life for all these kids, it's pretty damn impressive. You make the rest of us want to do our part."

"Stop it."

"It's true."

I saw a pack of gum in his center tray. I pulled out two pieces and handed him one. "Let's get this over with."

After moving past an area that was cordoned off with yellow tape, outside of which were about thirty folks—some of whom appeared to be recording us on video with their phones—we ambled across a patch of grass. It was about fifty percent brown, the Texas Bermuda nearly in its dormant stage. The wind slapped my face, but it didn't feel as cold as earlier. Or maybe my senses had dulled a bit.

I noticed a number of uniforms walking the grounds, their eyes searching the grass. Looking for evidence. Three more uniforms milled about outside the front door to the church, and each greeted Stan with a tip of the hat and a "Sir." Just as Stan put a hand on the mammoth wooden door, it opened. Detective Omar Moreno slipped outside.

"Hey, Stan. One thing you should know."

"Ivy's here too." Stan flicked a thumb in my direction.

"Yeah, right. Hey." I gave him a slight head nod. Moreno and I had a not-so-great history. From my perspective, he was to blame for that. He was a know-it-all ass, who had doubted my sincerity on more than one occasion. I was sure he had a different view of things, but I didn't really care to know about it. We'd basically learned to coexist, only because Stan had pretty much insisted on it.

"How bad is it in there?" Stan asked.

"It's bad." Moreno, who had a preference for wearing what Zahera and I called pimp suits, was following his typical fashion trend. The suit was brown and shiny, as if it were coated with plastic.

"Any IDs on the two girls?"

"Waiting to hear on that. The ME and his assistant are doing their thing in there. We'll know soon."

I wanted to ask if he could describe their physical appearance, minus any fatal wounds, but I knew that would do me no good. It would only increase my anxiety. I just needed to get inside and see for myself.

Moreno pulled out a toothpick and stuck it in his mouth. "Just a quick warning before you go in there. It's, uh, rather emotional on the other side of the door."

"Who's in there?" Stan pointed with his fake arm, his voice on high alert.

"The priest and his choir director. Oh, and I came across the caretaker too."

"They're potential suspects, Omar. Do I have to remind you of that?"

"Two uniforms are in there as well, so you've got nothing to worry about. I know Father Vargas. My aunt dragged me to church here a couple of times a year ago or so."

"So you can verify his alibi at whatever time these murders took place?" Stan's voice carried above the howl of the wind.

"Dude, I'm not his mother." Moreno shifted his toothpick to the other side of his mouth. "I'm just saying he's a good guy. You'll see. Feel free to grill him all you want. I just don't want us to spend time where it's not needed."

Stan put a hand on the door. "You coming back in to help out with the emotional issue?"

"I've been dealing with it. Your turn now."

I walked around Moreno and followed Stan inside. The first thing I noticed was the horde of folks in one uniform or another at the front of the sanctuary. They blocked any view of the bodies. Even though their voices were muffled, the sounds reverberated off the arched ceiling and stone flooring. The gold painted walls were illuminated by sconces, with crosses affixed to the wall every three or four feet.

"Rose, Rose, you must not take blame for this vile act." I followed the voice to two people in one of the middle rows, where a priest had his hand on the back of a woman with gray hair. She was kneeling, her hands covering her face.

Stan and I traded glances, then walked toward the front. Just as we passed them, that was when it started.

"You must help us," the woman cried out.

Stan stopped and turned around. I did the same, but not before I caught a glance of a bare leg on the floor near the altar. Someone wearing a CSI shirt stepped in my line of sight and started taking pictures with his camera.

The woman's cries turned into a hacking cough. She either had bronchitis or smoked on the regular. "Rose, are you okay?" The priest glanced up at us, a look of quiet desperation on his face.

"I'm fine," she said between wheezing breaths. "We can't pretend this is just another crime, Father Vargas. This isn't about a kid breaking into your office and stealing last Sunday's offering. This is the work of the devil. And we must refuse to give in to the devil." She smacked her hand on the back of the pew in front of her. Then she jerked her head upward and stared at Stan. "Are you going to rid our church of the devil who has laid his roots right here in our sanctuary?"

It almost seemed like she was asking him to perform an exorcism. I'm sure Stan had dealt with a lot of personalities over the years. As he'd mentioned in the car, he'd delivered bad news to family of murdered or injured loved ones before. But the bewildered look on his face told me he'd never come across someone like Rose.

"Rose," I said, taking a step toward the pew. I made sure my voice was set to calm, regardless of how she was about to respond. "We're truly sorry for the horrible things that happened to those girls. And the fact it happened in your church can't be easy." I couldn't help but turn and try to snag another look at the front. Just more law enforcement folks milling about. "Please know," I said, turning back around, a hand to my chest, "that we're just as human as you. It breaks my heart to see this. But Detective Radowski and his team at SAPD are dedicated to working this case and doing their best to find the person who did this." I put my hand on Stan's shoulder. "Just give him and his team some space, and that will help expedite the process. Can you do that?"

With the help of the priest, she got to her feet, grabbed my hands, and looked me in the eye. "Bless you, child. You knew exactly what to say to this old lady. To help me see light, where I only saw darkness. You are a blessing from above. God has plans for you. I can feel it."

My mouth opened, but nothing came out. I was at a loss for words. Her kind message touched me.

Her eyes shifted to the scene up front, and for a moment, I thought she might fall back into her sea of despair. "You and the detective need to go do your job. I'm sorry if I took your focus away. I need to go clean up and make myself presentable." She forced a smile and walked out of the sanctuary.

"Thank you," the priest said, shaking my hand. "I'll be available if you have questions."

"It won't be *if*," Stan said. "More like *when*. Give us some time to review the crime scene first."

The Father motioned his hand in the shape of a cross, and then Stan and I walked to the front of the sanctuary to identify the two dead girls.

Eleven

Before I stepped up to view the scene, I took a moment to look at the picture of Mia on my phone, my hand trembling. *Please don't let it be her.* I looked up to the larger picture of Jesus hanging on the wall behind the flurry of activity in the sanctuary of Mission Concepcion and pushed out a couple of breaths.

"Zahera would be proud of your breathing cadence." Stan, who was referring to the fact that Zahera was an OB/GYN, was trying to lighten the mood.

"Part of me wishes I was with her right now, wherever she is."

"Knowing her, she's probably drinking a Mai Tai on the French Riviera."

Out of the corner of my eye, I saw a man in a white coat lean over, and then I heard the sounds of metal dropping into a plastic toolbox.

"Okay, Detective, it's all yours." The man in the white coat removed his rubber gloves, then adjusted his metal-rimmed glasses.

"Thanks, PJ. Do you know cause of death yet?"

"Appears to be multiple stab wounds that probably severely damaged several internal organs. That and loss of blood. But I won't know the whole story—"

"Until you do the full exam back at your lab. Right," Stan finished for him.

"I know I sound like a broken record, but let's not forget, Detective, there have been murders where the killer's act of rage gives the appearance that was the cause of death, when in actuality the death was more subtle. Maybe he slipped them a pill that caused a fatal heart attack, or shot them up with so much heroin that they overdosed."

I was listening to all of this, thinking the ME had quite the imagination, or had just seen so many twisted, sick crimes carried out that he'd be a great candidate for writing horror stories.

"Can you stick around for any questions I might have?" Stan asked.

"I'll be right behind you and…" PJ looked in my direction.

Stan quickly introduced me to the medical examiner for Bexar County. PJ Frazier seemed to sense my anxiety. "I'm sorry for your loss," he said.

"I didn't know her personally." I was acting like it was a forgone conclusion that one of the girls was Mia. Part of me had, apparently, already gone there. Probably a subconscious internal defense mechanism to soften the blow once I was faced with reality.

"I thought you might be family."

"I guess I'm a representative of the family."

"Attorney?"

"Private investigator."

"Oh." He sounded surprised, and not in a good way. I ignored it as he stepped aside.

I took another look at the picture of Mia on my phone. Her smile made her seem so confident, as if her future was full of hope and promise. And not just aimless hope. She had an air about her that said she knew what she wanted to get out of life and she'd enjoy the ride along the way.

"Ready?" Stan asked, moving forward a few steps.

I glanced down and, after telling myself to ignore the blood, did a quick cursory scan of the two girls. One had blond hair and a nose ring. Not Mia. The other one had skin the color of wet sand, with lustrous brown hair. I could see she wore makeup. Her nose had a few sprinkles of freckles and sat atop a bloated face. The physical dimensions of her body were close to those of Consuela.

My heart fluttered. I tried to swallow, but it scratched my throat.

"Is it her...Mia?" Stan asked, a hand on my back.

I couldn't answer him.

"Ivy. Can you tell, or do we need to call her parents for confirmation?"

My eyes went back to the photo. That was when I noticed the hoop earrings in the picture. Mia had pierced ears. I lowered myself to the floor, my mind switching into a gear that an ME or mortician might have. I'd momentarily severed my emotions from what was all around me. I was looking for factual evidence.

"Hold on there, Ms. Nash," PJ said, moving down next to me. "You can't get near the body. You could contaminate the crime scene."

I didn't like being admonished, but I couldn't argue his point.

"I need to see her earlobe."

PJ pushed his glasses up the bridge of his nose. "You want to see if her ears are pierced?"

I nodded. "It's either that, or we have to call her parents and have them identify her. I'd rather not put them through that."

He rubbed his sizable forehead, as if I were asking him to cross some ME line.

"I want to do this for the parents, to find out if this is Mia."

Stan shuffled his feet. "Can you do this for me, PJ?"

The ME didn't say a word. He pushed himself to a standing position, walked a few steps to his toolbox, pulled out some type of metal instrument, and then put on a pair of rubber gloves. "Excuse me," he said to me.

I moved out of the way as he leaned down and, ever so carefully—as if a house of cards might topple if he actually touched the ear with the instrument—lifted a lock of hair.

I squinted. "I don't see anything. Do you see a hole in the meat of the earlobe?"

Stan had his hands—well, one hand and a fake hand—on his knees, leaning next to me. "I don't see a hole."

PJ agreed.

I took another glance at the picture on my phone, then I met Stan's gaze. "It's not her, Stan. It's not Mia." Tears welled in my eyes, and I backed up a few steps, away from the warm glow of the spotlights.

Stan and PJ exchanged a few words while pointing at the bodies, then Stan joined me by the front pew a few moments later.

"Are you relieved?" he asked.

"Yes. But it's still horrible. Their family and friends will be devastated."

"And I thought the scene at the field house was bad." Stan shook his head.

Taking in the full spectacle, I was suddenly struck at how similar it was to the crime scene at the field house. The bodies were at the base of an altar. They were also positioned at similar angles as the animals' bodies were, and there was a lot of blood.

I blinked a couple times then continued studying the bodies. That was when the differences between the two crime scenes became clearer to me. This was a church with an actual altar—not a makeshift one. The girls' chests weren't split open, although there was enough blood to make it seem like they'd been. They were fully clothed. The one who looked like Mia wore a dress that dropped to just above her knees. "Stan, do we know if the girls were sexually assaulted?"

"I just asked PJ that question. From his preliminary exam, no. But he won't give me a definitive answer until he does a complete exam back at his office."

For some reason, I felt better hearing that they likely weren't sexually assaulted, but I shouldn't have. The girls had still died a horrific death. And for what reason? What was their connection to each other? Race, gender, religion, other affiliations? Nothing at all?

I cleared my throat and quietly asked Stan the one question that would tie the two crime scenes together. "Were there any Satanic symbols?"

"According to the CSI guy I just spoke with while you were in your little trance, nothing. Now, maybe the killer did leave a similar clue, and it's just not as obvious as a scorched piece of artificial turf. So, they'll keep looking."

I followed Stan's gaze to the door at the other end of the sanctuary. Father Vargas was standing there, patiently waiting, staring at us. His calm demeanor freaked me out a little. I expected a little more concern. Maybe he was one of those who kept everything on the inside. Or maybe he was guilty of something and knew we would never figure it out.

Now, why the hell did I go there?

"Let's start the questioning," Stan said, signaling with his head for me to follow him. I scooted up next to him, and we walked down the aisle. "What are your initial thoughts?"

"It's really weird. On my way here, I was preparing myself to see Mia. Yet, before I knew this crime existed, my mind kept wondering if Mia had somehow changed overnight, or maybe she'd been duping her parents for some time. And maybe she might be involved in that scene at the field house, even though the two events—her disappearance and the sacrifice of the two animals—have no reason to be associated with each other."

"We still have hope that the video footage might turn up something," he said as we moved closer to the Father.

"The school video feed that Principal Peterson is looking over?"

He nodded. "And maybe even the one-camera footage at the field house."

Just as we reached the priest with his tight-lipped smile, a scream echoed through the sanctuary. It sounded like Rose. I ran in the direction of the scream—down an adjoining hallway.

"Ivy, wait," Stan shouted.

But I was already in the hallway and its incredible darkness.

Twelve

Rose's scream sounded like someone had just scared the crap out of her. But I couldn't be certain, given her earlier mental state. I hit a T in the hallway. Right or left? I couldn't see a thing either way. Another scream. But this one was choked off—as if someone did it for her.

The echo of her voice seemed to come from both directions. I chose left and quickly started losing my balance, raised my arms until my fingers slid across the stone. Where was the sconce lighting? Had someone turned out the lights?

"Rose?" I called out, still feeling my way down the hall. I paused for a moment, trying to get my bearings on where the sound had originated.

Then I walked straight into a wall. I released a muted grunt, reached up to my forehead, and felt blood. I saw a soft light off to my left, and I headed in that direction.

"Rose, are you okay?"

I could hear voices behind me. "Can't see a damn thing. Get me a flashlight." It was Stan and someone else. The Father possibly. I stopped moving again, squinted, listening for something up ahead.

"Rose, it's Ivy. Did something happen?" I held my breath, waiting and hoping for a response. Nothing. So I shuffled forward, the path still dimly lit. I began to wonder if the overwhelming anxiety of seeing the dead girls in the sanctuary had caused her to have a heart attack, maybe a stroke. That would explain why she wasn't responding. She could be lying unconscious in some hidden alcove in this two-hundred-year-old building that had the dampness of an ancient Egyptian catacomb. Yes, I realized the irony in comparing a Christian house of worship with that of a crypt, where sacrifices were usually kept inside the tombs of ancient kings.

"Rose, please let me know where you are," I said. "I want to help you."

More muffled voices behind me. I flipped around, but saw only darkness. Who'd turned off the lights? Hell, as old as this place was, they were probably off more than they were on.

I shuffled forward, but stopped suddenly when I heard a groan.

"Rose?" A chill crawled up my spine until I felt a tingle near the tiny hairs at the base of my skull.

The next few seconds came at me in slow motion, as if I had all kinds of opportunity to change the course of action. I froze amidst the flurry of incoming motion in the dim light. I first saw a hand the size of a catcher's mitt. The meaty paw took hold of my shirt, jerked me inside a room. A hot, wet breath in my face sickened me. I bumped into something. A high-pitched whimper. I reached out, tried to focus. I felt a curly mop of hair. It had to be Rose. Her body trembled with fear.

"Rose—" My words were cut off as the huge hand encircled my neck, choking off my air passage. I dug my nails into the man's arm. I could feel ligaments on his forearm, taut like steel wire. I caught a quick glimpse of him; he had to be a foot taller than my five-six frame. Just as he threw me backward, my thumb was sliced open. He'd been holding a knife of some kind. I hit the floor, landing on my elbow and shoulder. The jolt of pain only momentarily stole the pain away from my finger. The cut was deep, and I wondered if I'd severed an artery.

"Don't hurt her. She did nothing to you." It was Rose, her voice cracking yet defiant. I pushed up to my knees, saw the silhouette of the man or beast—some might say a manster.

"Shut up, Rose."

He knows Rose, dammit! Who the hell is this guy? There was no time for questions. He had a knife—he'd probably killed the girls in the sanctuary. That thought sent a surge rushing through my bloodstream. I leaped out of my stance, keeping my center of gravity low, and rammed my shoulder into the crook just behind his knee. He barked, then teetered backward, almost tumbling on top of me. I could see Rose slip away from his grip. "Get out of here, Rose."

She screamed and took off for the door. Just as quickly, the man regained his balance. "Come here, dammit!" he growled. He swiped at her with his free hand, grabbing her hair. She squealed, lost her footing, and dropped to the floor.

The glint of a swinging knife snagged my gaze. I just reacted, not thinking. Balling my hands together, I thrust myself upward, ramming my fists-of-a-club right into his testicles. He doubled over, screaming at a soprano level.

"Get out of here, Rose. Now!"

She scooted out on all fours.

I tried to make my way around the wounded beast, but he was so large it seemed like I was circling a domed stadium. I hopped over his leg, but before my foot hit the stone surface, he swung the knife at my shin. He miscalculated the speed of my leg, and the knife clipped my shoe, then sliced into the side of my leg. But it also knocked me off balance, and I dropped to the floor. In that extra moment on the floor, he used his foot to slam the door shut just as male voices descended down the hallway. I grabbed at my leg, writhing in pain as he got to his feet and wiped sweat from his brow. He smiled a crooked smile, and I saw more gaps than teeth.

"Enough games. It's time to play out my dreams again." Spit sprayed on top of me.

I covered my head.

Thirteen

His dreams. What did he mean by that?

The man dead-bolted the door, then turned and stood over me, huffing out breaths like a panting, wild animal. Two slices of lights from behind me, a covered window I assumed, put the man in full view. Slowly lifting my sights off his ski-size work boots, I noticed a slight paunch in his midsection, but his shoulders were as wide as the door, each arm the size of my leg. He had a patchy beard and a buzz cut.

"Emmitt, open up the door right now, do you hear me?" It was Father Vargas. There was pounding on the door.

Emmitt? The caretaker? Emmitt didn't move. His breathing cadence stayed at the same rapid pace. He acted as if he hadn't heard a word from the other side of the door.

Then I saw his eyes. They were liquid glass, some type of pale taupe color from best I could tell. I actually wondered if he was on something. He had that dazed look, as if he wasn't completely there. He flipped the handle of the long-bladed knife in his fingers.

More pounding at the door. "Emmitt, this is the police. Detective Radowski."

I coughed out a breath, then felt the sting of a thousand bees in the cut in my leg. It made my thumb wound feel like a paper cut. Blood seeped through the hole in my jeans. I squeezed the area above and below the gash, anything to reduce the level of pain.

"Open this door, Emmitt, and let Ivy go. Then we can talk about what you want to do with your life. You have friends. We can all help you get better."

Seconds ticked by, but Emmitt didn't move. He just stared down at me, his heavy breaths morphing into a high-pitched wheeze.

Suddenly, he lifted a boot, stepped over me, and walked to a table with a large book on it. He spread his arms, leaned over, and began to read…or chant, actually. I couldn't tell what he was saying. I turned back to the door, contemplating if I had enough time to make a break for it. Or even just unlock the door. Once unlocked, Stan would barge in, gun drawn. I would be safe.

I looked down at my leg. Blood covered my hands. I questioned how fast I could move. This might be a one-shot chance. If I didn't get the door unlocked, then Emmitt would stab me to death. Just like he'd done with the girls.

I nudged myself closer to the door, my eyes fixed on the caretaker. I repeated the same process three more times. On each surge, my heart thumped so loudly I thought he might hear it, flip around, and end my life with one swing of his arm.

I'd moved about a foot altogether. It might take another four feet to get me close enough to where I could lunge for the door before he'd have a chance to reach me. But I couldn't be certain.

"Emmitt, if you don't open the door, we'll have to force our way in," Father Vargas said, his voice stern. "Do you hear me, Emmitt?"

Again, no response from Emmitt, who appeared to still be reading the book. I wanted to call out, to yell at Stan to shoot the lock off the door. But would it work? This wasn't some Hollywood stunt. A lot could go wrong. "Forgive me, Lord, for I have sinned."

Emmitt's voice was suddenly distinct. I didn't breathe; I didn't swallow. I'd turned into stone, nothing more than a statue.

He flipped around and faced me, although his eyes seemed to be staring straight ahead. I followed his gaze to the door. There was a cross etched into the wood. I turned back to Emmitt. He mumbled something else and crossed himself. Then, he pulled out a necklace from under his shirt and kissed a cross.

I forced out a quiet breath and tried to think. Something was about to go down. I was the only other person in the room. I doubted he was ready to pull up a chair, kick back, and share everything that was on his mind. My pulse began to race, although I somehow still sat motionless. I wasn't sure what to do. What was my best chance at survival? Try to wait him out, hope that whatever drug he was on might finally subside and he'd start thinking normally? Or make a run for the door? I realized the latter option was even more far-fetched than before, as he was now facing me.

My eyes shifted to the knife again. He was rotating the handle forward and backward in his fingers. They were thick, but surprisingly nimble. The knife appeared to be an extension of his arm, as if he could effortlessly carve an intricate sketch. Had he fought in a war, been a chef? He used a knife like a painter used a brush.

Then the knife flipping stopped. I tried to swallow, but couldn't. I could see the ropes in his neck go taut, as if he were about to burst out of his stance and slice me into a hundred pieces. Fighting back would be useless.

I had no choice. I had to run. I jumped out of my stance—the gash in my leg sent an electric jolt of pain into my brain, but I ignored it. I reached the door in no time, grabbed the lock, and began to twist.

A roar from behind me. I cried out loud as my fingers fumbled with the lock—to no avail. He thrust his arm forward, the knife going right for my head. I jerked backward, and the blade jabbed into the door. I'd somehow escaped certain death.

With my entire body trembling, I reached for the lock again, but I was so jittery, I couldn't maintain a grip. Then his body slammed me into the door. Air poured out of my lungs, his jagged teeth up against my neck.

I was as sure as dead.

Fourteen

Emmitt's snarled grill was just an inch from my face. Waves of his rank breath seemed to invade my pores and it was everything I could do not to spit in his face, just so he would turn his head. Of course I didn't dare move. The shouts from the other side of the door—Stan, Father Vargas, maybe some others—became muffled and far away as I was forced to come to terms with my impending demise.

My breathing was shallow, and my brain begged for more oxygen as I tried hard to appear like an inanimate object, hoping Emmitt would somehow dismiss me as a chair or a lamp. He gave me a thousand-yard stare, and I wondered if he really saw me at all. Was he hallucinating?

The next thing I knew, he wrapped his paws around my shoulders and squeezed so tightly I thought he might crush some bones. Then I was airborne—actually, he lifted me up like I was in some type of couple's ice skating event. I yelped while bracing myself for the inevitable toss across the room, which would not involve a pirouette or graceful landing. This guy meant to do harm. Major harm.

But why me?

"Emmitt," I said through gritted teeth as he held me above his head. "Why do you want to hurt me?"

The question threw him off. He grunted and then lowered me to the floor, in front of a wooden chair. "Sit," he ordered. I did just that. He walked to the door, pulled out the knife, then turned back around. His face was again full of seething anger. I noticed his hand gripping the knife with purpose. He began to walk my way, raising his arm above his head.

"No, Emmitt, you don't want to do that," I said, covering my head—which I knew would do no good. My voice was eerily calm. Why I was having a conversation with this monster was beyond me, but it was the only thing I had left. He walked past me to the table and thrust his arm downward. The blade plunged deep into the book—it looked like an oversized Bible. He screamed at the top of his lungs, spinning around, clawing at his head and then his eyes.

"Why me, God? Why me?" he cried out.

There was a lot of shuffling and noise from the hallway. I heard only spotty words. "Lost." "Mental." "Crazy." "Death."

What were they thinking was going on in here? I had no idea. I had to focus on Emmitt and get him to calm down, join me on Planet Earth.

"Emmitt, please let me help."

"Shut the hell up," he barked.

He cried out again, then turned and swept his arm across the table, sending the Bible, a number of candles, and the knife flying against the wall.

"Emmitt, have you harmed Ivy?" Father Vargas yelled. "If you have, I will never forgive you. Do you understand me?"

Emmitt roared like a wild bear, ran to the door, and pounded it with his fists until he drew blood. "Shut up. Every one of you. I can't keep on hiding this. I have to let it all out."

Hiding what? Let what out? I had no idea what he was talking about, but my mind tried to find the reason behind this insanity. Was he in the process of releasing the demons that had led him to kill those two girls?

"Emmitt, we can help you," Father Vargas said. "Just let us in."

"No. Go away and leave me be."

"Emmitt, you know we can't do that. You have an innocent person in there with you. I'm assuming you haven't hurt her."

He looked back at me, as if he were noticing me for the first time.

"Emmitt, answer me!" Father Vargas sounded furious, the extreme opposite of his stoic demeanor thus far.

"If you don't open the door now, Emmitt," Stan said, "we will be forced to break down the door and subdue you by any means necessary."

"Shut the fuck up!" Emmitt screamed and turned in my direction. He lifted the chair, with me still in it, and then smacked it off the stone floor. My teeth rattled, but I was expecting much worse. It should have been much worse. I looked up at him, and he was staring at me. A strange sensation washed over me. I felt like he had suddenly connected with me and didn't want to hurt me. Not yet anyway. Crazy, right? "If you bust down that door," Emmitt said, his eyes still on me, "you'll leave me with no choice."

"What are you saying, Emmitt?" Father Vargas said.

"I'm saying you need to leave me alone. Go away. Leave me be."

"You know we can't do that," Stan said. "Either you come out, or we're going in."

"And I'm saying if you come in, I'm going to kill her, and then I'm going to end my own life."

Tears sprung to life, and I brought a hand to my face, but Emmitt put a finger to his lips. He was telling me to be quiet.

I heard more muffled voices, but nothing discernible. Emmitt scratched the back of his head as his eyes wandered a bit, then stopped at a point on the floor. *Crap.* He was staring at the knife over in the corner. I had to get his mind off the knife.

"Emmitt, do you know who I am, and what I do for a living?"

"Uh...no. Well, I heard them say your name is Ivy."

His eyes were stuck on the knife.

"That's right. I'm sorry we couldn't have met under different circumstances."

"Yeah. Well, I fucked up, right?"

"Hey, I've made a few mistakes in my life. Who hasn't?"

He turned his head ever so slightly, but he kept his gaze on the knife. "You haven't made the kind of mistakes I've made." His head dipped to his chin.

My ECHO instincts then came to the forefront. I wanted to confirm that he was the person who'd killed the girls. Where did he find them? Why did he choose them? This might be our best chance, our only chance to find out the truth before he lawyered up. Or before he ended his life. Maybe mine too.

I took in a breath and prepared to share one of my deepest secrets with a man I hardly knew. "Emmitt, if I tell you a secret, will you promise to keep it between us?"

He turned and looked at me. "Pfft. Don't tell me, you once stole a pack of gum from the grocery store."

"I wish that was it."

He did a double take on me.

"I once killed a man."

He didn't blink. He studied me, probably wondering if I was full of shit.

"You think I'm lying? I'm not. I didn't do it on purpose, but I had enough rage in me that I wanted him dead."

"Why did you kill him? How did he die?"

"He fell down some stairs. He'd tried to rape me, and I was escaping."

Emmitt's eyes became moist.

"Why are you crying?" I almost wished I had my phone on me, so I could record his confession right here and now. We'd have all the evidence to lock him up and keep him from harming anyone else.

"I have all of these crazy thoughts." His voice was cracking, and he wiped tears off his face.

"What kind of thoughts?"

"I can't say." He released a deep breath.

"Emmitt, there's nothing wrong with having a thought. No one is a hundred percent pure. Not me, not Detective Radowski. Not even Father Vargas."

I could hear more voices in the hallway. More people had shown up. A second later, "Emmitt, you need to open the door."

"Go away," he said.

"We'll give you thirty seconds. If you haven't opened the door, we're coming in, regardless of how we get in. Do you understand, Emmitt?"

He splayed his arms and looked at me, his eyes pleading for a reprieve.

"Stan, this is Ivy. I'm fine. He hasn't hurt me."

"Ivy, thank God you're okay." He paused a moment. "Ivy, if he's about to hurt you or even worse, just say the word. We'll storm the room and you'll be safe."

"Seriously, Stan. I'm okay. Just give us a couple of minutes."

Emmitt shook his head, then whispered to me, "I can't get arrested, Ivy. My family won't be able to deal with it."

"What's the alternative?"

His chin quivered. "I'll kill myself." His eyes shifted to the knife.

I gasped, and he looked back at me. "Don't worry. I won't hurt you. Well…" he said, looking off.

I waited for him to continue. He walked aimlessly around the room, then found another chair and dropped into it. I couldn't see the chair, he was so big. It was as if he were sitting in a chair meant for a three-year-old. He moved forward in his seat, his elbows on his knees. "Ivy, I hear things that other people don't hear."

"What kind of things?'

"Voices."

"Of people you know, or…"

"I don't know. It's almost like I hear myself, but another part of me. The bad part of me."

"What does the bad part tell you to do?"

He rocked back, rubbing his hands against his eyes. "Bad stuff, Ivy. Real bad stuff."

I swallowed and somehow managed to keep my expression even. "Remember, you're talking to someone who killed a man." I tried to snort out a laugh, but it never materialized. And he didn't seem to notice anyway.

"But you were acting in self-defense," he said.

Which told me that his act of violence—his multiple acts of violence—had been unprovoked, just as I'd assumed. We were so very close to him admitting to what he'd done. Just a little closer and I was certain he'd let it all pour out. "Emmitt, I'm not a cop."

He moved his hands from his face. "You're not? What are you?"

"I run this small PI firm called ECHO. We try to help kids who find themselves in trouble. I was one of those kids years ago."

"I did some shit back in the day."

I eyed his features. He looked to be in his thirties.

"Didn't we all. But, you know, I'm just trying to help make the world a little bit better for those who need it. Isn't that what you do here at the church?"

"I suppose." He exhaled. "I don't know if I can keep going on. I'm so tired. I can't ever sleep. Those voices in my head…they just won't go away."

"What do they tell you to do?"

His jaw flinched, then he said, "To hurt people. Girls especially."

"Why?"

"I don't know." He paused, started picking at his nails. "I think I'm being punished."

"For what?"

"Years ago, after one of my football games, I went out with my buddies. I drank too much, then got back in my car. I ended up running a red light, and I ran over a girl on a bicycle. It killed her."

Tears streamed down his face, and I sensed his sorrow.

"I went to prison for three years. When I got out, Father Vargas helped me. But I always wondered how God would punish me. And now I get these night terrors that I can't control…"

"And these are the voices that told you to do bad things…to kill girls?"

He tilted his head. "Yeah, but I never did anything. I wanted to. I thought about it a lot. I even followed a couple of girls home and looked through their window and all. Then I went back home and dreamed how I'd kill them. It's sick and twisted, which is why I hate myself. But I've never done—" He stopped short, then he lifted out of his chair, his hands rolling into fists. "You think I killed those girls in the sanctuary?"

"I wasn't sure, Emmitt. You did attack Rose, and then me. You were unhinged, uncontrollable."

He dipped his head to his chest. "I'll never escape my past."

He didn't say another word, didn't even move. I held my breath and slowly shuffled to the door. This time, I was able to flip the lock.

Stan walked through first.

Fifteen

Mia ran her fingers across the satin sheets on her four-poster bed, then waltzed over to the mirror and admired the diamond earrings that dangled from her ears. She felt their weight as she turned left and right. At every angle, they sparkled like…diamonds. Could they actually be real? These were the kind of diamonds that she'd ogled while watching all of the awards shows: Beyoncé, Ariana Grande, Rihanna, even an old entertainer named Jennifer Lopez. All of those women represented so much more to Mia, though— more than just fancy jewelry and designer dresses. They exemplified empowerment for women—even teenage girls who were looking for a gleam of light that would show them the way out of the darkness, the daunting tunnel of shame, and self-loathing.

Not wanting to smear her makeup, and not wanting to drag herself into another emotional recollection of the last year, she gripped the top of the leather makeup chair and fought back the tears. She'd cried enough to fill the San Antonio River. Amazingly, no one had noticed, or cared to notice. They'd been far too busy in their own worlds, trying to survive the game of life, to pay attention to a teenage girl who always seemed to be perfect. She was a master at presenting herself as a girl who had it all together.

She never forgot a homework assignment at school, studied for every test five times over, and even still, repeatedly showed up to tutorials. Anything to stay on top of her studies, to get the best grades, to try to make something of herself.

Something her parents never had the opportunity to do.

Under the same false pretense, she put a lot of effort into maintaining a positive and bubbly personality. She put herself out there to be friendly to everyone she met. She routinely sought out the new kids in school who were experiencing typical teenage jitters about finding new friends and acclimating to a different environment. She was the one who made introductions, met them for lunch, and generally took interest in their lives. If not for her, where would they end up? Isolated, for certain; depressed, most likely. It would shape the rest of their lives, and she didn't want to see anything bad happen to anyone.

She knew she was the girl whom everyone admired; to them, she was humble and, at times, self-deprecating even as she was popular. Money had always been an issue in her life, her parents' lives, but through a bartering process she'd developed—tutoring students—she'd ostensibly traded her brains to receive trendy clothes from the girl students, usually those who went to different schools. If that secret ever was exposed on Snapchat, her reputation at her own high school would turn to shit in mere hours. She'd become a laughingstock for convincing some other girl to give her the clothes off her back. They'd see her as nothing more than another homeless person begging from the street corner.

Her self-esteem, even though it appeared on the outside as an impenetrable force, was remarkably fragile. She had logged countless hours in the bathroom, trying to find the right combination of colors to ensure her makeup was tasteful, not slutty, and exuded an air of confidence. The same scrutiny was applied to her hair. She wanted a trendy style, but nothing too far on the edge.

She was a young woman who knew where she was headed, what she wanted to accomplish, how to treat people, how to be a leader, an example to all young girls growing up. She'd seen them looking at her, whether it was at basketball camp or speaking at a National Honor Society event. She was their role model. They wanted to be like her. They wanted to be her.

But how could that be, when she didn't want to be who she was?

More than any of that, however, she wanted to make her parents proud, to show the world what a daughter of immigrant parents could achieve. To show the world what she could accomplish.

She remembered her younger years like they'd happened an hour ago. Living out of the back of a fifteen-year-old station wagon with her older brother. Eating nothing but bread for one dinner after another. Being ridiculed by her classmates in elementary school for wearing the same pair of rust-color Levi's day after day.

"That's the nicest outfit. You look so pretty today," her second-grade teacher had told her on day three of wearing that outfit. Two weeks later, the same teacher who had noticed the hole in the knee of her jeans privately asked, "Is everything okay at home? Do you need help getting more clothes?" Mia had bit into the side of her cheek and debated how much to share. She didn't want pity. It would do her or her family no good. So she'd lifted her chin and said, "My mother is so busy running our family restaurant, she just doesn't have time to buy me clothes. I'm okay, though. She'll find time eventually, and when she does, she'll buy me a whole new wardrobe."

It had been a complete lie, but it had bought her some time, to not worry as much about what others thought. Eventually, the teachers noticed more and more, but not her fellow elementary school classmates. They were too worried about their own little worlds.

It wasn't until she reached middle school and social media exploded that the idea had begun to take root—to swap her knowledge for possessions. In fact, those roots had expanded greatly over the years as she took advantage of one opportunity after another to enhance her looks, wear nicer clothes, have *stuff*, all of which aided her ascension into the popular crowd.

She stared at the diamonds in the mirror, thinking about how she'd manufactured this persona over the years. While most of her steps in that direction were purposeful, she had refused to look at the big picture, at how she was pieced together, all attached by the thinnest of threads. Now, after considerable thought in the last twenty-four hours, she could admit with no hesitation that it was all a mask. A veneer to cover up the pain and guilt that hovered just beneath her beautiful skin. She'd grown weary of the never-ending battle to be someone she wasn't. In some respects, she felt like a two-bit con artist. *Look in this hand while I conceal what I'm really doing in this other hand.* All to have the privilege of being someone she wasn't.

She took in a breath, again feeling that emptiness inside her chest. She recalled that one moment when it really started to spiral out of control. It had been almost a year earlier, right around Christmas. Cheerful tunes played on every radio station, venues around the city were decorated with wreaths and trees, colorful lights blinked, and people were in a generous mood. Even her parents seemed to be happier. It was a time of hope.

But amidst the holiday cheer, she'd been tempted without even knowing it. His charm and wit were undeniable. He had those dreamy eyes that made her melt, where she lost all sense of knowing who she was...or who she'd become. While she couldn't deny having that tingle in her gut—the one that beckoned to the rest of her body to open up and share her heart, to trust him completely—it turned out to be a false signal. Actually, it wasn't a false signal as much as it was a mask.

He'd made her do those awful things. Things she couldn't repeat to anyone. At first, she did them out of loyalty. "You've got my back, so I've got yours," she remembered telling him. He'd smile, show off that twinkle in his eye. But then at the next opportunity, the cycle would repeat itself. Each time, it got a little more physical. A little more disturbing. She'd tried to trick herself into thinking it wasn't a big deal, that it didn't demean her or make her feel like she was less than human.

But it only got worse. And every time she saw that manipulative wink, she wanted to hurl. She'd tried to convince him that all of the demented, twisted acts weren't necessary. They could be a normal couple, enjoying normal things. Go to the drive-in, hang out at the mall, go to a concert. But he would have none of it. And then it got really physical—more than just during their twisted interludes. She lost weight as she worried, tried to find other things to keep her mind occupied, tried to keep busy so she'd have no time for him.

But everywhere she turned, he was right there, as if he were her shadow. The shadow from hell.

A shudder ran through her, and she swallowed back some emotion.

She picked up a shapely bottle of perfume and sprayed it on her wrists, then took in the musky aroma. The bottle probably cost more than all of her clothes back home combined. She ran her hands down the sides of the black suede dress. It was practically molded to her body.

Another glance in the mirror. She might only be seventeen, but she looked every bit of twenty-three.

That was the way he, the dignified man, wanted her to look. She called him Sal, because of his many salient qualities. Sal had saved her from the humiliation, the brutality of that silly, reckless boy with a pecker the size of her pinky. Perhaps he'd dabbled in all those creepy, hurtful acts to make up for his dick size. She'd read in a magazine that guys with small packages could be like that. It was all about control, the article said.

She looked around her room and saw nothing but luxury. Deep, rich palettes of color on the pillow-top bed—she'd had nothing more than a secondhand, piss-covered mattress during her years at home. Every beautiful dress a woman could dream of. All the finest makeup and creams and hair-care products. Fuzzy, warm robes. A library of classic novels and a catalog of every music tune she could think of. Luxurious furniture. Wonderful-smelling lotions and bath salts, and a two-headed shower. The list went on and on. Everything she could possibly want was in her suite.

It just happened to be a suite that she wasn't allowed to leave. The door locked from the outside. What was on the outside, she had no idea. She'd been "temporarily disabled" on the drive over. In fact, she couldn't say for certain how close to town she was. Five miles, fifty miles, five hundred miles? She had left her phone back at school, so she couldn't map her location. When she awoke, she found a lovely, welcoming note.

She knew life wasn't perfect. She missed some of her friends and, to a lesser extent, her parents. But this was about setting the course to a new life. One that didn't involve all the pressures of being Miss Perfect. She'd finally been able to start shedding some of her fake layers, the ones that were there for everyone else's benefit.

She had nothing to prove to anyone—he'd told her that during their first private moment a few weeks back when they met at the city library, sat in a quiet section, and just talked. They had rendezvoused another six times since then, each one giving her greater hope for a new life.

There was a knock on the door. She felt the corner of her full lips edge upward. She wondered exactly what Sal was expecting to see when he opened that door. She did her best to channel her thoughts into everything she knew about him, and then she quickly conjured up her new self.

She was a natural.

Sixteen

At first it was a half-snort. Over the course of a minute, it turned into more of an intermittent giggle. And then, finally, she rocked backward and guffawed. It wasn't long thereafter that Cristina adjusted the phone in her hands and texted at the speed of light.

If she'd bothered to look up, she would have seen my eyes unblinking in amazement at how she operated. Or perhaps it was her entire generation.

"Oh man, Paula, you won't believe what I heard."

That was Cristina having a conversation with an inanimate object, her phone, as we walked to the front porch of the Romero house.

I blew warm air into my hands. The sun had made a cameo appearance at the edge of the clouds in the western sky before dipping below the horizon. The blustery winds continued, and the temperature was dropping.

Again, I had no coat. Where was my mind? Oh yeah, still trying to make sense of how I'd been lucky enough to talk my way out of being sliced up by Emmitt, the caretaker at Mission Concepcion.

While I'd probably put on the best performance of my life, I was fortunate to be alive. The knife that slashed my leg hadn't severed anything important. Painful, yes, but it wasn't like I was going to have to live my life like Stan—minus a limb. A bandage was wrapped around my thumb—again, I'd been lucky. By the time all the hubbub died down at the church, where there had been a deluge of police officers, fire trucks, and paramedics, and an even larger contingent of onlookers, Stan and I had both learned more about Emmitt's background.

Father Vargas had said that Emmitt was telling the truth about killing that girl when he was a senior in high school. He'd driven drunk at an age when he wasn't legally supposed to get his hands on alcohol. Apparently, the beers had been supplied by one of his friend's parents.

From what Father Vargas shared with us, Emmitt had also suffered at least four concussions during his varsity football career. He played middle linebacker and fullback. He was his team's hammer. With his size and propensity for being physical, he was groomed at a very young age to be the headhunter. The one who made players on the other team withdraw their arms, or duck their heads, or simply run the other way.

He was fearless. He was fully prepared to give up his body for the team. But what coaches didn't know—or maybe didn't care to know—was that he was doing permanent damage to his brain.

The priest ultimately found Emmitt at a homeless shelter, unable to find a job after his stint in prison on the manslaughter charge. After hours of counseling, Father Vargas decided to give Emmitt a job at the church. Emmitt would often break down and cry during their conversations, tormented by the constant headaches. He never relayed any stories of the voices in his head. Nor did he ever intimate that he wanted to hurt anyone. Most of the time, in fact, he was quite the gentle giant. He received nothing but compliments from the small church staff, even the parishioners, Father Vargas said.

So, his outburst of violence shocked the priest, although we all acknowledged that if he'd wanted to harm Rose, or even me, he could have done so with very little effort.

Emmitt had been put in a strait jacket and taken to the local state mental hospital. As they drove him away, I told Stan, Moreno, and Father Vargas what Emmitt had shared with me. How he claimed to have had nothing to do with the murder of the girls in the sanctuary.

A day had passed since then, and while my leg was sore, I was able to walk on it. More importantly, Stan had been able to confirm that Emmitt had a solid alibi during the time the girls were murdered. He'd accompanied his brother and sister-in-law to go watch their daughter perform in her school play. He'd stayed over at his brother's house that night.

Stan, with the help of his colleagues at SAPD, had identified the two dead girls. One sixteen, the other seventeen. The blonde and younger of the two attended a public high school in Medina County. The older girl was enrolled in a private school in San Marcos. As of now, no one knew if they had been friends or had ever crossed paths, or how they had ended up in a San Antonio church that was also considered a historic landmark. And most importantly, law enforcement officials had yet to find any evidence that narrowed the suspect pool to a workable number.

"We still have hope the ME's report will give us something to go on," Stan had told me on the phone just before I'd hopped out of my car at the Romero household.

I leaned against the brick wall, relieving some of the stress on my wound. "Weren't they supposed to meet us here ten minutes ago?"

Cristina nodded and smiled and kept texting. Did she even hear me?

"How long has it been since you punched the doorbell?" She mumbled something, and I snatched the phone out of her hands.

"Hey, that's mine," she said, instantly sounding like she was five and someone had just taken her Legos.

"Just looking for a response." I handed it back.

"Yes, and five minutes ago?"

I turned my head. "Huh?"

"You think I wasn't listening. Yes, they were supposed to meet us here ten minutes ago. And I last punched the doorbell five minutes ago." She looked at her phone again. "Check that. Six minutes ago."

Just then, the front door opened, and Consuela appeared out of the darkness. Her face was so puffy I could barely make out her brown eyes.

Seventeen

I shot a glance at Cristina, then turned back to Consuela. She had two creases swooping across her face. "We didn't see you come home," I said.

"I...I fell asleep. I came home early from work, and I got online and continued reaching out to people, trying to see if anyone had any information about Mia." She pushed a lock of hair out of her face, but it didn't come close to reining in all of her crazy hair. "No one had any information, and I got upset, found it hard to breathe. So I took a pain pill." She turned and mumbled something, pointing inside.

"Is this a bad time?"

"No...no." She turned around so quickly she had to grab hold of the door to keep from falling. "Finding Mia is the priority, no matter how I feel." She pressed her fingers into the corners of her eyes. "Please, please come in."

We padded into the small foyer and paused a moment. The home was sparsely decorated, but with all the necessities. A plaid-covered couch and chair took up most of the space in a small living area. The kitchen was compact, with a basic fridge, a toaster, yellow counters, and a small dining table. One hallway went off to the right.

"I'll fix some coffee to help me wake up."

She walked three steps and grabbed hold of the couch, then wobbled a bit as she made it to the counter in the kitchen. She looked like a toddler learning how to walk. Cristina gave me one of those doubtful looks, as if she wondered if Consuela had taken more than just a pain pill.

"Can I make either of you a cup?" Consuela said from the kitchen.

"We're good," I said.

"Raul should be home shortly. Trying to fit in work at the same time we're searching for Mia has been trying on both of us."

"I wish it was different, Consuela. I'm sorry you're not comfortable in going to the police. Any chance of you and Raul reconsidering?"

She turned for a moment. "I don't think so. Raul isn't very trusting right now. We've heard so many stories of good, hard-working friends being picked up at their work, like a construction site, and being carted off, sent back across the border, separated from their families. We can't take that chance."

I planned to make another attempt at convincing Raul to go to the police once he got home, although he seemed more paranoid than Consuela.

As she made her coffee, we moved into the kitchen area. The unpainted and unfinished wooden table was covered with flyers of Mia. Since this was still a grassroots effort, I wondered how they were managing the information that was coming in. "When we spoke earlier this morning, you said you and Raul had received somewhere in the neighborhood of twenty calls."

"Twenty-two as of this morning at seven. Now…" She sipped her coffee and shuffled to her right, ran a finger down a legal pad. "Now, we're up to twenty-seven."

"How does that work?" Cristina asked, dropping her phone hand to her side. I wondered why she didn't put the damn thing away. It seemed like she valued that phone more than anything in her life. I knew it was a connection to her friends, but still… What about her music? She used to be into playing her guitar, performing at small venues. Maybe that was a trend that had come and gone.

"How does *what* work?" Consuela asked, a hint of annoyance in her voice.

"So the number on the flyer is your home number. But how do you know when someone calls if you're not here?"

"We have an answering machine. I dropped by in between two of the homes I clean and checked messages. Raul isn't allowed to leave his work. It's not a perfect system, but it's the best we can do."

"Hmm." Cristina walked over and picked up the home phone. "Maybe I can make this work a little more efficiently for you. Can I take a look at your cell phone?" Consuela grabbed her purse off a kitchen chair, pulled out her phone, and handed it to Cristina, who quickly went to work.

Consuela shuffled closer to me, downing the coffee in quick order. She seemed more lucid. "You said earlier that you had information about these two other crimes, the one at Mia's school and the one at the church. Two girls were actually…?" She looked off, took a hard swallow.

I gave her the limited information I had. "But the SAPD is still hoping the full report from the medical examiner will turn up a solid lead." What I didn't share was that I'd spent a good portion of the day studying up on Satanism. There had been no evidence at the church that connected the murdered girls to anything related to devil worshipping. But I couldn't get past how similar the two crime scenes were, as well as the fact that both crimes occurred during the same basic window of time.

A thought hit me. Was there a chance that the same person could have committed both crimes? On some levels, the premise didn't work. One had created a makeshift altar, sacrificed animals, and purposely left a symbol that emphatically connected the killings to Satanism. The double homicide at the church didn't go there. Still, though, could someone be playing games, maybe just to keep investigators guessing? Possible, but the more I thought about the idea of one person committing both crimes, it seemed like a stretch.

Maybe the perpetrators knew each other. Or maybe they're rivals. That theory held my thoughts for an extra moment. I'd originally believed that the perps who sacrificed the animals at the field house were high school kids. It was still possible, of course. At the same time, how many adults and teens interacted online through video games? It wasn't my scene, but I knew online gaming was practically an obsession. "What are you thinking about?" Consuela said, shaking me out of my daze.

"A few things. Nothing solid."

She then asked about what I'd witnessed at the high school. As I updated her, I realized we'd yet to hear back from Principal Peterson on the video footage. I would contact him or Stan right after we left the Romeros' home.

"Killing animals, devil worshipping symbols. I'm not naïve. I know this kind of thing happens, but here, at Mia's high school? If she wasn't missing, I'd still be upset." She glanced down at the flyers, then shifted her eyes back to me. "Do you think Mia's disappearance is somehow connected to the sacrifices at the high school?"

"I've wondered the same thing. But it's just a guess right now." I explained how the principal was looking through the video footage.

"What the hell is taking him so long?"

"I can't argue that. I'll be making some calls after we leave here."

As she poured herself another cup of coffee, I sent a text to Stan asking if he'd received feedback from Principal Peterson yet.

"Well, I know your time is valuable," Consuela said. "I know you want to take a look around Mia's room. Let me take you there."

I waved my hand to get Cristina's attention. She was still fiddling with the two phones, but looked up and said, "I'll be right behind you."

Consuela led the way down the hall. It was dark. The light bulb on the side of the wall was either not working or just not on. The carpet under my shoes was frayed, and I saw at least a couple of holes in the wall along our path. Just before the end of the hallway, there was a closed door with a poster of a motorcycle on it. I pointed at the room.

"That's Daniel's room." She sighed, placed her hand on the door. "We've yet to go through his things. Every time we think about it, we delay it a little longer. And now…" She flipped around to the last door on the left. "Mia." That was all she said. Nothing else was needed. Her torment was obvious, like a thousand-pound weight.

She pushed open Mia's door. My eyes did a double take. Her room was full of color. Pinks and purples mostly. My eyes were drawn to a shelf full of trophies and medals. Photographs attached with a string were affixed to the wall above her bed, strung at least fifteen feet. I moved closer. "This is Mia," I said just above a whisper.

"And her friends, yes." She paused a moment. "She's so unique. Most girls have the same group of friends throughout high school. Mia doesn't. I mean, she's friendly with everyone, but her core friends have changed over time. I guess it just shows how confident she is."

Cristina ambled into the room. "Nice setup," she said, nodding. Then she handed Consuela her phone. "Every time you get a call on your home line, it will call your cell phone." She then explained to Consuela how to add Raul's phone to the group.

"Thank you, Cristina. This is very helpful."

"Sure thing. I also set up a group text with you, Raul, me, and Ivy. If you get any clues that you think are valid, just fire off a text to us, and then we'll contact the person who gave you the tip."

"Wonderful." She took in a deep breath, but one that had little energy to it. "I'll leave both of you in here to look around. Nothing is off limits. I'm going to jump on my computer and see if anyone has offered further information online."

She disappeared, and I went back to the pictures on the wall, shuffling across the room. "Interesting."

"What?" Cristina asked, moving up next to me.

"So this is basically a chronology of friends and events of Mia's life in high school. But I don't see a single picture of a guy. Which means no pictures of her boyfriend."

I looked at Cristina, who was back on her phone, texting and grinning.

"This is kind of important, you know," I said to get her attention. She kept her head down, her thumbs peppering her phone screen. "We could learn something here. Maybe we already have."

She finally lifted her eyes. "I see two options. Either Mia was lying about having a boyfriend, or they had one ugly breakup."

Eighteen

Now that I finally had Cristina's attention—or rather, she had mine—I tested each theory. "Okay, so let's suppose she was lying about having a boyfriend."

Cristina held up her phone hand. "Let's remember, the only people who confirmed she had a boyfriend were her parents."

"True," I said, tapping my finger against my chin. "That's something we should be able to verify if we can talk to any of her classmates." I lifted both eyebrows.

"You want me to do that?"

"I guess I could go to the principal and ask if he could bring a few of her friends to the office and I could quiz them there."

"I thought you said that guy was kind of a prick."

"Not kind of. He just is."

She smirked. "You do something like that, and word will get out all over the school that you're snooping. You'll either start getting the fringe offering up crazy conspiracy theories, or people will just go mute. If there's anything going on that's connected to Mia's disappearance, then we might never find out. Not quickly anyway. And doesn't Stan always say that the longer someone is missing, the chances at finding them alive drop like a dead weight?"

I glanced at the door. "Keep it down, will you? And tell me you didn't purposely try to use that distasteful pun."

She shrugged. "I'm a teenager. Sometimes I say shit I don't mean. What can I say?"

I arched a single eyebrow.

"At least I admit it when I screw up."

"Okay, so it sounds like you're actually agreeing that you're the best person to reach out and try to locate a friend of Mia's. Someone that Consuela and Raul may not know."

She swiveled her phone between her finger and thumb. I kept thinking it would slip out of her hand and drop to the floor. She seemed unfazed by the potential risk of ruining an expensive gadget. "I've already been asking around…in a casual way, where no one would notice."

"Any leads?"

"Nope."

"Any weird rumors about whether she left on her own, or if someone took her?"

"Nope."

"Have you interacted with anyone who claimed to know her?"

"Uh…maybe."

I folded my arms across my chest. "And when were you going to tell me about this connection?"

She mimicked my folded-arms act. So sassy. "The minute I verify this person actually knows Mia."

I gestured toward the phone. "What are you waiting on? Verify away."

"Look, Ivy, I know we just said that time is uber important, but I can't walk in and start swinging a baseball bat…virtually, of course."

"Yeah, I get it. How long do you think it will take you?"

"Well, this one person I met in a chat room last night…she doesn't use her real name, of course. Her online name is NSBitch."

"I'm sure her parents are proud," I said, rolling my eyes.

"I'm sure her parents have no clue she uses that name. And we want to make sure she doesn't think I'm affiliated with anyone of that type."

I turned my head.

"You know, old parent types, like you."

I shook off her categorization. "NS. Wonder what that's all about."

"Probably her initials."

"I bet we could get a school directory without too much effort. Maybe we could ask Stan to do a favor for us. I don't know. He's pretty damn busy with that double homicide investigation."

Cristina shook her head. "Doesn't she know," she said, pointing a finger down the hall, "that they're making it ten times more difficult by not going to the cops?"

"They're afraid, Cristina. And as much as I'd like to convince them, I don't think they're going to change their minds."

"All they have to do is file a missing-persons report, or whatever you want to call it."

I held out my hands to signal for her to take it down a notch. "We're lucky that Stan is helping us out. And now that there's been a crime committed on school grounds, he has another reason to be there."

Cristina began to look around the room, opening Mia's desk drawer, searching through books on her bookcase. I fired off another text to Stan, asking if he could pick up a school directory the next time he was at the school.

Before I'd even put my phone away, I received a response.

Not much time to focus on school crime. Taking late jog, then going to ME's office to review final report. He expedited the request.

I curled my lip, assessing the good news/bad news. Good to see at least some progress and focus on the murders of the girls at the church. But the animal sacrifice and Mia's disappearance seemed to be taking a back seat.

I thought about another avenue and thumbed a quick text back to Stan. But before I hit send, I paused. What if he didn't agree with my idea, for whatever reason? Then I would have used my best card—maybe my only card. I deleted the text. "Better to ask for forgiveness than ask for permission," I whispered aloud.

"Where did that come from?" Cristina asked, as she thumbed through a book.

"Nowhere."

"I like it. I might have to use that sometime with ECHO business."

I silently cursed myself as I made my way over to Mia's nightstand. It wasn't full of disorganized junk. She had a basic clock radio, a couple of bracelets, three hair barrettes—yellow, pink, and purple—and a stack of index cards. I picked them up and read the first one. "Big Rules for Basketball" was the title at the top. There were six so-named rules under the title, finishing with "Keep butt down on defense—don't take the fakes."

Sounded like she really knew the game, which made sense if she was the captain of the team. I moved on to the second index card. "Big Rules for Physics" was the title of this one. Sifting through the remaining cards, I found similar Big Rules for not only every class, but every important topic a teenage girl might have in her life: Big Rules for Being a Leader, Big Rules for National Honor Society, Big Rules for Staying Positive.

This girl was amazing. It was like I'd stumbled upon a cheat sheet on how a teenage girl should approach life. I found two more cards. Big Rules for SAT. It had only one rule and it was written in all caps—STUDY LIKE YOU'RE GOING TO COLLEGE.

"Check this out, Cristina," I said, holding up the card so she could see it. She'd just opened the top drawer to Mia's dresser.

She turned in my direction. "I can't see it."

"It says, STUDY LIKE YOU'RE GOING TO COLLEGE."

"I can't hear you."

She was bullshitting me. It was difficult enough to get her back into high school. Asking her to think about college, apparently, was like asking her when she planned to travel to Mars.

I changed the topic. "By the way, all your texting earlier. Was that to—"

"Yes, to Leo, *Mom*." I had a feeling. But what I wasn't sure of was the nature of their relationship. Had they reached the boyfriend-girlfriend status, or was it more of Cristina having a crush and Leo keeping her at arm's length? It was difficult to imagine anything other than the latter. Not that Cristina didn't have plenty to offer…at least to a boy who was closer to her age. Leo was twenty-one. In Hollywood terms, that put him almost at middle age.

I couldn't help myself. "Are you planning on dating guys who are in your generation?"

She froze for a second, then slowly turned to look at me. "You can't help yourself, can you? Always trying to be my mom."

"Sorry, I shouldn't have said it." At least I was quick to back off.

"Sheesh," she said, riffling through the dresser drawer. "By the way, just so I don't get the third degree here in a couple of days, Leo and I are setting up plans for the weekend."

"Plans," I repeated. At least she hadn't used the term "quickie," like she had when talking about the last time he flew in from LA.

"Yeah, he's saying he has some big news to share. Something he wants to ask me."

We turned our heads to look at each other at the same time, but I somehow managed to stay quiet.

"You want to say something, I can tell."

"What can I say…good luck?"

"Why are you saying that?"

I pretended to lock my lips and toss the key aside.

"And now you clam up." She paused a second, then giggled. "You don't think he's going to ask me to—" She stopped short.

"To take you to a Spurs game? It's possible."

"Funny." She went back to looking through the dresser drawers, and I finally got to the last index card: Big Rules for Boyfriends. Again, there was only one rule, and this one made the hair on the back of my neck go straight. It said, "Boys are punks. Real men are forever."

"Hey, check this out," I said, holding up the last card.

"No." Her eyes were riveted to something in her hand. "Check this shit out." She held up a piece of paper. "It's a Bible verse." I sidled up next to her to have a look as she read, "From Proverbs 12:7. An excellent wife is the crown of her husband, but she who brings shame is like rottenness in his bones."

We looked at each other. We didn't say anything or move until I realized I still held the index card in my hand. I showed it to her. We knew we had gold, but weren't sure how the two pieces of evidence were connected, or exactly how it might lead us to finding Mia.

But I knew one place I wanted to start.

Nineteen

I sat in my car, a dinged-up Honda Civic I'd aptly named Black Beauty because she was exactly not that, and tried to keep myself from staring at the front door of Lee High School. For whatever reason, I flashed back to my high school days when a friend and I had waited outside a grocery store for her older sister to bring out our stash—a six-pack of black cherry wine coolers. At the time, it felt like I was living on the edge… What if the cops came out of the grocery store instead of my friend's sister? And then from there, my imagination had hit the alarm, and I began to envision being handcuffed, put into a squad car, and locked up. All for trying to procure alcohol.

Thankfully, I'd grown up since then.

In this instance of the waiting game, I was looking for a tall redhead—Detective Brook Pressler—to waltz out of the school with vital information on helping us find Mia, or at least a step in that direction.

I redirected my attention to my cell phone and spent more time studying a couple of websites dedicated to Satanic rituals and symbols. Some of the graphics that depicted how sacrifices were carried out sent a chill up my spine. I focused on one particular picture that showed a person who was apparently already dead.

The perpetrator was using a knife to carve something into the victim's chest.

I started to touch my chest, but I stopped myself. A flood of memories was sitting at the precipice of my conscious thoughts, and this recollection was far more disturbing and painful than wine coolers. It involved torture.

I picked up my half-empty can of Diet Coke and took a sip. I tried to block out the images by focusing on happy thoughts—sharing a good laugh with Zahera, jogging with Stan, an intimate moment with Saul. But I couldn't hold off the power of evil.

Each picture hit me as if I'd been forced to touch a live wire over and over again. Chinese water torture, where I felt like I was drowning one painful drop at a time. Blaring music that made my skin crawl, playing for hours on end. A room of all white, making me believe there was no floor, no walls, only a white expanse of nothingness. A video loop of gruesome acts of torture…watching real people die while the perpetrators laughed about it. Snakes, bamboo torture, a guillotine. On and on it went. Milton Weber would haunt me until I died.

My entire body tensed. I could hear the crackle of the metal can in my hand as I started to put more and more pressure on it, but it couldn't match the pressure in my mind. I was stuck in this mental replay, and I couldn't stop it. I was suddenly powerless. And that scared the shit out of me.

I flinched, then realized someone was knocking on my window. I gasped, startled, and the can of Diet Coke was crushed in the grip of my hand, spilling over the side. I set it in the cup holder and used a sticky finger to roll down the window to see Brook's green eyes wide with astonishment.

"Are you okay, Ivy? I've been knocking for a good minute."

"I'm fine. It's just…" I wiped my eyes, which, of course, spread the syrupy goo to my face.

"Seriously, did you black out? Do I need to get you to an emergency room?"

"No, no. It's not that. I just have these episodes where I recall the times I was tortured."

She nodded slowly. "Milton's funhouse, when Stan had his arm…" She didn't want to say it.

"Yes, that." I swallowed back some tears, trying to keep myself from falling into an abyss of guilt for allowing my friends to be hurt by that monster.

I pushed out a few breaths, let the chilly wind hit my face. "I'm doing better now."

"What started this latest episode? I mean, you're just sitting here in the parking lot."

"The mind is a dangerous place. Well, mine is."

She gave me a straight smile. "Unfortunately, you don't own the patent on a mind that dwells on the negative. I've been there a lot after my divorce. It's all relative, though. We feel sorry for ourselves because we think no one has experienced what we have."

I looked at her without any expression.

"Okay, your situation is a little unique."

We both chuckled, and I could feel my body relax. "How'd it go with Principal Peterson?" I noticed she was holding a book against her chest.

"Painful, as you might imagine. I've been conducting interviews with his staff about the animal sacrifice in the field house."

"I guess no one has raised their hand to say they did it?"

"Hardly. But plenty of opinions of who could be involved— all the nominees are students. I have a list of about fifty kids to investigate further."

"Cool, I guess. And the video footage?"

"Nothing."

I was about to bang my head against the steering wheel. "Why?"

"Wait, I'm sorry. Not the Mia footage. I'm talking about the field house footage. There's nothing there. So it just makes my job ten times more difficult." She let out a sigh.

"That sucks. What about Mia?"

"That's where our favorite principal is dragging his feet."

"Why would he do that when a student has been missing for over two days?"

"He's still stuck on the fact that it's not an official investigation and that he's seen countless kids walk out of school and end up partying with a cousin in Louisiana."

I was about to say that he must not know Mia, but after what Cristina and I had found in her room, I wondered who really knew Mia. "But he did review the video?"

She nodded, then moved a lock of hair away from her face. "He even showed me the clip."

"And?"

"Not much there, but I did see her. She walked out of the south entrance, near the band hall. Really wasn't much to it."

"So no struggle or argument with anyone else?"

"Not many others were in the hallway at the time. I think it was close to the bell going off, from what Peterson said."

"Was she running out of the school? Did she show any signs of stress? Did you watch the video long enough to see if anyone followed her?"

"It was a non-event, but you can see for yourself." She pulled a flash drive out of her front pocket and handed it to me through the open window.

"For real? You convinced Peterson to give you this, even though he's acting like Mia's disappearance is nothing?"

She smiled so wide I saw nothing but straight, white teeth. She looked like she could be on one of those toothpaste commercials. "Peterson stepped out for a moment, and that's when a student aide popped in. He seemed a little enamored with this older woman." She buffed her nails on her sleeve. "I just asked a simple question: what would it take to get this thirty-second video clip onto a flash drive. Apparently, he thought I was asking him to do it. Next thing I know, he's handing it to me, and then he said he had to run off to his next class."

"Nice. I'll send you and Stan a video file, just so I'm not the only one with a copy."

"Sounds good." She tapped her hand on the car. "I need to head back to the station and start running checks on these fifty names. Hoping something turns up and I can bring in the punk who did this for questioning." She stepped away from the car, then flipped around and handed me the book.

"More gifts?"

"It's the yearbook. Found it in the reception area."

I fanned through some of the pages. "This is perfect. Thanks. Do I need to pay someone for it?"

"Eh, I doubt anyone will know it's missing. Hell, they don't even think Mia is really missing. But if you're feeling guilty, you can give money to the Quarterback Club."

I turned my head. "And that is?"

"Some stupid name for their football booster club." She waved and walked off.

The more I hung around Brook, the more I appreciated her.

I held up the flash drive and yearbook and allowed myself to feel a glimmer of hope. Mia might have walked out of school without anyone thinking much of it, but that didn't mean she was in control of her own destiny. My firsthand experience as both a child and adult victim told me that we can all be fooled, even if we think we're level-headed and capable of making wise decisions.

More than anything, my haunted memories reminded me why I'd started ECHO—to help kids with little or no voice. If you're being held against your will, or even worse, being tortured, every minute that passes is filled with a fear that eats away at your desire to live. And I'd do anything to keep Mia from suffering like I had.

Twenty

Over the next four hours, I received three text messages from Consuela with new tips that had come from the flyers that were all over the city. Cristina's idea was working like a charm. While sitting in the corner booth at Smoothies & Stuff—our old, unofficial ECHO office before we'd procured real space down near the MACC—I took those three tips plus the original list of twenty-seven that Consuela had on her notepad and started making phone calls. She or Raul had already attempted to contact most from the original list and had concluded there was nothing worthwhile there. A quick verification wouldn't hurt, I told myself, especially since I had a few hours to burn until my next appointment.

I sipped a healthy smoothie, adding to my pool of energy, and worked my way through the list, starting with the three most recent tips. The first sounded promising, at least initially.

"I saw a girl who looked just like that Mia person on the flyer." The woman sounded as if she were gargling pebbles, one of those raspy, smokers' voices. "In the corner drugstore at Laredo and Brazos."

I sat a little taller. "When was this? Who was she with?"

"Late last night. About three, maybe four customers, one of whom was very rude to her."

"Customers?"

"Yeah. Looks like she was working the morning shift."

My excitement quickly waned. "Did she look like she was being held against her will?"

"Would you work retail in this day and age? It's frickin' brutal out there. This one asshole was jumping all over her because the donuts were stale. Like it's her fault."

"Are you sure the person you saw matches the picture? If so, then I'll need you to meet me at the police station so we can get the cops involved." I was lying, but it was necessary to root out the fiction-tellers.

"Eh. Now that I think about it, this girl at the drugstore was a little hippy."

"As in...?"

"You know, she had those wide, birthing hips."

The opposite of Mia. I thanked her for the call and moved on to the next person on my list. It didn't last long. He was vague about what he'd witnessed, supposedly seeing Mia at a bus stop by the Alamo. When I continued peppering him with questions, he said, "Listen, sweetie. In this day and age, information is worth something. Dinero, if you know what I mean. So, I'll turn over everything I know—and believe me, it's some juicy stuff—for five thousand bucks." In the background, I heard a bell ringing and dogs barking.

"Are you at the track?" He hung up before I could ask another question, which would have been, "Are you trying to extort money to pay off your gambling debt?" I tried not to waste any more emotional energy, and I forged ahead.

The third call was a 1-888 number. I was a sucker and called the number and instantly regretted it. The solicitor tried to convince me that the world would stop spinning if I didn't purchase life insurance. I hung up in the middle of his sales pitch.

I plowed through the other twenty-seven calls. Many of the tipsters seemed to have good intentions, but their stories were a stretch. Still, I made notes of four possible locations where Mia had been seen, all in different parts of the city. I opened up the map app on my laptop and plotted out the locations. In doing so, I recognized something that I should have realized about thirty-six hours earlier—she could be anywhere in the state of Texas, which, from my history class back in the day, I knew was over a quarter million square miles. Whoever had her—and yes, that was where my mind was going—could have easily gotten lost in a neighboring state. And who was to say she hadn't been smuggled across the Mexican border? I'd read stories of girls being traded to drug cartel leaders in exchange for paying off debt.

I could feel my gut tighten into a knot. I wasn't naïve. Finding a missing girl wasn't easy, even when law enforcement was fully engaged. The Romeros had done an admirable job of circulating Mia's picture in the San Antonio area, but that didn't come close to matching the resources of spreading the word across all police departments in the state. I'd seen multiple reports about Amber Alerts, where the kid and their abductor were found within a few hours.

But to make our odds even worse, we had no specific clues as to her whereabouts. And certainly nothing as solid as a make and model of a car.

I plugged the flash drive that Brook had given me into the USB port of my laptop. I located the .mov file and opened it up. It was thirty-two seconds long. I clicked play. The video was in color, but not the highest quality. Every couple of seconds, the picture would flicker, but I could follow it. As Brook had pointed out, it was rather uneventful. Just a handful of kids loitering in the hall. Then a few started moving toward the right part of the screen, away from the exit door I could see on the far left.

"There she is," I murmured. Mia moved in from the right part of the screen. She had on black jeans with holes near the knees— the kind that were made that way—and a burgundy shirt and gray sweater. She was holding a binder, very typical for a high school kid. Her hair was similar to the picture her mother had given me, shoulder length, some natural curl, with two locks pulled to the back of her head.

Her pace was even, nothing rushed. By the time she made it to the left side of the screen, no other kids were visible. She put a hand on the exit door, turned to look over her shoulder, and then disappeared.

I leaned back, put a hand to my chin, and pondered if there was any significance in what I'd just seen. I clicked replay and watched it all the way through again. This time, I clicked pause just before she reached the door.

"Her hand is moving to the top of her shirt," I whispered to myself. I clicked play again and closely watched her hand movement as she turned to look over her shoulder.

"That could be something." My eyes, anyone's eyes, would normally be drawn to her head turning to look back into the school. It seemed obvious that she didn't want anyone to see her leave. But I focused on her hand. I replayed the clip another three times to verify what I thought I saw. She was pulling a necklace out from under her shirt.

No big deal, right? But my mind didn't think that way. Why was it under her shirt? She could have simply forgotten to pull it out from her shirt when she dressed earlier that morning. Possible. But I doubted that notion. She seemed to be the type of girl who was very conscientious about the clothes she wore, how everything had to be *just so* to give off the right vibe. Of course, that didn't exactly set her apart from most girls her age.

Think about all of those index cards with the Big Rules, Ivy.

Mia might come across to her parents, and even all of her classmates, as easygoing, cheerful and pleasant, but something told me that she was actually a high-strung person. The index cards, to me, didn't come across as reminders to complete certain tasks, but more as a reminder on how to stay in character. Her life was all a fabrication. A performance of sorts. But to achieve what goal? To simply be accepted?

Back to the video and her necklace. Something told me she had been hiding it. She wanted no one at school to see it. But, apparently, she wanted it in full view when she walked out. She must have been planning to meet someone.

A thought came to mind. And I knew I needed another favor from my favorite SAPD detective.

Twenty-One

Leaning against a red pickup, which probably didn't have more than five thousand miles on it, in the Lee High School student parking lot, I waited for the final bell of the day to ring. My phone buzzed, and I looked down to see that Cristina has responded to my text.

Sup?

Three letters was all she could manage? I know I sounded like I was eighty-eight instead of twenty-eight, but this whole texting business just seemed to be burning brain cells at an alarming rate. Yet…here I was, engaging in a text conversation so I could do multiple things at one time—wait on another text reply from Stan, hope that I had the owner of this red pickup figured out, research, survey, rinse and repeat. I'd also spent a few minutes looking through all the names to see if I could find a girl with the initials of NS. I'd made it through the two oldest grades and, astonishingly, found no one with those initials. Perhaps the person known as NSBitch was younger. Or maybe those weren't her initials at all.

I tapped a response back to Cristina.

Any progress with your friend?

She shot back another text before I could blink.

Which friend? I'm working a lot of angles.

Hmm. I didn't know about her numerous angles.

NSBitch. Isn't she the one who you think might know more about Mia?

Cristina: *I'm pretty certain.*

Me: *How certain?*

Cristina: *Do you want to know the odds or something? I should know in about an hour.*

Me: *What's the plan?*

Cristina: *I convinced her to meet me at the MACC. A lot of shit going on in her life. So, I'm kinda acting like her big sister.*

I would have chuckled had she been right there next to me. And the whole "Lol" response would have been lame—I didn't want to draw her snobby, cool, teenage wrath.

Me: *I'll meet you at the MACC.*

I counted to three, knowing she'd respond quickly. I reached two.

Cristina: *Please don't. I don't want to scare her off.*

Me: *Don't worry. The MACC is huge. She won't know I'm there. I'll visit with Dr. Amaya until you're done. Then, we need to talk through everything we've learned today. Gotta run.*

I looked up to see a flood of students invading the parking lot. I put a few feet between me and the truck and tried to look nonchalant. I wasn't sure what to do with myself, so I put the phone to my ear and pretended to be in a conversation while casually pacing. Out of the corner of my eye, I saw two guys moving in my direction. One was tall, lean, had blue eyes that could have been seen from the moon. Brandon McCarthy, Mia's ex-boyfriend, looked just like his picture from the yearbook.

"I'll tell you what, motherfucker, ain't no way in hell I'm going to practice today. That motherfucker can suck my—" He stopped midsentence. I was pretty sure he saw me, but he just continued heading to the driver's side door. His buddy, a shorter kid with glasses, continued walking past the truck. I assumed he was parked in another row.

I felt Brandon's eyes on me, so I said into the phone, "As an insurance company, we're not in the business of giving away money just because someone files a claim. Yeah, I get what you're saying, but tell your adjuster to reverse his decision."

I heard an electronic chirp—he'd unlocked the doors to his pickup. I quickly shuffled over, pulled open the passenger door, and dropped into the leather seat. Brandon was halfway in the pickup when I saw his eyes practically pop out of his head. He got in and held up both hands.

"I didn't mean no harm when I filed that claim. Some kid hit me, and that's the God's honest truth."

Who would have thought he'd tried to commit insurance fraud? "I don't work for your insurance company."

"Who do you work for then?"

"I don't work for any insurance company."

He looked out the front windshield as if he were still trying to piece it all together. He swiveled his head to me. "Who are you? What are you doing in my truck?"

"I have a few questions for you, Brandon."

His eyes scanned me, then he took a swallow. "What kind of questions?"

"Just a—"

"It doesn't matter. I don't know you. You're obviously not a cop, so I don't have to answer any questions. I know my rights. So get the hell out of my pickup," he said, flicking his wrist at me like I was a pest.

I supposed I was. But this pest wasn't easily scared off. "I'm not going to leave until you answer my questions."

He looked out the window, his brow furrowed. "Listen, lady, you're, uh, making people look at me. Just get out. Now."

The boom of his voice rattled inside the small compartment, but I kept my composure. "You can yell and scream like a two-year-old, but I'm not going away."

He squeezed the steering wheel and grunted. "You're invading my privacy. It's completely within my rights to come over there and throw your ass out."

He was trying to convince himself, but I'd brought along a little insurance policy of my own. I made sure he had my gaze, then I lowered my sights to my purse sitting on my lap. I tapped the side, hoping he could see the outline of the Luger LC9s.

I could practically see the air leave his body. "Okay," he said steadily. "I'll answer your damn questions, but can I meet you somewhere?"

He thought he could pull a fast one on me. What a punk. "Drive."

"What?"

"If you don't want to be seen with me, just drive."

He huffed out a breath, didn't say a word. He pulled to the edge of the parking lot and turned right. "Okay, go ahead with your stupid questions."

Twenty-Two

The muffler rumbled as he increased his speed.

"We're in a school zone, you know."

"You sound like my damn mother," he said, lifting his foot off the gas.

Cristina would have said the same thing. She didn't have her license yet. Up until a few months ago, she wasn't sure where she was sleeping on any particular night. Eventually, she'd want to take that next step. San Antonio wasn't Boston or Chicago, where rapid transit was a way of life. For now, though, she could use her skateboard or bike. Maybe I'd hire someone to teach her how to drive. Otherwise, I wasn't sure our professional relationship could survive.

A car drove by, honking its horn. Two girls leaned out the side windows and waved at Brandon. He responded with a quick wave.

"You're rather popular," I said.

"I hold my own."

He made it sound like popularity was a sport, and one that he intended to be successful at. "Do you play football?"

"I'm on the team, yep."

That seemed like a loaded response. "On the team, but you're blowing off practice."

"Yep."

He kept his eyes on the road, then he turned to see me looking at him. "Do you work for Coach Rossi? Did he hire you to follow

me around, to babysit me?" He started to laugh, but it was the kind
of machine-gun laugh that made him sound like he was about to
lose it. "Oh, please tell me that you work for Coach Rossi. That
motherfucker…I'll drive back to school, walk out on the practice
field, and tell him to go straight to hell."

His bravado was quite impressive. And likely a load of crap.
"First of all, I don't work for your football coach or anyone
associated with the football program or the high school. So relax."

"Yeah, whatever. If you were me, lady, you would have
thought the same thing."

He had a major attitude toward his coach. Again, typical
teenage stuff. Although his grudge seemed like it had roots that
went on for miles. What I found most intriguing was that his
thoughts didn't go straight to Mia, a girl who'd been missing for
two-plus days.

"I'm not really into the drama around your football team. I'm
more concerned with finding a girl you might know, Mia
Romero."

He shot me a quick glance before executing a right turn. We
found ourselves in another school zone in bumper-to-bumper
traffic. He was forced to drive ten miles per hour.

"So are you some kind of private detective hired by her
parents?" He'd already lost some of the steel in his voice.

"Yes. Do you know where she is?"

"How would I know?"

"You two were a couple, right?"

"Sure, I guess."

"I guess? The way I understood it, you were boyfriend and
girlfriend. Is that different than how you remember it?"

"No," he said with a sigh. "But that doesn't mean anything. I
have no idea where she is."

He'd already settled into a defensive posture. I needed him to open up, not close down. I changed my approach. "Her parents are extremely upset. I guess you know what happened to her brother, Daniel."

"Yeah," he said. "Kind of sucks."

"Did Mia talk much about Daniel?"

"Not really. She didn't want to get all sad and everything. But I could tell it was tough on her."

"Did you help her during those times when she was upset?"

"I suppose. I'm not really good at that stuff. But we talked some, yeah."

We'd made our way through the school zone, and he increased his speed, but only to thirty-five. He steered with one hand, scratched his chin with the other.

"Mia's parents—"

"I know, I know. They're upset. I get it."

"Actually, I was going to say that they really liked you a lot. Thought you were good to Mia." I got the feeling that Raul had a stronger positive feeling about Brandon than Consuela did, but that could be because Raul might have looked at Brandon as a replacement for his son. Not completely, but at least in sharing common interests, as in sports and caring for Mia.

He shifted in his seat. I couldn't determine if that was normal for him or if he was uncomfortable with the discussion. "I guess that's cool and all."

"Something wrong?"

"No, it's just that we broke up, and you know, I've moved on. So has she. Her parents were cool."

He paused, and I waited for him to continue. When he didn't, I asked, "Was it an amicable breakup?"

"Are you asking me if we had a big blow-up or something and that's what ended it?"

I tried not to roll my eyes. "Yeah, that's what I'm asking."

He cleared his throat. "We were cool. We agreed to be…" He paused, using his finger to form quotes. "Friends."

"Why do you phrase it that way?"

"I mean, that's what most people say, right? But it's awkward. And you know, like every couple, we had our issues."

"Yeah, we're all human. If two people spend enough time together, then after a while you realize that thing you like about your partner is also the thing that bugs you." I couldn't say where that insight came from. Had I subconsciously thrown in my feelings about Saul? Doubtful. I didn't have any hidden issues with him. At least none that I'd uncovered thus far.

"I mean, yeah…" He scratched his chin again. "Mia and I weren't perfect. She was hot and all, but we argued like normal people."

Hot and all. Why had I thought he would be any different than most teenage boys? Maybe I was hoping that Mia's parents really knew him. Apparently, they'd been snowed. But I still hadn't been able to determine if that meant he had anything to do with her disappearance.

I continued the good-cop approach…for now. "Yeah, I've been dating this guy for a while, and sometimes, you know, we just lose it on each other. Gets kind of ugly." This was a complete fabrication, of course. Saul and I, to a degree, were so amiable it was almost too good to believe. I was sure eventually there would be something about him that would annoy me to high hell. For now, it was smooth sailing, at least as long as we kept our relationship in this committed-but-refuse-to-put-a-label-on-it mode.

"Fuckin' A," he said, with a slight chuckle. "I mean, Mia was cool and all, but she was kind of a nag. 'Dress this way. Put your arm around me this way. Dance with me this way,'" he said in a whiny voice, obviously trying to imitate Mia. "And what did I get in return? Nothing. She didn't even put out for me."

Again, I tried not to roll my eyes or, better yet, backhand him across his smug face. I had to keep up the act, hoping he'd give me something to go on. "Yeah, well, we can't always get what we want." I almost chuckled, hearing myself quoting the Rolling Stones song. It was, nonetheless, applicable.

We drove another mile in silence. Then, finally, he said, "I don't know your name."

I turned to him. "Ivy Nash."

"Ivy. Strange name."

"I've been told."

"And Mia's parents are paying you? I didn't think they had much money."

I looked around his truck, noticing all of the bells and whistles you might see on the vehicle of someone who'd worked his way up the corporate ladder. But Brandon was only seventeen or eighteen, and here he was. He'd arrived, or so he probably thought.

"They don't have a lot of money, Brandon. But they can't find their daughter, and they're absolutely distraught. I'm sure you've seen the flyers around town."

Just then, we reached an intersection. Stapled to the electric pole was a picture of Mia. "They're everywhere," he said, his eyes staying on the flyer for an extra second.

"Do you still care about Mia?"

He pulled away from the stop sign. I could see we'd made a giant loop around the school and were nearing the entrance. He pulled in and stopped in the front parking lot where the administrators and teachers parked. "What's that supposed to mean?"

He was back to being defensive, but I still couldn't get a bead on his motivation. "It's a pretty straightforward question, don't you think?"

"She's cool, I guess. It's just that, you know, we had our issues, like you said earlier."

"Brandon, she's been missing for two-plus days." I let that linger a bit. He looked out his window. Did he get distracted by a squirrel, or was he pondering whether or not to tell me more?

Teachers were starting to walk into the parking lot. A couple of them glanced in our direction. Brandon didn't seem to care or maybe just didn't notice, lost in his own thoughts. Who knew?

I decided to work on his oversized ego. "What position do you play on the football team?"

He flipped around to look at me. "Why do you want to go there?"

"Just humor me."

"Quarterback. Why?"

"That's a leadership position."

"And your point is?"

"Kids, your teammates, they all probably look up to you."

"Eh. Some do. But others don't like me skipping practice. They think I'm a rebel."

"So you think you're just a conscientious objector?"

"What the fuck is that?"

I tried not to smile. "Whatever you're doing by skipping practice, you think it's a justifiable cause. You're doing it to make a point, not just be a rebel."

"Now you're reading me," he said with a half-smile.

"Like I said before, I'm not really into the political issues with your team. But my point is, if you wanted to find out about something that's going on at the school, you probably have a lot of different people who will listen to you. Am I right?"

"Maybe." He looked off, scratching his chin yet again. I slid my business card out of the side pocket of my purse and handed it to him.

"ECHO. Sounds like some type of ghost-hunting company." He tried to chuckle but never quite got there.

"My number is on the card. Call me, text me. If you find out anything about Mia, even if it's a rumor, let me know, okay?"

He flapped the edge of the card against his few whiskers. "Yeah, for sure. I can do that." He tossed the card toward the center tray, which was full of junk. The card fell to the floorboard. He picked it up and shoved it in the tray. When he did, my eyes were drawn to the chain of a necklace and what looked like the edge of a pendant. I felt a click in my breath.

He shuffled the stuff around in the tray, as if he were trying to keep the necklace or the pendant concealed. I tried not to stare.

"Is that all? I think I need to go check in with the coaches. Or maybe I'll just head home and get started on my homework."

I pulled on the door handle and stuck a foot out. "Just remember, Brandon. I don't care about all of the petty school stuff. Mia's life could be in danger. And if you put some effort into it, I think you can help her."

He shrugged. "I'm no Five-O, but I'll ask around." He motioned for me to close the door. I did and he sped away, not toward the back of the school where football practice was being held, but instead toward the parking lot exit. And, as if he were trying to make a statement, he punched the gas as he turned onto the road and laid some rubber.

Twenty-Three

$\mathbf{F}$rom where I was standing next to the glass door of Dr. Amaya's office—one that was framed in purple, the dominant color throughout the MACC—I could see Cristina crumpled into a bean bag chair, her eyes focused on her cell phone as she thumbed in letters faster than any human I'd seen. She and I had already given each other the not-so-subtle head nod that signified we'd seen each other. But I knew not to approach her, in case NSBitch was one of the dozens of kids roaming around the community center. We didn't want to scare off a potential source of information on Mia.

I peeked at my phone for about the tenth time in the last five minutes. My screen was blank, and I let out an exasperated breath. I'd sent a text to Stan and then decided to send one to Brook too—trying to work both sides of the coin, so to speak. I was desperate to get some movement on Mia's disappearance and I had an idea, one that probably would have already been executed had the Romeros officially filed a report with the SAPD.

The door opened, and I had to jump out of the way so it wouldn't smack me in the arm.

"Oh, hi, Ivy," Dr. Amaya said. "So nice to see you."

The man to his left had a distinguished look. Business-casual attire—brown slacks, blue button-down shirt, and loafers. Silver tips on his sideburns. And an air about him that said he was quite confident in who he was, what he did for a living.

"I don't mean to interrupt. I was just going to pop in and say hello," I said, clasping my hands in front of me, suddenly feeling slightly underdressed in my jeans and one of my comfy but worn T-shirts.

"No worries. Clifton and I were just crunching numbers, going over some board business." The doctor tapped his mouth with his hand, feigning a yawn. "All of the stuff involved in running this place can be a little tedious. But I guess it's been worth it."

"It's been a huge success, Doctor," I said. "Because of your generosity, your vision, the MACC—uh, the Mandy Amaya Community Center—has become a great place for kids of all ages to come have some fun."

"By the way, I'm fine with calling it the MACC. I can see Mandy smiling every time someone uses that term. And, frankly, this place has grown so much, I can't begin to keep it all going on my own." He did a double take as the third person in our space gave me a tight-lipped smile. "I'm so out of it. You two haven't met?"

I shook my head.

Dr. Amaya introduced me to Clifton Hines. I was ready for him to end his name with "the third," using some type of snobby British accent, but he stopped at Hines. Clifton stepped forward. He kept his eyes on mine, and we shook hands. A smile played on my lips as I imagined Cristina whispering in my ear, *"Does he have a son named Duncan?"* As in the cake mix company.

Now I was starting to think like Cristina. That was worrisome.

"Did I miss the joke?" Clifton said with a self-deprecating smile.

"Oh, it's nothing. I'm just thinking about someone I know." I could feel my face reddening. *Busted!* We made small talk for another minute or two, then Clifton said he needed to run.

"I can walk out with you if you're leaving, Ivy," Clifton said, removing a key fob from his pocket. It had a logo on it that looked familiar, but not familiar enough to where I'd know the name.

"Oh, I need to stick around. I have a little bit of business to get done myself."

"Is Cristina around here somewhere?" Dr. Amaya craned his neck. I didn't want to draw attention to her specific location, in case she was speaking with the NSBitch person.

"She's around here somewhere. She might be in the skateboarding room." They had this cool room that had risers and benches and other obstacles for experienced skateboarders.

"What business are you in, Ivy?"

"She's a private investigator," Dr. Amaya said before I could speak. "Oh, I'm sorry for jumping in. Really, though, I have to brag on Ivy every chance I get. She's done so much for this community, for this city. Her main focus is helping kids, those who are in trouble, or simply troubled themselves."

"Wow, Ivy, that's quite an endorsement," Clifton said. "I don't hear Delmart...Dr. Amaya gush over many people or businesses like that."

I shrugged and grinned. "Dr. Amaya is my paid spokesman."

We all laughed, but I took another quick peek at my phone. Nothing. *Dammit!*

"Seriously," Clifton said, taking a couple of steps toward the exit, "you don't have a family you need to run off to? We're not exactly in the best part of town. And I think I counted three busted lights last time I was here this late."

"Oh, that's not necessary." I was flattered really. For some reason, I felt compelled to hold up my left hand and show that I wasn't wearing a ring. But then again, it wasn't like I was on the market. Saul and I were a…thing. *Why was I constantly thinking about him today, especially in these awkward moments?* "Thanks for the offer, but I can take care of myself."

"And then some," Dr. Amaya said.

Clifton waved goodbye and walked off, and then the doctor ushered me around to make sure I'd seen all the latest things at the MACC. I had, but I needed to kill some time anyway.

We stopped at a large, open room where three ping-pong tables were set up. There were probably two dozen kids in there, with three games going on, each one drawing an equal amount of attention from onlookers. "We've got a tournament going on tonight. It brings out the real competitive folks."

"Right," I said. I then noticed one of the MACC employees in the signature purple T-shirt. He was a youngish guy with a beard. Probably a college kid, although, these days, age seemed more difficult to determine. I then realized I had seen a purple shirt in every room so far. "So did something change? Seems like you have a lot more staffers milling around."

We started to walk again. "Ah, you've noticed."

I nodded.

"We've had a few instances where some kids were causing problems, bullying other kids, just being jerks. So, that's one of the things I've been working on with Clifton. Trying to find more funds so we can make sure we're adequately staffed. I want every child here to feel safe and comfortable, and still allow them to have fun."

I put a hand over my heart. "I'm really glad to hear that. I think it's important for every kid to feel safe."

We came upon a room that had the Star of David on it. "Now this is new," I said, pointing at the door.

"Believe it or not, we've found out that several kids have been ridiculed for having their own religious beliefs, so we set up some basic things for each of the religions represented in our community. One of Judaism here, then..." he walked down the row of rooms, "we have our Christian area. One room for Protestants, one for Catholics, then Islam and Hindu, and then finally Mormonism."

"And no protests so far?"

"Not a peep, thankfully. But most of the kids go to school together and understand what it's like to be in a diverse environment. So if it's not their thing, then I think most of them just look past it and find something else to do."

We waved at a couple of folks with purple shirts in the various religious rooms. "And are those people just MACC employees, or do they have some type of training in that particular religion?"

"They're volunteers from their local temples, churches, mosques, whatever. We wanted to make sure we have the right kind of people in each religious room. They gladly give their time, since they have an opportunity to interact with kids in a more relaxed setting."

"Damn, you continue to amaze me, Doctor."

He pointed at the cross on the door next to us. "You sure you should be saying that word right now?"

He had a point. We made our way back to the center part of the building. I saw a girl talking to Cristina, and I stopped in my tracks.

"You look like you've seen a ghost," the doctor said.

"Uh, no...I just—" My thoughts were interrupted by the buzz of my phone. It was a text from Stan asking me what was up. I excused myself and stepped away from the doctor to call Stan.

Twenty-Four

Stan let out an exhaustive breath. "And you have a favor you want to ask."

"Oh, I assumed it was, more or less, implied." I tried a lighthearted giggle, but it came out more like a snort. Silence, and then a sudden thud.

"What was that?" I asked.

"The two-by-four that's attached to my stub. I'm actually working from home. Bev helped me set up a home office so I could be closer to her and Ethan at night when I have extra work to do and I don't have to be in the office. I'm a little out of my element, which means I move around with the grace of a dinosaur."

"Funny, Stan."

"Anyway, sorry for the distraction. No solid leads have come in from the flyers?"

"No, nothing." I considered sharing a burgeoning theory after my conversation with Brandon, but to say it was far-fetched would be an understatement. "But I need you to search for the GPS on her phone."

I was about to bite my nails—an old bad habit of mine—when Stan said, "Sure. Just have the Romeros come in and file a missing persons report and then we can do a lot of things."

"Dammit, Stan. I've tried over and over, but they won't budge. They only see the worst-case scenario."

"I won't let that happen."

"Thank you for saying that, but they don't trust anyone. And I kind of see where they're coming from."

I heard what sounded like lips smacking. Was he back to eating candy bars? "Are you stressed about the murdered girls?" I asked.

"Just got back the ME's report, and we're learning more about them. And by the way, I'm chewing a piece of gum," he said as if he'd read my mind.

"Can you share what you know?"

"Eh, I guess. But first things first. Mia. I'm thinking we might be able to put in the GPS tracking request because we think she's connected to the animal sacrifice crime."

"So the only way to make this happen is to implicate an innocent girl in a crime she didn't commit?"

"To make this quick and easy, yes. If you or the Romeros want to still keep her name out of the investigation, we can take it up the chain and make our own case. It might take four or five business days to get approval."

I thought about calling the Romeros, but I knew their state of mind, and it was near panic. "Do what you need to do, Stan. And make it quick."

"Let me put in the request right now."

"Then you'll call me back to give me the scoop on the ME's findings on the double murder?"

"Sure. It couldn't hurt to get your take on it."

I hung up just as Cristina approached. She raked her fingers through her hair, which signaled that something wasn't right.

"I thought I had her," Cristina said, flipping her head left, then right.

"NSBitch?"

She didn't respond. I followed her gaze to a flock of teens huddled near the ping-pong room. One of the girls in the group—a brunette with a head of curls—looked in our direction for a quick moment.

"Do you think that's her?"

"Maybe. Who knows?"

"So the girl you were talking to earlier wasn't her?"

"Nah. She was just asking me where the bathrooms were."

"So did NSBitch tell you what she looked like or how to pick her out from the crowd?"

"Never got that far." Cristina typed a quick note into her phone.

"Sending NSBitch a text to see if the curly-haired girl responds?"

"That's what I'm hoping. I'm not going to turn around, so you need to tell me what you see, okay?"

I was positioned perfectly, where my eyes could peer just over Cristina's shoulder and look in the direction of the girl. Sure enough, she reached for her back pocket.

"You see something, don't you?"

"Yeah, hold on. She's looking at her phone."

Just then, the girl put her hand on her friend's shoulder, then broke through the pack. I took a single step to the side of Cristina.

"What's going on?"

"I think she's headed for the exit."

"Crap. This has gone on too long." She broke into a jog and headed straight for the main exit. Seconds later, as Cristina approached a guy in a purple shirt, he held his hand up and said, "No running. You should know the rules."

Cristina swatted his hand out of her face and picked up her pace. Two other purple shirts came out of nowhere and began to converge on my ECHO employee. This, I could see, wasn't going to end well.

I took off in that direction.

All of the purple shirts were focused on Cristina, so my jog went unnoticed. I caught up to Cristina just as she, four purple shirts, and NSBitch reached the exit.

"It's time we had a talk…in person." Cristina reached out and a put a hand on NSBitch's shoulder.

"Excuse me?" she said, pushing Cristina's hand off her shoulder.

"You're NSBitch. You can't hide it any longer."

"What did you call me?" She turned to face Cristina. I could see her nostrils flare.

I tried to push my way to the middle, but one of the purple shirts beat me to it and stepped in between the girls. "You should both know our policy. No fighting or even arguing in the MACC. "And you," he said, nodding at Cristina, "that kind of language will get you suspended from the MACC for a good month. Dr. Amaya has a zero-tolerance policy on bullying."

I made my way up next to Cristina just as she was about to retort. I put my hand on her shoulder and squeezed.

"Guys, everyone, it's just a misunderstanding," I said to the group. "Cristina thought this girl was an old friend, and they used to call each other those names. She's sorry." I looked at the curly-haired brunette, who may or may not have been NSBitch. She glared with her lips pressed tightly shut. I turned to Cristina. "Right, Cristina?"

"Yeah, I guess," she said, her eyes locked on the other girl, assessing her. I nudged her in the arm.

She peeled her eyes away and looked to the MACC employees. "Okay, you're right, Ivy. I was just messing around. And sorry about running too."

Everyone seemed to take a breath. "You cool, Nat?" The lead guy in the purple shirt asked the girl. *Nat.*

Cristina and I shifted our eyes to each other.

"No problem. We all have our issues," she said, stuffing her hands into a pair of ultra-tight jeans. "I'm late getting home."

She walked out the door as the rest of the group began to break up.

"We need to go after her," Cristina said under her breath.

I hooked my arm in hers and guided her away from the door. "If we go out that door, we'll have a dozen purple shirts all over us. And even if we catch up to Nat, it doesn't sound like she wants to talk right now."

"Dammit!"

"Text her later. See if she'll even reply to you. Then maybe you can find out why she got cold feet." I saw the snack room and moved in that direction. "Are we a hundred percent sure that girl was actually your source?"

"You heard the guy say her name. Nat. It has to be her."

"I'm just saying we don't know until we get confirmation. So when you text your source later, you might want to play it cool, not give anything away. If it wasn't her, you don't want to scare her off. She might have her own reasons for not showing up."

"True." Cristina walked straight to a bin of candy. "You got a couple of bucks on you?"

"I guess. I need to tell you what happened earlier with Brandon."

"Throw two bucks into the jar, and then I'll sit and listen while I chew on some Twizzlers."

And we did just that.

Twenty-Five

Benito Alvarez walked across the open expanse behind the old church, known by many as Mission San Jose. Clouds had parted just enough for a bright moon to drench the area around him in a pool of light. It only added to his mounting anxiety. He could practically feel the crosshairs of a rifle on his chest. He knew that was a metaphor—he was prone to being overdramatic anyway. And now, heading for a dark church in the middle of the night, the creep factor had tripled.

He forced out a breath and watched the fog curl into the sky. Before he knew it, or even wanted it, the edge of the back of the church was right in front of him. After another few steps, he stopped and rested his hand on the stone wall. He could see the silhouette of the cross at the top of the church's tower, which now blocked the moon. The sudden absence of light brought another rash of anxiety. He knew why—he was close. So very close to irreversibly altering the course of his life in a way that he never thought possible. In his most private moments, he would question whether he wanted to follow through with this…transformation.

A shallow exhale. His airflow was restricted. It felt like one of these enormous stones from the church had been carved out and strapped to his chest.

Maybe that's what happens to your body when you're about to go through an exorcism, Benito. Tears pooled in his eyes. He thought more about why he was here, why he would put himself through such a ritual.

It's because of your so-called condition, Benito. You've known it ever since you were a little kid.

"But there is a way to fix you," he said out loud, quoting the holy man who'd convinced him that there was indeed a method to rid his body of... What had he called it? Oh yes, a disorder.

A disorder. A popular name used throughout the years, depending on the level of paranoia of the community in which he lived. His parents had moved across the country before settling in San Antonio during Benito's freshman year in high school. It was rough at first, being the new kid and all. Especially since he was carrying this extra burden that he wanted to share with the world but knew that he'd only shame his parents. Things had settled a bit. He'd found some friends who were supportive. But then came this year's football season. He was a starting linebacker, one of the key members of a defense that was considered one of the best in the area. Somehow, seemingly out of nowhere, rumors had started circulating. The same kind that had emerged at his previous schools. He felt like he was being exposed, thrown into the middle of a coliseum, stripped of his clothes, the world's eyes boring holes through him.

Which is why he had reached out and sought help. It was either that or commit—

He stopped himself before uttering the "s" word: suicide. He'd promised his mother years ago to never use that word. She'd found him crying in the corner of a hot attic, petrified to show his face to anyone in the neighborhood. The hateful slurs, the sarcastic comments, even a simple sneer, all had made him feel like he wasn't deserving to be called a boy, nor even a person. He couldn't face the kids at school any longer, and the park wasn't much better. The ridicule was nonstop, and as he'd told his mother, it very often turned violent. He was punched and kicked by gangs of kids just looking to humiliate someone. He was the easy choice because he was always outnumbered, five to one, or even ten to one. Once, they had even thrown stones at him.

When his mom had found him curled up behind a row of boxes, he told her that he no longer wanted to live. She hugged him that day for what seemed like an hour. She told him he was special and that no one could define what he thought of himself. "Don't give them the power," she had said.

And then she made him promise to never, under any circumstance, reject the gift of life. He did as she wished, and then he made a quiet promise to himself: he would work his body into a physical specimen and be able to defend himself against anyone. And once he had done that, he then made his father proud by playing football. He turned out to be pretty good, especially when he was the one doling out the punishment. With each crunching tackle, he would envision snapping the neck of one of his hecklers. It had bolstered his confidence, even gave him a little bit of swagger.

Until football had started this season. And now, even despite his intimidating presence, the hateful deluge of social-media bullying had hit an all-time high. Even a couple of the coaches had made hateful slurs.

Which told him he had no choice. This was it. The end of the road. And hopefully the beginning of a new way of thinking...of feeling. This exorcism had to resolve his disorder, once and for all. He was ready.

Or was he?

"Fuck it," he said, pushing off from the stone wall. He walked through the shadows of the outdoor walkway, itself made of stone, looking up at the windows of the church as he went. He saw no lights on. But the holy man had told him to expect just that. Nothing to be concerned about. He knew this wasn't a normal practice. He knew that most had shunned the practice of exorcisms. But there were experts who still performed this ritual, those who were endorsed by the Pontiff himself for the most extreme cases.

And he'd been told his disorder might be one of the most acute. But because of his age, there was a belief that he could be transformed. And that gave him hope.

He pressed the door handle—it was unlocked just as he'd been told it would be—and walked inside. A faint light from up ahead guided his path, but he ran his fingers along the stone wall to maintain his balance. He reached a dead end, turned right, and then saw shadows flickering on the wall leading into the sanctuary.

He felt a tingle inside. Nerves. From excitement or from fear, he wasn't sure.

He pushed his doubts to the side, allowing his curiosity to take over. He padded forward and stopped at the threshold. He could see candles burning at the altar, where a book was open—presumably the Bible—and next to it, a set of instruments. Those had to be the tools the holy man referenced in their final conversation, when they'd set up this clandestine meeting.

"Good evening, Benito."

The holy man appeared from behind a pillar. He wore a dark cloak, appearing more like a monk than a man of the cloth.

"Hi." His voice quivered, and he cleared his throat.

The man walked toward him, pulling back the cover over his head. His face was solemn, his jet-black hair slicked back, forming a widow's peak. Benito noticed a cross pendant on the end of a chain around the holy man's neck.

The man reached Benito and then gestured toward the altar.

"You want me over there?"

The man nodded.

"That's cool," Benito said, slowly moving in that direction. "I've never done this before, but I guess you know that."

He reached the altar and saw the flames from each of the four candles pointing toward the ceiling. The sanctuary was made of limestone. He'd read that much in his history book. He turned and spotted the Rose Window. A carver from Spain had created that window to honor his beloved sweetheart.

For a quick moment, his mind went elsewhere, to someone who'd captured his heart. But that would be no more, not after this ceremony.

Just as he was about to turn around to face the holy man, to start the ritual, something caught his eye. He focused on the second row of pews. Was that a leg and a shoe?

A trigger went off somewhere in his mind. But before he could take action—and dammit, he was about to take direct action—he felt a stabbing pain in his torso. He staggered a bit, looked down to see an arrowhead sticking out the front of his stomach. He tried turning his head, but the agony was unbearable. Blood pooled around the exit wound. He wrapped his fingers around the shaft and caught his finger on the arrowhead, slicing it open. But he didn't feel pain from the cut. Every tentacle of his nervous system seemed to be attached to his stomach. It was on fire. He heard himself crying out.

His mind swirled, as a few sane thoughts mixed with delirium. It was difficult to tell fact from fiction, especially considering the lie he'd been living most of his life. He crashed to the unforgiving stone floor, landing on his side. He coughed up blood, but the rest of his body was unmoving. The man walked in front of him and allowed his robe to fall to the ground. He was naked. He had a round, ornate pendant attached to the chain around his neck. It was a symbol he'd never seen before.

Where was the cross that had been there before?

As his lungs filled with blood and the oxygen to his brain came in short bursts, he thought about the irony. The last thing he would set his sights on would be a naked man. Yet, he now had clarity like never before. He was looking at pure evil.

The end came, and he was finally at peace.

Twenty-Six

For the first time that I could recall, Stan had not only beaten me to Smoothies & Stuff, but he'd also ordered his drink and was seated at the old ECHO corner booth. He looked my way and, using his prosthesis, held up his cup in greeting—he might have been trying to impress me—while speaking into his phone with his good hand.

The door dinged open behind me, bringing in a rush of cool wind. I rubbed both of my arms. I could hear Saul in my mind, saying, "And where's your coat?" I really needed to keep one in my car or something. This was getting a little ridiculous. I had even checked the weather on my way out of my apartment this morning. The app said the temperature was fifty-two. I didn't believe it.

I made my way through the line, picked my smoothie of choice—a double strawberry and banana—and scooted in opposite Stan.

"Will do," he said, before ending his call.

"Who was that?"

"Do you ever hear me asking you who you're talking to? Why is everything fair game with me?"

He seemed stressed, but I had to give him credit that he was still on the wagon, eating healthy, looking fit. "Good point. None of my business. I guess it's just because I know you, and you'd definitely share anything that was important to our investigation."

"Ha ha. Funny. Which investigation?" He held up his fake hand to keep me from responding. "That was a rhetorical question. We have three investigations going on, although only two are official."

"You know which one I want to ask about first."

"The unofficial one, of course."

The door chimed again, and I glanced in that direction. "The Romeros are supposed to meet me here for a quick debrief before they head off to work."

Stan opened his mouth to speak.

"Don't say it," I interjected. "I know, it's frustrating as hell. I'll try to convince them today. But I'd love to give them some good news. The GPS triangulation...any movement on that front?"

He held up his phone. "I had to bring Brook into the loop, since she's leading the investigation of the animal sacrifice at the high school."

"That's good to get her in the loop."

"Turns out you already have," he said, taking a pull from his straw, which forced both of his eyebrows upward.

"Yeah, well, she was available. I didn't want to pull you off the murder investigation just to check up on Principal Peterson."

"I appreciate that. By the way, I'm sorry I never got back to you last night. I worked until late, and then Bev came into my office and dragged me to bed."

"Oh, Stan, you don't have to share your intimate details," I said with a wink.

"You've seen the video of Mia leaving the school?" he asked with a straight face.

"Yep."

"Brook said it was nothing special. What's your take?"

I took a breath, then explained what I thought I saw after I'd replayed it several times—Mia pulling a pendant out from under her shirt.

"And you think that's the smoking gun to this whole thing?"

"Never said that. It's a possible piece of evidence."

"Which we don't have because it's on her."

"True." I debated telling him about my conversation with Brandon.

"So what did you use the yearbook for?"

"She told you about that?"

A single head nod.

I gave him only the essential information on my Q&A with Brandon. "Essential" being that he was a tool, had no love for Mia, and only cared about himself and his little football issue.

"Teenage drama."

"There's a missing girl, Stan."

He held up his fake arm again. "I'm not downplaying Mia's disappearance. I feel the opposite of that, in fact."

"So, did your team figure out where Mia's phone is?"

"Not yet. One way or the other, we should know something by noon at the latest."

I nodded, took another sip of my drink.

"I also have more information on the double homicide," he said.

I flicked my fingers, signaling to him to let me hear it.

"It's the ME report. When he cleaned away all the blood, he found a symbol carved into both their chests."

I squinted, my thoughts momentarily flashing images of the etched letters on my body. "Do you have a picture?"

"No need to look at it. He's already done the research. And once I saw it, I knew without him telling me a thing."

I tilted my head.

"It's the same symbol we found at the field house, the circle with what looks like an A in the middle. Turns out that's the Satanic symbol for human *or* animal sacrifice."

Both of my palms smacked the table. "The crimes are connected?"

He shook his head.

"You don't think so? How can you say that? Talk about smoking guns."

"No, no. I'm in more disbelief than anything. It's just that..." He looked off for a second, then turned back to me, rubbing his mustache. He was looking at me, but I could see the wheels turning in his mind. I found myself in the same mode, thinking through the details of the two crimes.

"It doesn't add up," I said.

He chuckled just once. "You're flipping worse than a politician."

"The crime at the field house seemed to be hastily put together. A few boards, using animals, the symbol burned into the turf. It comes across as more of a teenage prank. A sick prank."

He nodded, but didn't say anything, so I continued.

"And the double homicide had all the trappings of a horror film. The setting, the ritual seems to be very important to the perp. And now we know the precision with which the perp carved the symbols." I paused as I searched my memory banks for another fact. It wasn't there. "So the actual cause of death?"

"The knife wounds. Loss of blood, plus the perp made deep holes at each point where the inside part of the symbol intersects with the circle. Those punctured key organs."

I strummed my fingers. "But how would he—"

"You're assuming it's a he."

"True. How would the perp keep the girls secured? Wouldn't they try to crawl away? Did he not use something to keep them in place? To make that kind of detailed carving, they couldn't be moving."

"All good questions. And there was no trail of blood. I asked the ME to take another look at the toxicology report and see if he found any traces of a substance to knock them out."

"And there were two girls. Wouldn't they try to work together to fight back? Even if this perp had a size and strength advantage, wouldn't it at least be very messy? Unless…"

He gave me a second, then leaned into the table. I'd never seen Stan do that before. Usually, his gut got in the way.

"Unless the perp either killed them in another place and brought them to the church, or he—and I mean this in the generic sense—cleaned up the mess."

He nodded. "Interesting theories. But we already discussed the fact that the perp got off on the whole setting. So…"

"Maybe the perp is a janitor and knows how to clean up the most disgusting messes."

Stan picked up his phone and used his left hand to punch in a note. "I sent a text to my team, asking the crime scene guys to do another check of the floor and look for cleaning substances in particular. Thing is, that's not an uncommon thing to find."

"That's the point, right?"

He twisted his lips. His phone buzzed, but he kept his eyes on me. "We learned more about the girls who were murdered."

I waited for more. "And?"

"Don't jump to conclusions."

I could feel my pulse tick up. "Now I'm on high alert."

"Sorry. Anyway, we talked to the two girls' parents, and they were both recently in trouble."

"How?"

"Both were caught drinking at a party."

"A party. The same party?"

He shook his head. "Different parties, and somewhat different situations. One girl supposedly had sex that night, losing her virginity in the process."

Every time Stan added another data point, the case, or cases, became that much more disturbing and confusing. "This is a strange twist. But the real question is what about the other girl? Did she lose her virginity the night of her party?"

"According to her parents, no. Her mother showed the detective her birth control pills. She did go a little crazy the night she got drunk, though, and destroyed a coffee table, broke a number of glasses, threw a coffeemaker across the room. Pretty much lost it, according to reports."

"A mean drunk."

"I guess."

"But two very different situations, like you said. Did these occur on the same night?"

"About a week apart."

"You think Mia could be involved, or be a victim herself and we just haven't found her yet?"

"It doesn't totally fit, I know. Up to now, the perp or perps, haven't kidnapped anyone."

"But we don't know if the perp has kidnapped her or anyone else. Maybe the perp is saving her for some type of special ritual. Or, like you said, maybe she's been dead for a couple of days."

My whole body tensed. I took another drink and felt the coldness slide down my chest.

"Brook and I are meeting at the office to compare notes." His phone buzzed again. He picked it up as I felt the presence of someone to my left. I looked up to see the Romeros. They both had dark circles under their eyes. They looked at Stan, then back to me. It seemed like they were holding their breath, as if Stan might cuff them and throw them into the back of his car. Of course, that was nonsensical. Stan would never do that. But how could they trust anyone right now? Their son's death was still a fresh wound, I would imagine, and their daughter was missing. And after talking to Brandon and watching the principal drag his feet, my faith in humanity to do the right thing was waning.

"Another teenager murdered in a church?" Stan lifted his head just after he spoke. He quickly realized who was standing nearby. He mouthed "sorry" to me, then lifted to his feet, gave a respectful nod to the Romeros, and walked out of the shop.

I looked at the Romeros. Consuela had a hand to her face. It was quivering, her gaze locked in a state of fear. Raul was doing something on his phone and didn't seem to notice. Or had he disconnected from his wife as the sobering reality of a missing child had numbed his ability to show compassion? I quickly got to my feet and put my arm around her. She buried her face in my shoulder and sobbed.

Twenty-Seven

With a handkerchief covering his mouth, Stan came through the front door of the historic church just as I reached the yellow tape. He gave the cop the signal to let me through, but then held up an arm.

"You don't want to see it." He took a hard swallow, then turned his face into the northerly breeze.

"You know my stomach can handle it, Stan. You know I've seen worse."

He turned and pointed to the door. "Whoever did that is not human."

I tried to keep my imagination in check, but I could feel a pit in my gut. "Stan, your ME found the Satanic symbol on the two girls—just like what they found at the field house. You told me that just this morning. We talked about the very real possibility that Mia could be wrapped up in this."

He nodded.

"For now, just talk to me. Tell me what you know."

"Two dead. One teen, and one lady who looks to be in her sixties."

"Did they find—"

He nodded before I finished the question.

"What? What was it?"

"Another Satanic symbol. This one looks like the Star of David, but it's not. It's a hexagram, something that's really popular in that bizarre world, according to the ME."

"Where was it found?"

"Lower back. Carved into his skin."

Again, I had to resist the urge to reach around and touch the scars on my lower back from my captivity almost a year earlier. I remembered hearing my skin peel apart as Milton etched the words: *This Is My Space.*

I shook myself out of the past, but it was too late to catch something he'd just said. "I'm sorry. I was thinking about something."

He pocketed his handkerchief, turned to face me. "He was basically skewered by an arrow...right in the middle of the hexagram."

"As in a bow and arrow?"

He nodded, his chin quivering just a bit. "That's not the worst of it," he said.

I wanted to reach out for a handrail, but there was none. "I'm ready."

"This...monster." He paused, wiped a hand across his face. He was definitely rattled by this crime scene. "This monster cut off his, his...junk and his testicles and stuffed them in his mouth."

My chin practically bounced off my chest. Then the church door opened, and I heard a shrill coming from inside.

"Who is that?"

"The twin sister of the lady who was killed. They both went to the church. The victim was the office manager."

I could only shake my head. "How was she killed?"

"Bludgeoned to death," he said with a heavy exhale. "I don't know what or who we're dealing with. This sick, twisted pervert just—" He stopped short, as if he had to cease talking before his emotions bubbled over the edge. A moment passed, and he was calmer, but not by much. "This guy, and yes, I'm saying a guy did this…the violence he's shown from the first homicide two nights ago to this one. If I hadn't seen it for myself, I'd say it's inconceivable."

"Could we be looking at two different killers?"

He scratched the side of his nose. "I can't think straight right now, but I suppose it's possible. I just know that with Satanic symbols now part of two murder scenes, it won't take long for this to go public. And when it happens, parents at Lee High School will go shit crazy, connecting the murders to the animal sacrifice. And standing here right now, I can't blame them."

"But your team will have some evidence to work from, right? The arrow. You can find the manufacturer and try to figure out who purchased it. And somewhere in that church, there has to be some type of blood or hair from the killer. He can't be that perfect." Suddenly a realization hit me square in the head. "Unless the killer is a priest or another worker of the church."

He tilted his head, a look of disbelief on his face. "What did you just suggest?"

I wasn't fond of his tone, but I didn't back away from my theory. "You're probably thinking my instincts are off because of the situation with Emmitt. But that's behind me," I said, swatting a hand. I realized I was in the way of two law enforcement officials carrying toolboxes toward the church, and I scooted into the grass and faced Stan. "It makes too much sense. There are countless pedophile stories in the ranks of the priesthood, and—"

"Ivy." His voice had a snap to it, which caught me off guard. He never used that tone with me. Maybe he was at his breaking point.

Another bluster of wind blew across my face. I pushed aside a wayward lock of hair, then Stan continued, his voice subdued. "Look, I don't want to completely dismiss your theory. Anything is possible. And we'll follow all the leads and see where they take us—even if they take us to the Pope's front door, I have no problem busting it down. But the priest in that church is grieving more than anyone right now. I can see it in his eyes. And, oh, by the way, he's eighty-four and moves like someone who's a hundred and four."

I wanted to dig further into the idea of someone connected to the church—any church—as being the killer. Stan was already working through the same angle apparently, but he seemed truly shaken to the core, so I let it go.

Brook stopped by the crime scene and had only been on site for a few minutes when Stan got the call: the tech guys had the location of Mia's phone. That was when she'd jumped into her car, and in no uncertain terms, told me to follow her.

It was one of the strangest sensations I'd experienced as an adult. The late-afternoon traffic parted like a zipper being pulled open. Even stranger, I was in Black Beauty, cruising at fifteen miles an hour above the speed limit while following a cop.

We made our way to Lee High School in record time to meet with the SAPD tech team. They believed they had figured out the general location of Mia's phone, somewhere at the high school. For the first time since Mia's parents sat in my ECHO office and unloaded all their grief, past and present, there was some positive news coming our way. Or at least a piece of solid evidence. I pulled into the high school parking lot behind Brook. The flashing red light on her unmarked car drew the attention of students. I saw a lot of open jaws and kids breaking out their phones. We met two SAPD techs at the front door. One was holding what looked like a tablet. He was tapping the screen as we dodged students on our way to the front of the school. Principal Peterson walked out of his office and put up a hand. "Where do you think you're going in my school?"

I saw Brook set her jaw. This was going to be good.

Twenty-Eight

Brook slammed him hard with a barrage of harsh words before Peterson could even take a breath.

And then he did a deep inhale and exhale. "Do you have a warrant?" He folded his arms across his chest, stretching his coat to the point where I thought it might rip at the shoulders. He was actually trying to pull off a smug look, but it didn't work. In fact, if anything, he looked fearful. As Brook proceeded with gouging out his eyes—metaphorically speaking, of course—I wondered what the hell his problem was.

"Do I need a fucking warrant when we're searching for the whereabouts of a missing girl?" Brook's skin was as smooth as butter, but at this moment, the butter had red dye in it. She was fuming. I thought about stepping in, but she was doing a fine job of cutting Peterson off at the knees.

"I thought she wasn't officially missing," he said, now jabbing a finger. "On top of that, I do believe a little birdie told me she was now a suspect in the field house crime."

How the hell did he know that? Did he actually have a contact on the inside of the SAPD? But more importantly, I still couldn't get past the fact that this tool was trying to obstruct us from a piece of evidence that could help us find Mia. Why would he do that?

Did he have something against her? I could feel heat moving up my neck, and I knew if Brook didn't put this asshat in his place, then I would.

Brook got right up under his chin. "If you believe that I'm doing something wrong, then you can file a complaint. But for now, you need to move out of the way and allow us free access to the school. Understood?"

A short woman with a beehive hairstyle shuffled closer, clearing her throat. "Mr. Peterson, I hate to bother you at this time."

He turned in her direction while rolling his eyes. "Yes?"

"Assistant Superintendent Meg Burton is on the line. Says it's urgent."

He took in a breath as if it might be his last, then he looked at Brook. "Be quick about it. School just ended and kids are milling about. I don't need you to cause me more of a PR headache."

He walked off with the short woman.

"Come on," Brook said, waving us forward.

The tech guys took the lead; Brook and I were two steps behind them.

"Can you believe that guy?" I said to her.

She was still seething. "No wonder people are upset with public education. That man doesn't give a rat's ass about the kids. He's only concerned about the PR hit." She groaned.

"Call me a cynic, but I'm wondering if there's something more to it."

She flipped her head in my direction. "Like?"

"I don't know. I can't put my finger on it."

The tech guy holding the tablet motioned his arm to take a right. Kids and teachers were all watching us like we were in a parade. I felt tension in the air as we turned left and our pace slowed down. There were just a few kids down this hall. Lots of lockers, a couple of classrooms. Then I saw a sign that said *Band Hall*.

I looked straight ahead, and it all came back to me. I nudged Brook's arm. "I think this is the hallway and exit from the video clip."

Her eyes shifted. "I think you're right."

A moment later, the techie with the tablet stopped in his tracks. "It's right in here." He waved his arm in a circle, facing a bank of lockers, two rows.

"How big of a radius are we looking at?" Brook asked.

The guy shrugged.

"I need to know how many we need to get access to."

"Crap," I said. "Now we have to rely on Peterson to open the lockers? He could drag this on forever, and even then he might claim it's not our right to search all of these lockers."

Brook turned to the tech who didn't have the tablet and asked if they had bolt cutters in their van. He nodded somewhat nervously. "Get those here in two minutes. Can you make it that fast?"

He nodded, then ran off. I looked up and located the camera that must have been the one that captured Mia's last moments in the school. Then I glanced at the wall of lockers. "One of these lockers could be hers."

"Or it could be a friend's locker," Brook said. "Or it could be the locker of someone who had it out for her. We'll soon find out."

It took less than two minutes when we heard the squeak of the tech's shoes as he cut down the hallway toward us, bolt cutters in hand. Peterson and his squatty assistant were close behind him.

"Do not under any circumstance deface school property. That would come out of my budget, and I don't have room for it," Peterson said, pulling up next to us, out of breath.

Brook ignored him, taking the bolt cutters from the tech guy.

"Did you hear me?" Peterson moved in front of the lockers and held up his arms, as if he were a protester.

She snapped the bolt cutters at him, just below his belt. He quickly moved his knees together. "Are you threatening to…?"

"If I could find it, I might."

I tried not to laugh. But damn, that was a good one.

"Get the hell out of my way before I cuff you."

He removed a set of keys from his pocket. "Just let me unlock the lockers, okay?"

"Sure. Thanks for being so *helpful*," she said with as much sarcasm as she could muster.

The tech guy gave Peterson the parameters of which lockers to open. It appeared to be about forty, twenty on both the top and bottom rows. He opened the first, and Brook searched through it. After a couple of minutes, she shook her head. She asked the other tech guy to make a notation of the locker number and the primary contents and waved at Peterson to move on to the next locker. I wanted to jump in, to ask Peterson and his assistant if Mia's locker was in this group, but something told me to keep my mouth shut. Brook was a seasoned detective and surely had a reason for not asking that same question.

As more lockers were opened, I watched Peterson more closely, looking for signs of stress or apprehension. Part of me wanted to see it. But I didn't. He seemed impatient and annoyed, rolling his eyes every time he opened a new locker, but, strangely, he didn't say another word of protest.

My gaze shifted to the floor. Why did I feel like Peterson was hiding something? And what would that be? Was he a pervert and had somehow convinced Mia to leave school on her own, meet up with him later, and then he killed her or was holding her captive somewhere? Possibly. It had been done before by men whom no one had suspected. Then, after the horrors were revealed—a

woman held in captivity acting as his sex slave for years—
neighbors would say, "He was a simple man, quiet but cordial. The
last person I would think could do something like this."

Quiet and cordial? That wasn't Peterson on his best day.

Playing it out in my head, that right there made me think
Peterson wasn't the perpetrator. But why had he, at least up to now,
acted so paranoid? Why had he been so callous, so uncooperative,
when he learned about a missing student, one who, despite all of
her Big Rules and such, still appeared to be one of the good kids?
Could there be some secret in Mia's life that Peterson knew about?

"Bingo."

I looked up and saw Brook holding a phone in her rubber-
gloved hand.

"Oh my, it's like a ghost speaking to us."

All eyes went to Peterson's assistant.

Peterson wiped a hand across his rubbery face, then said,
"Really, Marilyn? You think that was appropriate?"

She cowered a bit, and I moved closer to Brook. "Whose
locker is this?"

She opened the door wider, and I saw Mia's name in pink cut-
out letters. I also noticed a lot of pictures and quotes about
motivation, hitting your goals, keeping your focus.

Brook placed the phone in a baggie and handed it to one of the
techs. "That's the first step. Now, we'll see if there's anything
relevant on it."

"You can check her phone records, too, with her wireless
company, right? Oh, also, I was thinking if we can figure out her
handles, we should be able to dig into all her social media
channels."

She peered over her shoulder. Peterson had stepped down the
hall and was speaking with Marilyn, perhaps giving her a teaching

moment…coming from a guy who was a walking, talking example of teaching moments. Oh, the irony.

Brook turned to me, kept her voice down. "I'll do some more digging in her locker, but unless I find a note or something, we still have no evidence that a crime has been committed. Searching through her phone is still probably a stretch, according to the rule of law, but I'll sanction it. Let's hope we find a trail."

I moaned softly, then said, "To state the obvious, since the Romeros still haven't filed the report, there's only so much you can do legally."

"That, and Principal Asshat apparently knows someone in the department, so I can't push this too far."

I made a few mental notes on things to get from the Romeros, starting with Mia's social media handles, if they even knew them.

"You're going to start digging more into her online life, aren't you?" Brook asked. "I can see it in your eyes."

I thought I was showing nothing more than a straight poker face. "No offense, but someone has to."

"Good. Let me and Stan know what you find out."

I just hoped we wouldn't be too late.

Twenty-Nine

Texting and walking was apparently one of the great new dangers of the modern world. At least for me.

I'd just walked out of the ECHO office and was heading up the street to visit Saul before meeting the Romeros at Crockett Park. Cristina and I were in a rapid-fire text conversation about the social media information we'd just received from the Romeros through our group text. My head was buried in my phone as I tried to match Cristina's response time with quick texts of my own...all while walking on the city sidewalk.

I heard the whine of a little boy too late, yet it still seemed like it all happened in slow motion. My swinging thigh ran into the toddler—at under three feet tall and holding a sippy cup, I guessed he was around two years old or so—and he fell backward. I instantly pulled back my leg to reduce the force of the blow while trying to avoid stepping on him. I was no ballerina, so my balance was thrown off by my twisting body. I actually tripped over my own feet—amazingly, I was still able to avoid stomping the little guy—and plunged face first into a street sign, then toppled backward to the concrete.

I found myself lying right next to the kid, who was now crying. I looked up to see his mom acting as if he'd been drawn and quartered. It took a good five minutes to calm her down. He stopped crying the instant she replaced the sippy cup in his hand with a handful of Goldfish. I apologized a dozen times and watched them walk off with the mom shaking her head in disgust. I couldn't blame her really. I wasn't happy with myself for being so self-absorbed in my own world.

Then I realized two things. I had an egg-sized bump on my cheekbone, and I'd dropped my phone during my graceful performance.

"Great," I said, picking up my phone to see cracks splintered across the screen.

As I gently opened and closed my mouth, I could really feel the extent of my injury. It hurt no matter which way I moved my facial muscles. Before I took another step, I read Cristina's last text.

Parents usually don't know squat about their kid, especially on social media. Lots of kids have alter egos, sometimes many of them, just to play out some fantasy. It's crazy. I'll take what they gave us and start digging. Later.

Cristina's raw insight into how the teenage mind worked never ceased to surprise me. She had the maturity to view her own age group from a higher level and make valid assessments. It was impressive, especially since she was in the very midst of those age-related issues herself. Of course, her maturity ebbed and flowed, so I was happy when it appeared. I typed in a quick response.

Thanks. Heading to park to share video footage with Romeros.

I made sure to pocket my phone before walking, and then plodded down to Saul's office, now looking for a little sympathy for the bump on my face in addition to wanting to share everything I'd learned today about Mia, the latest Satanic murder, and my thoughts about that shithead, Principal Peterson.

The glare of the low western sun made me question what I was seeing. That and the foggy, dirty glass on the front door of Saul's office. Or maybe I'd suffered a concussion and my vision was off.

I leaned closer to the glass, rubbed my eyes. All I saw was cleavage. A woman wearing a leather, thigh-high skirt and a tight V-neck sweater that amplified her chest tenfold, was leaning over the lower drawer of a filing cabinet, organizing papers and folders. Had someone broken into Saul's new office? Maybe she was his client, and he'd stepped to the back and she decided to be nosy. I put my hand on the door.

"Boo!"

I knew instantly that Saul had walked up behind me. But it didn't matter. I couldn't help but gasp and jump into the air. And to top it off, I inadvertently slapped myself in the face—right on my bruise.

"Ahhh," I said, turning around, holding a gentle hand against my growing cheek.

"I'm so sorry." His eyes bulged open. "Wait, did you just give yourself that bruise?"

"That fine work was done about five minutes ago when I was walking and texting." I stuck out my lower lip, waiting for his arms to embrace me. But he didn't. Because he was holding two cups of coffee. "Sorry, my hands are full."

I reached out to grab one of the cups. "How did you know I was dropping by?"

"I didn't," he said, glancing over my shoulder. I followed his gaze and realized the other coffee was for the busty brunette in the office.

"Is she a new client?" I tried to act excited, but my acting job was less than convincing.

"Oh, that's Kyra. She's my new legal assistant," he said with a little too much enthusiasm.

"You have a legal assistant?" I'd pointed at him without even knowing it.

"You sound shocked."

"No, it's just that…well, I didn't know you had any clients yet. Wait, did you actually do it?"

"Yes," he said. His beaming smile morphed into a nervous chuckle.

"You gave your two weeks' notice?

He nodded, but I could see there was a story there. "And?"

"And it didn't take two weeks."

"I'm not following."

"Ross fired me on the spot. Told me I was traitor, to pack up and get out."

"Fuck him."

"I'll drink to that." He sipped the coffee in his right hand.

I turned back to look through the window of his office.

"Right, so…" He paused, cleared his throat. "Kyra minored in marketing in college, and she has some great ideas on how to get the word out."

"She graduated college? That's good. Any professional experience?"

"Professional? What do you mean?" he said, taking another sip. Then, it looked like he had one of those *aha* moments. "Wait, she did work for an ice cream company."

"Doing marketing or helping out their legal department?"

"She scooped ice cream. Says she always got the size of the scoop to the right specifications according to company policy. That was her example of being detail oriented."

I blinked a couple of times, wondering if my concussed brain had sent me into some type of alternative universe where Saul had lost his frickin' mind.

"Come on in, I want you to meet her. She'll be part of the family." He nodded at me, but I was still stuck at his last comment. *Family?*

"Do you mind getting the door?" he asked.

"Right. Let me help you."

We walked inside, and Saul handed Kyra the coffee while I got my first full-on view of the ice cream scooper. I thought they might have accidentally done a chest bump like the ones I'd seen athletes attempt, but Saul would have bounced into the wall. So far, though, I'd yet to see his sights go to her chest. He was looking into her eyes, which were like prized jewels. Were those even real? Was anything about her real?

"Ivy, I'd like to introduce you to—"

"It's Kyra, right?" I stuck my hand out first. Her smile was far too alluring, just like the rest of her.

"That's what my mom and dad named me," she said, popping her eyebrows at the end to emphasize something I apparently didn't understand. She giggled, and then snorted once as she took in a quick breath.

Yeah, she snorted. Finally, a flaw.

They tried to engage me in small talk, but it was meaningless. All I wanted to do was spill my guts to Saul, but he was too enamored to notice my needs. And yes, I had to admit, I was feeling sorry for myself. Finally, probably a second before I was about to pick up a pen and see if I could pop a hole in those puppies, Kyra excused herself to the restroom, in her own cutesy, albeit annoying, way.

"Hey, I'm late meeting the Romeros at the park, so I need to head out," I said, motioning to the door.

"Oh, how's that going? The missing girl case."

"If I told you one thing, I'd have to tell you a hundred, and we'd be here all afternoon. Let's catch up later, okay?"

"I almost forgot, Ivy. I got a text this morning from the PI looking for your parents," he said, walking behind his desk. He found his phone under some papers, then looked up at me. "The

PI says she has someone she wants you to meet. Says she might have information on your parents."

"That's odd. Isn't that her job to meet with the people and figure out if they know something first, so I don't have to keep getting my hopes dashed?" Even as I asked the question, I could feel my expectation level rise. I tried like hell to keep it under control.

"Yeah, I guess so. But something tells me this is different."

The office phone rang, and Kyra the ice cream scooper bounced in and answered it, stealing Saul's attention.

"You can ask her to set something up," I said, but his attention had been diverted.

Wearing a smile a mile wide, his eyes were focused on Kyra as she spoke on the phone, as if he were watching his very own invention take life form.

Didn't they make some teenage movie about that?

I turned and walked to the door.

"Oh, right, Ivy. I'll get her to set up a time and place."

I heard footsteps behind me, then his arms were wrapped around my waist. He kissed the nape of my neck. "You can't get out of here without giving me a kiss."

He was going for the late-in-the-game save. And it was working. I turned around and we kissed. I put my hands on his chest. "Just in time, buddy."

He turned his head. "Before what?"

"Before I kicked you to the curb," I said, glancing over his shoulder.

He smiled, knowing I was kidding. "Meet at my place tonight?"

"I might be late. Real late."

"I'll wait up. Maybe we can share some pillow talk."

"You're thinking you might get lucky?"

His dimples came out in full force. I left his office in an improved mood, thinking luck was back on my side.

Thirty

The scene before me warmed my heart. Standing near a gazebo in Crockett Park, the Romeros were conversing with members of the Lee High School basketball team, about eleven girls in all. They all wore their school sweats, a shiny red and black, sharing funny stories about Mia. Both Raul and Consuela wore big grins.

To a degree, I almost wished I could freeze the moment. Once I gave them the update on Mia, it would launch them back into the present, a morose feeling of emptiness, and I knew their grief would return with a vengeance.

Although the group mostly had their backs to me, one girl appeared to be the alpha of the group. She was high-fiving her teammates, leading the storytelling, getting everyone engaged. All I could see was her head of curly, brown hair roped together on top of her head. Given her height, I had to guess she played small forward.

"Boo!"

It was Cristina. I turned and saw her giggling like a little girl. I shouldn't have to remind her about my aversion to parks, especially when darkness set in.

"You're pissed," she said, her big, brown eyes scanning my face. "It was just too easy, though. I walked through those trees, and *boom*, there you were."

"*Boom*, that's the second time someone has done that to me in the last hour."

"Oh." She stuffed her hands in the pockets of her tight jeans. "Well, at least there's some good news."

"What's that?"

"I don't know how you did it, but somehow you got NSBitch to show up at the park."

I flipped around and the girl from the basketball team, the one with the big hair on her head, was up on the first step of the gazebo, now facing her teammates and a few others who'd joined the throng.

"Holy shit. That is her."

"How'd you do it? I mean, she'd gone completely mute since we had our little run-in at the MACC."

I shrugged. "Luck, I guess." I found myself shuffling closer, trying to listen in.

"Don't scare her off, Ivy. We don't want to have to chase her down again." A momentary pause, then, "Hey, is she on some team?"

I put up my Cristina filter and caught a few words from the girl we only knew as NSBitch. "Our teammate, our friend, Mia, hasn't been seen in over two days. Mr. and Mrs. Romero here know we've been doing our best to search for her online. Because Mia means so much to each and every one of us, I know we'll all keep spreading the word." She punched a fist into her opposite hand, as the onlookers started chanting, "Mia, Mia, Mia." Then NSBitch pumped her fist in the air and the others followed suit.

In some respects, the whole scene didn't feel appropriate. The vibe was more like a pep rally than a gathering of people to organize and hand out flyers. But, hey, they were high school kids. Maybe it was the only way they knew how to deal with the heartache. I glanced over at the Romeros. They were nodding, chatting with the girls. The youthful energy seemed to have rejuvenated them.

I turned to face Cristina. I told her about finding Mia's phone in her locker. Then she asked me about the murder scene at Mission San Jose. I started to share what I knew, then she stopped me.

"Hold on, before you get into that, you have to tell me how you got *that*." She pointed at my cheek.

"Oh." I touched the bruise. It was still very sensitive. "It was Saul...well..."

"What? The motherfucker put his hands on you?" She pushed her sleeves up to her elbows. "I'm going to rip out his eyeballs."

"Hold on. I misspoke. I was walking to Saul's new office. That's when I got the bruise."

Her face looked like she'd just eaten cold spinach. "You walk and get a bruise? I'm not understanding something here."

I explained the whole story about running over the toddler and then face-planting into a street sign.

"Do you need to see a doctor?"

"I'll put some ice on it later." I looked over at the crowd.

"No, not for the bruise. I mean for being so slow and uncoordinated. You're old, Ivy, and I think it's time you got some help. Maybe you need to wear one of those panic alarms around your neck."

I shifted my eyes to her for a second. "Your old jokes are getting...old."

"Who says I'm joking?"

"I do." I nudged her arm. "Before the girls break away to start handing out more flyers, why don't you go talk to NSBitch, while I touch base with the Romeros. I'll join you in just a minute."

"She might run again. And I'm not sure what I'll ask her."

"Start with her name. Her *full* name."

I approached the Romeros, who were handing out packets of flyers and hugging each of the girls.

"I'm sorry I was so upset earlier at the smoothie shop." Consuela reached out and grabbed my hand for a couple of seconds. "To hear that detective talking about another murder, it just made all of my emotions boil over."

"It's okay, Consuela. I think you and Raul are showing remarkable resilience considering everything you're going through."

They both nodded, looked at each other, then back at me. That was the signal to provide the update. Looking around to ensure no else could overhear us, I saw Cristina talking to NSBitch. Oddly, Cristina didn't seem to be paying her much attention. She subtly shifted her sights to two other girls speaking near them. It was good that NSBitch hadn't run off or created some type of confrontation.

I got back to the Romeros and reviewed everything that was pertinent to their daughter. Understandably, they had lots of questions.

"Did they find anything on her phone?" Consuela had her hands pressed against her cheeks.

"Remember, this still isn't a real investigation within the SAPD, but Detective Pressler is going to call in a favor and try to get their tech team to conduct a thorough search." I went on to say that Cristina was reviewing Mia's online accounts and we'd get back to them with more information. Part of me wanted to get into the Satanic killings at the church and the animal sacrifice at the school, but I knew it wouldn't help them. And I had no evidence to connect Mia to any of it. Besides, my feelings were just that: feelings, though sinking ones. It was probably just me.

I also gave them a high-level overview of my discussion with Brandon.

"I'm glad you reached out to him," Raul said. "He's one of those kids who knows everyone. Did he give you anything helpful?"

I debated giving them my assessment of his attitude and demeanor, which at times had been overly aggressive and paranoid. But again, I had no evidence—just feelings.

I finished our conversation by showing them the video of Mia when she walked out of school. I'd waited until the end because I was almost certain of the reaction they would have. I was right. They both broke into tears. Consuela touched the phone, as if she were trying to touch her daughter. "I need my baby back, Ivy. Please bring her back."

I swallowed hard. "We'll continue to put all our focus on this case. But it would be easier if the full resources of the SAPD were formally engaged. Detective Radowski, the man at the smoothie shop and a friend of mine, assured me you have nothing to worry about."

Consuela and I both looked at Raul. "You know how I feel, Consuela. I thought you felt the same way," he said, turning his palms to the darkening sky with a shrug.

"I know, I know." She rubbed her eyes. They were hollow. She looked over at Mia's teammates still milling about. "It's just that, even if we're apart, isn't that better than not finding our Mia?"

He closed his eyes for a moment, then released a shaky breath. "If we're not here, then who would ensure they were looking for her anyway? And then she'd get deported too."

"But—" I started.

"Ivy, I don't expect you to understand. It's just the way it has to be. We have more flyers to hand out. Please let us know when you learn more information."

I watched them walk off. It was heartbreaking, but also maddening.

Thirty-One

I then turned to Cristina and saw she was still talking to NSBitch. That had to be a good sign. As I began to walk over, NSBitch's eyes snagged my gaze. She said a couple more words to Cristina, motioned for her teammates to follow her, and scampered away, all of them again chanting, "Mia, Mia."

"What's up with her?" I said, pulling up next to Cristina. She responded, but my mind did an instant replay of what I'd just witnessed. Lots of subtle signals. NSBitch obviously had something against me, but there was more. When she flipped around to head off, she put her hand to her upper chest…as if she were holding something in place. Something that wasn't visible, something under her T-shirt.

"Did you hear me?" Cristina said.

"Sorry, I was thinking. Does she know anything about Mia?"

"We never got there."

"Why not?"

"I pressed her on Mia, asked if she'd been stringing me along. She then asked who I was, who you were, what we were doing. I finally got her to calm down some, to let her know we were PIs working for the Romeros."

"And?"

"She, uh, Jasmine—"

"That's her name? I thought it was Nat. So what's up with the NSBitch handle?"

"Apparently her nickname is Nat. Something to do with her being a real pest on the basketball floor. You know, like a gnat, the bug."

That sounded plausible. "You didn't press her about why she's called NSBitch? And if she told you all this, why did she run out on you at the MACC?"

She grabbed my arm. "She's dealing with her own shit. She's pretty stressed. I think she's more comfortable around her homies."

"What's bugging her?"

"Some type of sexting scandal involving her and two others. Said it could really screw up her life."

"Coming from a girl whose online handle is NSBitch."

"Not sure how many people know her by that name," she said.

"Still, that's a normal-day issue, comparatively speaking. Can you tell if she's legitimately concerned about Mia?"

Cristina pressed her lips together. "I think so. I'm pretty sure."

"You sound less than convinced. I mean, a moment ago, she looked like she was the lead singer of a band, getting everyone into the mood. She definitely seems like the alpha of the group."

"Yeah, I suppose." Cristina watched them disappear at the end of the park.

"Something on your mind?"

"Probably nothing, but I heard those two other girls complaining about their coaches."

I snorted out a fake laugh. "That goes hand in hand with being a high school athlete, doesn't it? Coaches will do anything to put a state championship on their resume."

"This hatred," she said, turning to face me, "was over the top. It sounded as if they were almost planning some type of payback."

"I can remember a few teachers who fell into the category. How about you?"

She didn't respond right away. I nudged her shoulder. "Earth to Cristina."

She sighed, then raked her fingers through her hair.

"So, back to the important work. Mia. We still think NSBitch, a.k.a. Jasmine, might know something."

"Maybe. She's wearing me out, I'll tell you that much. She kind of drains me."

Interesting to hear Cristina speak like that, as if she were a mom of a toddler. "You'll try her again later, after they've delivered the flyers?"

"I'm sure I'll be up late digging for Mia information through her online accounts."

"Good. Jasmine might feel more relaxed now that she knows you're being transparent about why you're asking her all these questions. Hey, any reason she was freaked out by me showing up?"

She twisted her lips just as my phone buzzed. I pulled it out, but didn't look at it until she answered my question. "And?"

"You said you don't like the old jokes."

"She doesn't want any part of me because I'm old, as in twenty-eight years old?"

"I tried telling you, Ivy, once you're over about twenty-one or twenty-two, old is old. You don't have to walk with a cane or have gray hair."

I didn't allow myself to get pulled into another pointless discussion about her age discrimination. We stood there for a moment as the sun's last rays disappeared behind the live oaks. The temperature felt like it had dropped a quick five degrees, but it still wasn't cold. The park now was mostly void of people, but I was somehow able to keep my demons at bay. I found myself trying to make sense of everything I'd witnessed and heard. The Romeros' refusal to formally file a missing persons report on their daughter was at least partially understandable. But with every passing hour, it seemed like their anguish was only growing. Would they ever reach a point where they'd give in to their worst fears and file the report? Then again, I knew it wasn't a given that, once they filed a report, Mia would show up at their doorstep an hour later. And while I welcomed all the help we could get from the SAPD, even the FBI if it was possible, the further away we moved from the time she had walked out of school, the odds of her being found alive and well were getting worse.

Then all of the other data points, visual and otherwise, flooded my mind: Brandon's who-gives-a-shit attitude, Brandon's necklace, the video of Mia reaching for what I thought was a necklace, Peterson's paranoia, finding Mia's phone in her own locker, Jasmine, who was a member of Mia's basketball team, failing to reveal anything pertinent about her friend. Oh, and then there was the whole coach-hating thing.

Wait. Brandon had mentioned the same type of thing—issues with his coach.

"You going to see who texted you?"

I looked at Cristina, then lifted my phone. "It's a text from Stan."

I blinked a couple of times, but the words never reached my lips.

"What the hell did he say?"

"The dead teenager at Mission San Jose? He was a football player at Mia's school."

Thirty-Two

"That's a notch," he said, finally releasing her head.

She shrieked as tears poured out, and she put a napkin to her mouth. She didn't ask what he meant, but he told her anyway,

"Any time you screw up—and I understand, because of your age, you will screw up—I will cut you. We'll start real small at first. But over time, you'll begin to see a pattern. If you're smart, by the time you leave here, you'll have all of your limbs, your ears, and your nose."

They were sitting at the dinner table. He had invited her to join him for dinner in his massive dining hall. All she had done was ask why he wasn't married. It was an innocent question. She trembled with fear and was afraid to make eye contact. "When will that be?"

"I thought you knew that. No?" He sawed off a bite of steak, popped it in his mouth, and then placed the utensils next to his plate. He laced his fingers together and stared at her. Attempting to drown out the piercing sting in her lip, she gave a quick shake of the head, but braced for a violent response.

"You'll leave when I move on to the next life or when most of the world incinerates itself."

She was still processing what he'd just relayed when he tapped a button on his cell phone screen then slid it into the front pocket of his sports coat. It looked to be cashmere. It was refined. Like he was. Like she'd *thought* he was.

The twenty-foot, floor-to-ceiling curtains opened, revealing a breathtaking view. An orange sunset behind the distant hill, and a horse galloping across the open field. A few trees were sprinkled across the setting. She inhaled to steady herself, then glanced around the room. When she'd walked in, she'd seen the fancy chandelier, the finely crafted woodwork of the dining room table, a colorful painting at the far end of the room hanging above a stone fireplace. But now she looked at the Persian rug. There were some frayed edges at the end, and it was a bit discolored. She noticed a thin layer of dust on the chair next to her. This man, who had radiated confidence and charm, was, on one hand, both cultured and sophisticated. He came from money, old Texas money. Yet, after closer examination, she began to feel he was simply playing out some type of fantasy. As if he were nothing more than a squatter on someone else's abandoned property.

He raised his glass of red wine, which was the sign for her to do the same. Still with her napkin at her lip, she picked up her glass. He swirled the wine in his glass and said, "What do you think?"

She could feel her pulse drumming in her lip, but the rush of blood lit a fuse in her brain. She had been naïve. No, it was far worse than that. She'd been a fucking fool. Ashamed of her clueless lack of good judgment, she found herself wrapping her ankles around the legs of her chair to keep her whole body from shaking. From unmitigated fear and sheer anger. At this man for holding her captive, for treating her like an animal, and at herself for being so self-absorbed that she thought his promises of all the trappings of wealth and travel would sweep all of her pressures and petty high school scandals aside.

They would travel the world, he'd said repeatedly, sail across the aqua waters of the Caribbean, ride elephants on a real African safari, hike across a glacier, take in all the incredible museums and castles and cathedrals across Europe.

But he'd meant none of that. What had she been thinking? She would have bit her lip had she not tasted blood in her mouth from him making his first "notch."

"Of what?" she responded timidly.

"The wine, the view," he said, turning in his seat while taking a drink. "This is the life, isn't it?"

She looked once more at the beautiful scenery and then turned, staring at him. Sal had the kind of perfectly chiseled profile from which they could mint a coin. But, apparently, the man who had a presidential appearance was truly demented. And what could she do about it? Absolutely nothing.

"It sure is." She pretended to sip her wine as she thought more about what he'd said. "Do you think there is going to be a war, or are you aware of some type of meteor hitting the earth, or some other natural catastrophe?"

He lifted from his chair, walked to the windows, sipping his wine. Then he turned and faced her. "Mia, my dear, very few things in this world are as perfect as you."

There he went with the charm again. For the first time since they'd first met a month earlier, his charm was meaningless, hollow. Hell, he'd cut her lip, threatened to put more "notches" in her every time she didn't follow his set of rules.

"Thank you," she said, not wanting to upset him.

"But the rest of the world…it's really fucked up. People making the decisions are so self-centered and, frankly, crazy. It will lead to the destruction of the world. Some might live, maybe someone young like yourself. But most of us will perish. And it won't matter how much money any of us have."

She narrowed her eyes. Was this guy for real? Was he really one of those people who thought the end of the world was not just imminent, but had a clear vision for how it would happen? And because of that, what kind of world had he set up on this so-called estate, which seemed more like a prison? Yes, she was eating, or more like nibbling at, a five-star meal. She drank wine from a bottle of a name she couldn't pronounce. But that had nothing to do with her. That, somehow, only fed the irrational desires of this man. She was a prisoner. His apocalyptic view of the world was something he'd conjured up to justify his actions. She was sure of it. But what else had he done? Surely, there was more to his plan than kidnapping a high school senior and eating nice meals and sharing a bottle of wine.

What's on every boy's mind? S-E-X. Where the hell have you been, Mia?

Her eyes shifted across the table, finally landing on the fork. She picked it up, put her thumb at the end. She glanced in his direction. Could she somehow run at him and stab the fork in his eye before he could react? It may not kill him, but it would give her enough time to figure a way out of this house, off this estate, and find someone, anyone who could help her escape.

He downed the last of his wine, walked back to the table, and poured another glass. He held the bottle near her glass. "By the way, I'm a black belt in karate. I might be older than you are by a good three decades, but any attempt you make at harming me will not end well. Not for you."

She placed the fork back on her plate. "I'll take some more wine, thank you." He poured it and she took a small sip. A silence draped over their space. Then, a shrill ripped through the air like a reaper's scythe.

Someone else was in the house? The scream was that of a woman. Where was she? And what had made her scream?

Sal jerked his head to look over his shoulder. "It's time for you to go back to your room."

With her senses on high alert, she slowly got to her feet. He ushered her down a series of connected hallways. She now saw three other doors that were shut, all with padlocks on them. Was the screaming woman inside one of those rooms?

When they made it to her room, she turned and said, "Is it possible for me to ride the horse sometime?"

"I don't know. Maybe. You'll have to improve your behavior. I have a lot going on. A lot to prepare for. Honestly…" He ran his fingers across her face, then stroked a lock of her hair. "I had hoped we could continue our lovely evening together." He shuffled in his space. "I need to go take care of something. You'll get your turn again. Maybe tomorrow."

Her turn.

She wanted to continue the discussion, to show she was buying into his new world view. "Are you sick? Have you received bad news about your health recently?" To a degree, it was an honest question. If someone were at his death bed, what would he want his last days to be like? Had he created this weird sense of reality to give him some sort of peace before he passed? "I'm in good health. Thank you for asking, Mia." He touched her face again.

"So, you're not going to die?"

"I don't like that word. But eventually, we all shall pass. Between now and then, I plan to live life to its fullest. And I can't wait to share it with you." He kissed his fingers and gently touched her lips. Then he shut the door and locked it.

She went to the bathroom and turned on the sink water to tend to her wound. Sal's words replayed in her head like it was on some type of infinite loop. *"You'll leave when I move on to the next life or when most of the world incinerates itself."*

The sound of the water rushing from the faucet brought her back around, and Mia focused on her face in the mirror. She blinked to make sure she wasn't hallucinating. She didn't just have the large raccoon eyes and lips like that of a clown. She looked like the star of a horror movie. The star who would ultimately die in the end. The good girl who meant well, but was unable to recognize the real monster until it was too late.

A gasping breath passed through her lips, and she fought off more tears. Her parents had taught her so many things over the years, most of which, she had to admit, never really resonated. She'd heard the basics—watch for cars while crossing a street, don't chew with your mouth open, and behave like a young lady. She never really understood that last one, and even in the middle of this nightmare, it didn't make a lot of sense. Were they asking her to be better than everyone else? Smarter? Modestly cute? What else?

Her brain was too scrambled to think through everything she'd screwed up to get to where she was. Somewhere along the way, her parents had probably given her the proper advice. But they were parents. Who really listened to their parents? She certainly hadn't, not after turning fourteen. She'd been a so-called good girl, but she'd always thought she knew more than they did. And maybe more so because they were immigrants and didn't really understand how American teens should act, what was socially acceptable.

Damn, she wished she'd listened more, applied their teachings. She would give anything to be back home, safe in her mother's arms.

She washed her face, but winced when the warm water touched the corner of her lip.

She shut off the water, tied her hair back into a tight ponytail, and forced herself to remove the heavy blanket of fear for just a few moments. She had not heard another scream, she realized. But she would not soon forget the terror in that one scream.

She prayed the cops would find her. Her parents were probably worried sick. An image of her brother, Daniel, came to mind. Again, her perception had been skewed as to how her actions could impact others. Sure, she'd lost her brother a year ago, but her parents had also lost a son. And now, they might lose their daughter too.

Guilt wrapped her body like a strait jacket. She'd been selfish, on top of being clueless.

She had to figure out something before Sal returned and forced himself on her.

She jumped in bed and tried to formulate a plan.

Thirty-Three

After stopping by Saul's apartment and sharing some late-night sushi, I told him I'd be back later, probably after he'd fallen asleep. I had some late-night surveillance to do.

The outdoor light on the corner house flicked off. At just after midnight, it was the final home in the neighborhood to go dark. The only visible light came from a single street lamp two blocks away, which illuminated the light rain falling from the dark sky. My black Civic blended in with the night, just as I'd hoped. I checked my rearview one more time to ensure the street was barren, just as it was in front of me. It was. I slid out of my car, shut the door with a quiet click, and then hopped onto the sidewalk and began the two-block trek to Lee High School. I'd initially considered doing some surveillance at one of the three remaining mission churches—Mission San Juan, Mission Espada, and the most famous of them all, the Alamo. But Stan had let me know the SAPD brass had posted armed guards around the clock at all the missions—the two where the murders had been committed and the three others. So that left me with an easy decision, Lee High School. We knew there was a common element between the homicides at the two missions and the animal sacrifice inside the field house: the use of Satanic symbols. Did that mean the same person committed all the crimes? As Stan and I had conferred following the gathering at the park—just before he was about to take off for his evening jog—it seemed highly unlikely, but not impossible. He said he'd once worked a case where the felon had purposely committed a similar crime several miles away. Once he was caught, he admitted that he'd done it to try to make it look like a copycat crime, to add more confusion to the investigation.

The key difference in these crimes was how the Satanic symbols were used. The first two crime scenes included the symbol most closely associated with human and animal sacrifices—the circle with the letter A inside of it. So, the usage of the symbol made sense. In the killing at Mission Concepcion, the killer had carved the symbol into the flesh of both girls, while the field house crime scene had the symbol burned into the artificial turf. At Mission San Jose, however, the killer had used a different symbol, the hexagram. It was carved into the victim's back with the arrow shot right through the middle. In addition, the victim of the third crime, a teenage boy, had his junk cut off and stuffed in his mouth. The level of violence alone made it seem like there were two different perpetrators, Stan had surmised.

I tended to agree, but I was still curious to learn more about this unknown world of devil worshipping. I'd spent a good couple of hours researching the topic, and what I learned surprised me. Satanists were mostly spiritualists who worshipped Satan as a deity. Some believed that Satan, also known as Lucifer, was the creator of humanity. The Church of Satan was established in 1966 by a guy named Anton LaVey, who made it clear that the church did not believe in the devil, and considered that more of a notion created by Christians and Muslims. While LaVey was the author of what is considered to be the Satanic Bible, it was actually nothing more than a collection of essays, rituals, observations. I found a record of him saying, however, that there were many people who smeared the name of Satanism, usually to only further their own cause, to shock their community, or to justify their own demented actions.

I'd also perused the web looking for more information on the Satanic symbols. When I found a site that provided definitions for each of the symbols, two things captured my attention very quickly. First, the symbol that looked like the Star of David, also known as the hexagram, and sometimes referred to as the Seal of Solomon, was the most powerful symbol used by occultists. Second, the sacrifice symbol, the one that had an A in the middle of a circle, apparently stood for anarchy.

Who are the biggest rebels in society? Teenage kids.

The homes in this middle-class neighborhood were as cookie-cutter as they could get, and so were the lots. One-story, brick, three windows across the front, a standard outdoor light, two thin trees in the front yard sitting on a lot that would barely fit my Civic. I saw a sign in about every third yard showing that a kid in that home was associated with Lee High School. Some were band members, a few used the term "orch dork" to show their affiliation with the orchestra, a handful were either cheerleaders or drill team members, and there were a good number of athletes—basketball, football, soccer, volleyball, just to name a few.

I crossed the street and heard a dog barking. Sounded like it came from one of the backyards. I wondered if the homeowner had a lock on the gate. And I also wondered if that would stop someone who was motivated to kill an innocent animal. Probably not. But was sacrificing animals the real purpose of what went down at the field house?

I knew I was questioning everything. This wasn't a quality born from running ECHO; it was my survival instinct growing up as a system kid, where I'd logged time at seventeen different foster homes. I trusted very few people.

My Spidey sense nibbled at the back of my mind after hearing both Brandon and, through Cristina, the girls at the park, bitterly complaining about the coaches at the school. What better way to get even than to desecrate their precious field house with the remains of a dead animal all in the name of Satan? I could practically see the worst element of the teenage community laughing hysterically, fist-bumping each other, after pulling off such a feat.

When I learned that the victim of the Mission San Jose killing not only went to Lee High School but was also a football player, I felt like the intersection of all of this crap was, for now at least, Mia's school, even though the two murdered girls hadn't attended Lee. How Mia's disappearance or kidnapping, or whatever it was, fit into all of this was still baffling. In fact, part of me was worried that I'd become so desperate to find clues on her whereabouts, I'd mistakenly clung to these murders with the hopes they would lead me to her.

I knew there were more holes to my theory than actual pieces. In fact, I didn't really have a working theory—that was how far behind I felt I was. All I could do was dig and ask questions until something popped up. And something would pop up. It had to. For Mia. For her grieving parents.

I could see the top of the school just over the row of rooftops at the end of the block. A light mist fell from the sky. It quickly matted my hair and sent a slight chill through my core. Part of me wished I was snuggled up with Saul in his apartment. But who was I kidding? I would never be able to sleep if I knew I wasn't doing everything humanly possible to bring Mia home. There was a chirp from my jeans pocket.

Thirty-Four

I continued walking and took out my phone to see a text from Cristina.

You still up?

I thought about walking and texting, but even with no one in sight, I didn't trust myself from twisting an ankle or doing something else equally as graceful. I pulled to a stop just at the corner of the last fence before the high school. I wondered if she'd found anything about Mia online.

Me: *Just out taking a stroll near Lee HS. Find anything new about Mia?*

Cristina: *Not really. She's either the biggest square, or she's better at hiding it than most.*

Me: *So nothing?*

Cristina: *Not even a reference to her old boyfriend, Brandon.*

Me: *Odd.*

Cristina: *And then some. But I told you before, she might be playing all of us. I only checked the accounts her parents gave us. She could have different accounts on the same social media sites using different login creds, even a different email address. Some people get off on how many personalities they can be. Of course, these are usually the same people who play video games 24/7 while cramming ten different kinds of junk food in their mouths.*

I quietly laughed at both her character description as well as the speed in which she spit out text messages. It was something to behold. But her point was solid. The only thing we really knew about Mia was that she was almost obsessed with trying to be a perfect person. Her Big Rules. I could see someone like that creating a different online persona, if only to feel like she wasn't boxed in.

Me: *Anything else?*

A splash of light caught my eye. It looked like it came from behind the main building of the school. I hopped across the parking lot, put my back against the brick wall on the east side of the school, and began to scoot closer toward the back. I glanced at my phone.

Cristina: *I'm kind of dead. Need a little sleep, then I guess I can start searching for the mysterious alt personality of Mia. Although I might have better luck in winning the Chinese lottery.*

She wasn't making much sense, but I understood her frustration. We needed someone to give us more information. Someone had to know more about Mia's whereabouts.

Another flash of light. Yep, it came from the field house. I typed in a quick text.

Get ready to call 911.

I made it to the northern edge of the building. Another text chirp, but my attention was focused on the field house. More than one beam of light, and they were moving. Without looking at my phone screen, I flipped it to mute and kept it in my hand.

I could see the dim outline of the field house, and then, a couple of seconds of light illuminated the far side. I didn't move for what seemed like a full minute. The coaches had probably made the building impenetrable by now, given what had happened there, so it made sense for the perps to be performing their ritual just next to it. Was there another animal sacrifice going on? I had to act. I couldn't just sit here and watch from afar.

I quickly measured my options. If I had Cristina call the cops, by the time they arrived the people could very well be gone. And what if they were nothing more than late-night walkers?

Assume the worse, Ivy. I hated to think that way, but the thought of animals being killed just to satisfy some bizarre ritual made my whole body tighten.

Another option: move in close enough to see if they are actually harming an animal, and then scare them off. The downside, of course, was that they'd get away.

A thought hit me like a bolt of lightning. What if they were killing a human being? What if these were the same people, or at least people from the same group, who'd killed the two girls and the boy at the missions?

I pushed off from the brick wall and scampered across the parking lot to a small brick enclosure for garbage bins. I peeked around the edge, waited a few seconds, then saw the lights flash across the sky from the same location as before. They hadn't run off.

I wiped water from my face—the rain had picked up—then plotted my next move, which was, essentially, running so quickly and silently that I could make it all the way to the field house without being detected. I'd aim for the closest position to where I stood on the western side of the field house.

I started giving myself a countdown, then I said screw it and just took off. I ran low to the ground, my sights looking for any movement of a person in the darkness on the side of the field house from where the lights were shining, or anywhere else. I stumbled over the curb—my teeth clamped down on my tongue—and then slammed my back into the brick facing of the field house. I was panting like a dog, my heart peppering my chest.

I glanced around the edge of the building and didn't see anyone. As I took a quick peek at my phone, I tasted blood. There was so much of it I could feel it swirling in my mouth like a fine wine. I read the text from Cristina.

Were you serious? Are you actually at Lee HS?

In checking the time stamp, another text came in a few minutes later, probably while I was taking a chunk out of my tongue.

Hello? Should I call 911 or not? Dammit, don't do this to me.

I didn't have time for her drama. I slowly shuffled down the side of the building, glancing at the ground for something I could use as a weapon, if it came down to that. I found a couple of small rocks, but that was it.

My gun. *Dammit!* I so rarely carried my Luger that I'd forgotten to bring it. Probably for the best. If it was just a couple of kids hanging out, doing nothing wrong, I'd scare the shit of them. Literally. I could question myself and my methods a hundred different ways, but it wouldn't change a thing right now. I amended my plan: I'd get just close enough to see what they were doing, and if needed, I'd send a quick note to Cristina to go ahead and call the cops.

I shuffled about fifty feet, then stopped the moment I heard voices. They were young. At least one girl and one boy. I couldn't hear what they were saying. Then, against the dark sky, I saw the lights again. I took a hard swallow and continued moving forward. At about ten feet from the end of the building, I heard a swooshing noise. It sounded familiar, but my mind couldn't place it.

And then I smelled something. It was rancid, as if my face had been stuffed into my cat's litterbox. I plugged my senses just as my mind connected all of the dots: they had killed an animal. Or a person! Maybe they were high on acid and dancing around their victim. For some reason, the story of Charles Manson and his crazed group of followers came to mind.

I had to get the cops here. I tapped my phone, which, of course, made the light come on. *Crap!* Then I remembered the camera on my phone. That was it. I had to get a picture of them. Sure, they would likely run away, but I'd have the image that would convict them of this horrible crime.

I jogged around the corner while I opened my photo app—which meant I wasn't looking where I was going. My foot slipped on a patch of grass, and I went airborne. People scrambled, shouting things like "get the hell out of here" and "teach that bitch a lesson," all before I hit the ground, knocking the breath out of me.

I clawed at the mud, trying to pull myself upright. A flash of light swept across me, and a shoe was swinging right at my face. I pulled back, and the shoe glanced off my shoulder. I cried out, fell back to the ground.

More yelling and people running. Then, two people jumped on top of me and started slapping and punching me. I crawled into a ball and tried to protect my face and head, but the blows still connected. I could feel the sting when one shot broke the skin on my forehead.

"Come on, man, let's get out of here before the cops show up," a boy said.

More footfalls all around me. I lowered my arm from my face and saw two people running away—in robes, the kind a monk might wear. I blinked a couple of times and pushed myself upright. I'd survived the mugging. Where was my phone? I needed to get a picture, call the cops.

I didn't see the fist until it was too late. It came out of nowhere and connected squarely with my jaw. Lights flickered as I teetered for a couple of seconds. I lost my balance and dropped back to the ground. On my way down, the guy who I thought had been the one to throw the punch jumped in front of me. Another flash of light.

What was that?

Something round and metal dangled from the guy's chest.

"Should we kill her, or is she dead already?"

Those were the last words I recall hearing.

Thirty-Five

More lights flashed in my eyes, and I pushed the paramedic's hand away. He sighed, then looked over at Stan and Cristina, who were talking quietly off to the side of the red truck. I noticed the rain had dialed back to just a light mist.

"Will you let the man do his job, Ivy?" Stan said. He sounded more irritated than compassionate.

"I'm not doing anything." I wiped my face and realized I sounded like a whiner. "Okay," I said to the man with the nice-sized tire around his waist. "I'm ready."

It seemed like I'd been on the gurney for a good couple of hours. He'd already treated a number of my cuts, including one on my forehead that made him say, "That sucker's going to hurt for a few days." That comment had upped the pain meter another couple of notches.

He went back to shining the light in my eyes. He lowered his little flashlight just a second before I was going to smack it out of his hand.

"Both eyes are dilated," he said. "More than likely you have a minor concussion. You sure you didn't go unconscious?"

I thought about where this answer would lead me—straight to a hospital where I'd be held hostage for hours, if not a day or more. "I'm okay."

He lifted an eyebrow. Perhaps I wasn't convincing enough. I said, "Seriously, don't you think I'd know if I went dark?"

"Don't believe her," Stan said as he and Cristina moved closer. I gave Stan the eye.

"If you think she went unconscious and you think she should make the trip to the hospital, then by all means, put her in the back and take her. Even if you have to strap her down."

"Stan, that's not your decision," I said with an air of defiance.

He turned to look at Cristina, who was staring right at me. I lowered my chin just slightly.

"She always looks like this," Cristina said, trying to make a case for letting me skip the trip to the hospital. But it came off like she was either blind or covering for me, the latter being the truth. Stan just shook his head.

"Look, guys, I got beat up. That's rather apparent," I said, pointing at my face. "It hurts, especially that last punch. But I'll live. There's no need to follow some antiquated protocol."

"Stubborn…" Stan put his head down, reading his notepad as he mumbled something else. I didn't bother asking for clarification.

"Wait. I found another cut on the back of your neck," the paramedic said.

Good. Something other than my brain to occupy his time.

As I turned my head so he could treat the cut, I noticed a purple glow on the horizon. It had to be close to sunrise. I thought about Saul.

"Has anyone contacted Saul? He might be surprised to not see me when he wakes up."

"I've texted him a dozen times," Cristina said. "I think he's a deep sleeper."

At least he couldn't say we didn't try. "Are you guys finally going to share with me what we've got?"

"A dead raccoon, for one," Stan said.

"And some sloppy graffiti," Cristina added, looking beyond the front of the truck, out of my line of sight.

That swooshing sound. That must have been spray paint. "What does it say?"

"Eh, we're trying to decipher it," Stan said.

"Is it some Satanic reference?" I sounded a little too eager.

"Maybe. Can't tell. The light rain made it all smear. So, there are letters, maybe two words, maybe sixteen or seventeen letters, but there are a lot of possible combinations."

I asked Cristina to go take some pictures of it with her phone, which she did. When she returned, she plopped her phone in my hand. I tried to focus on the small screen, but it made my head hurt. I kept that to myself, of course.

"Hmm." They were right. The words looked like some type of Egyptian hieroglyphics. I started to swing my legs to the side of the gurney.

"I'm not done yet," the paramedic said.

"Where do you think you're going?" Stan said, on the heels of the paramedic.

"I'll have a better chance of determining what the graffiti message is if I can take a look for myself."

Stan shook his head. "Do you ever give up? This isn't happening. Not now. You have a concussion, and he's in the middle of treating a wound."

I huffed out a breath and tried to again focus on the picture from Cristina's phone. It felt like a nail was being driven into my skull with each passing second. I handed the phone back to Cristina. "I'll be a good patient and just wait a few more minutes."

Stan was called away by a couple of uniforms, but said he'd be back to ask me more questions. Cristina began to tap her phone screen.

"Still trying to dig up something on Mia, or is NSBitch—excuse me, Jasmine—reaching out to you again?"

"Neither. I'm playing a video game," she said, her eyes peeled to the small screen.

Video games? Now? Without turning my head, I took a closer look. She seemed intense, if not stressed. "Who's winning?"

"I don't know. Just playing. Doing something to occupy my time."

"Are you bored?"

She lowered the phone, looked off for a moment. "Ivy, you could have been hurt really bad. You could have been killed."

"It was just some punks. They're not killers." Just as I said it, I realized how naïve I sounded.

"They killed an animal, and you told us that someone yelled out something about killing that bitch."

I didn't recall sharing that information. Not that I wanted to withhold anything. "That must have been when Stan first showed up. I was still a little groggy."

The paramedic stopped what he was doing, looked at Cristina, and shook his head. No other words were spoken, thankfully.

"Cristina, these things happen in this line of work."

"But you know you shouldn't have tried to jump into the middle of it. You should have asked me to call nine-one-one, and then wait for the cops to show up. You know it." Her tone had some bite to it.

Ow. "Looking back on it, you're probably right."

"Probably?"

"Okay, you're right. Good enough?"

She started laughing.

"What's so funny?"

"You. Me. Didn't they make a movie like this where the daughter and the mom somehow switched personalities?"

"Now you think I'm old enough to be your mom." I tried to keep a straight face, but a grin finally won out. Until the paramedic made me jump. "Ouch."

"Sorry. I'm almost done, so bear with me a moment."

I heard a loud voice over the din of the engines. "Who's that?" I asked Cristina.

She walked a few steps, then came back. "Some dude blowing a gasket with a cop. Looks like he's headed this way."

A few seconds later, Principal Peterson appeared just on the other side of the paramedic. He cocked his head and crossed his arms. "Why am I not surprised? Every time something bad happens on my campus, you're right there. Am I wrong?"

A jolt of pain hit me in about ten different places, as if alcohol had just been poured inside each wound.

Thirty-Six

I lifted my hands, but they quickly felt heavy and they dropped to my lap. "I wasn't the one who defaced the side of the field house or killed another animal. I was actually trying to get a picture of the people who committed this crime. It just didn't quite work out."

"What were you doing on my campus anyway?" He narrowed his eyes.

"I was in the neighborhood and was curious. Ever had that feeling?"

"I have no idea what you're talking about. All I know is you were trespassing, and I'm getting sick and tired of you acting like you run this place." He rolled up his sleeves, started jabbing his finger at me. "This is my campus and—"

"Put a sock in it, Peterson." Stan appeared out of nowhere, standing in front of the gurney. He held his prosthetic arm in front of Peterson, keeping Peterson from further intruding on my space.

The school principal, who I'd just noticed was wearing some type of suede jogging suit, smacked his lips a few times. He glared at Stan. "What is this about one of our prized student athletes being murdered at that mission?" He put a hand to his chest and coughed.

"Just got an ID earlier," Stan said. "It's very sad. We're investigating every possible angle."

"Sad? That's all you can say?"

Stan took in a breath and somehow kept a measured tone. "We have an entire team focused on finding the person or persons responsible for those killings, as well as what's going on here at the field house. Are they related? Can't say for sure."

"I understand you found Satanic symbols now at all locations." Peterson paused, giving us ample opportunity to take in his smug look.

Again, he had information that had not yet been released to the public, which I knew annoyed Stan. Me too, for that matter. Peterson, in general, was beyond annoying.

"I can't discuss specific pieces of evidence that may or may not have been found at the crime scenes," Stan said.

"But this is impacting me, do you hear me? Me, me, me!" he shouted.

Not his students, but him.

"I've got to go give an update to the assistant superintendent." Peterson took two hard steps, then stopped and looked Stan in the eye. "You, that redhead detective, all of these cops…you all need to find out who's doing this and lock them up. I never knew we had such an incompetent police department until this crap went down." He walked off before Stan could offer a retort.

Stan flipped around and tried scratching his chin with his fake hand, but he basically punched himself in the jaw. He was pissed. He flipped a few pages on his notepad. I could see he was giving himself a minute to cool down. Meanwhile, the paramedic said he was done with me, but he encouraged me to rest on the gurney for the time being. I was about to push back—I had a strong urge to see this graffiti for myself—and then Brook showed up, asking Stan all sorts of questions.

He looked at me. "You ready to go over all this again?"

Considering I had little to no memory of our first Q&A session, I was game. "Hit me."

Cristina looked at me with a blank face, and then she cracked up. It took me a second to catch on to what I'd just said. "I'm a piece of work right now. I think I need a little sleep."

"You look like shit, by the way," Brook said. She looked like a million bucks, even at this hour of the day, but I was too tired and my head hurt too much to care.

"Thanks. You should see the other guy."

I wasn't sure if she'd picked up on my sarcasm. I wasn't even sure where it had come from. Probably because my brain was operating like I'd had one too many lemon drop martinis.

"Just glad you survived the mugging." She looked to Stan. "Any Satanic symbols on this one?"

"Good question." I was glad someone's brain was functioning properly.

"Nothing we can find thus far. Not unless it's somehow painted in that mess of graffiti on the side of the field house. Not sure what the hell they're saying."

"But that's the key here, Stan," I said in a moment of clarity. "They're saying something. They might be high school kids getting off on killing animals and vandalizing the building, but they want us...someone to hear them."

Outside of the paramedic putting his gear back into containers, our space was quiet for a moment.

"I'm glad you pointed that out, Ivy. I mean, it's rather obvious, but even the obvious clues can be disregarded as just another piece of evidence." Using his left hand, Stan scribbled something on his notepad. He then asked me to start from the beginning with what I had seen.

I wasn't a minute into my answer when Brook interjected another question. "How many were there?"

I took in a breath, looking away to try to resurrect my memory. "Hard to say. It was chaotic. It was dark. Six, seven. Maybe more."

"Girls too?"

"Yep." A few images came to mind. "Did I tell you about the robes?"

Stan shook his head, so I gave them the details.

"Like a monk?" Brook said, putting a hand to her face as if she were about to laugh.

I shrugged. "That's the first thought that came to me." An image flashed across my mind, but it was so fast I couldn't determine its origin.

"So, you never told me why you decided to show up here at the school," Stan prompted.

I could feel Cristina's eyes on me. I was about to share ECHO secrets…the kind that made me sound borderline crazy, or maybe just desperate.

"It stems from two conversations. One that I had with someone, and one that Cristina and I overheard."

Stan moved his fake arm, a robotic gesture for me to get to the point.

"Both conversations were with kids who are in athletics here at the school. They sounded really pissed at the coaches."

As expected, Stan and Brook looked at me like I was borderline crazy. "I didn't think you'd take me seriously."

"Guys, wasn't her hunch right?" Cristina said. "I mean, we don't know for certain, not unless we can get a student athlete or coach or administrator to enlighten us. I bet if we figure out what's painted on the side of the field house, we'll have a better idea if her theory is valid or garbage."

"Thanks…I think," I said with a wink. A pain shot through my head, then that same image flashed across my mind. This time, I saw something metal, shiny. I was lying on the ground, looking up. Was it after that asshole had punched me?

An officer walked up and handed Stan something.

"Is that my phone?" I asked. He handed it over, and I saw the screen had been cracked even more.

"Is it usable?" Cristina asked.

I opened my text app and sent a test message to Cristina. She gave me the thumbs-up. I then called Stan. He pushed a button on his phone without looking at the screen. "That could have been Bev asking if you were coming back to bed," I said, grinning.

He tilted his head, then checked the time. "Hell," he said with single chuckle, "this is almost the time I get up to take my morning jog. Not sure I'll get to it today. Might have to go twelve miles tonight."

He was serious. It was still hard to believe this was the same guy whose sugary snacks were considered appetizers before a four-course meal of pure fat.

A moment later, my phone rang. Everyone looked at me. "It's Saul." I answered the phone as I heard Stan say, "Now who's acting like the old married couple?"

Saul initially was relieved to hear my voice. He had just awakened and seen Cristina's text messages. I wondered exactly how dire she'd described my condition. It was kind of cool to have someone care about me like Saul did. This was new territory for me, so I wasn't sure how to take it. I only said, "I didn't mean to worry you."

He then convinced me that I needed to get to his place and he would make sure I was as comfortable as possible.

"Okay, I'll be there soon. Sorry I wasn't there to wake you up in that *special way*."

He laughed, then said we'd have plenty of special opportunities in the future. After I ended the call, I used my powers of persuasion to get a ride over to Saul's. Brook volunteered and even grabbed one of the uniforms to drive my car behind us so it wouldn't be stuck in the neighborhood.

Back on my feet, the terrain seemed a lot less even. I knew it was me and my physical instability, but it would pass eventually. On the way to Brook's car, we walked by the field house to view the graffiti.

"Any ideas?" Cristina asked us.

"I haven't learned how to read Chinese yet."

Brook looked at me. "Now that you're seeing it in person, what do you think?"

I studied the series of letters—which looked more like a two-year-old's chicken scratch—for a good couple of minutes. They were starting to blur together, so I used my phone to take a few pictures.

"Does your camera even work?" Cristina asked. "You've got an old model anyway. Might need to throw it in the gadget junkyard. Your car should have been there a long time ago." She gave me a toothy grin.

Smart ass. I tried to arch an eyebrow, but that tugged at the gash on my forehead. A moment later, the skies opened up and unleashed a heavy, chilly downpour. We scrambled to the car. From the passenger-side window in Brook's car, I watched the white letters dissolve into nothing. Save for the few pictures Christina and I had taken, I wondered if our best clue to date had just gone down the drain.

Thirty-Seven

Who knew that Saul had the culinary skills to cook homemade chicken noodle soup? Not that it required years of training and hours in the kitchen, but it was the most delicious bowl of soup—actually, I had two bowls—I'd ever downed.

I reclined on Saul's comfy couch after taking my second catnap in the last three hours. While I missed my Zorro—he was probably tearing through a roll of toilet paper back at my place—I felt remarkably revitalized by the soup, the rest, and Saul's compassion. After a look of shock on his face when I'd showed up at his door, he'd asked me one probing question: "Why do you keep putting yourself in danger like this?" I'd told him he should know by now, and he'd dropped it. From then on, he was the ultimate caregiver.

What else could a girl ask for?

I had to practically push Saul out the door so he could head off to work. Because of his caring hands, I even convinced myself to not worry about Kyra, the centerfold ice cream scooper.

My headache had subsided into the normal range. While my cuts and bruises were still pretty fresh, the pain meter only hit the red zone when I accidentally brushed against something. Like earlier, when I'd turned onto my side, I draped my arm over my head and clumsily bumped the gash on my forehead. I could have bitten through steel at that moment. Instead, I unleashed a string of expletives that would have put Cristina to shame.

I grabbed my cracked phone off the coffee table, opened up my photos, and studied the pictures of the graffiti. The first showed an entire word, or letters, or artwork, or whatever. And that was the real problem. It was impossible to determine if it was nothing but letters that had been disfigured by the rain, or if there was a graphic in the spray-painted mush. And if I was looking at an image, not words, was it Satanic? And what did it mean? What were the perpetrators trying to communicate?

After coming face to face with at least one of the monk-looking perps, I was still vacillating between the two options: devil worshippers who had a specific message they were trying to communicate, or punks who were just going for the shock factor.

I swept through the subsequent pictures, pausing to study each letter or blob. Some were connected, but it was difficult to tell if that was by design or because of the rain. The ninth and tenth pictures appeared to be related to each other, though they also looked very similar. I opened up a browser on my phone, and in between the cracks in the glass, I clicked on my favorites list and found the website I'd referenced earlier with all of the Satanic symbols.

My eyes went straight to the two symbols that had been used at the three different crime scenes, the anarchy symbol and the hexagram. I was almost certain that neither of those images were represented in the graffiti. I scanned through two dozen other symbols, continuously flipping back to my photos to see if there was anything that matched.

I came up empty. But if there was no Satanic symbol at this crime scene, what did that tell me? Had the objective of the group who committed the first crime at the high school changed? Of course, they'd killed an animal this time too, albeit a raccoon. The creature probably wasn't a pet, but to kill a living thing like that was just sickening. And for what? Kicks? To incite fear? Make a statement about Satanism?

Another thought: what if this group wasn't involved in the first sacrifice? They could be copycatting the crime. Teenagers mimicking bad behavior of other teenagers was pretty common. Follow the leader, that type of thing.

My mind then went in yet another direction: what if this group of teenage thugs was behind all of it—the other animal sacrifice, the brutal murders of the teens at the missions? After all, the football player killed at Mission San Jose had been a student at Lee. Who knows why he was killed or why he was at the old church? The two murdered girls were high school age, although they went to different schools. But that didn't mean they didn't have a connection to someone at Lee. Maybe from the parties they attended? Seemed like a stretch.

A sudden throb of pain shot through my head, and I got that same mental snapshot I'd seen earlier: right after that asshole had sucker-punched me. I'd looked up from the ground and noticed a glint of metal. It was round, hanging from the guy's chest. My brain then hopped to the next image: the links in the chain around his neck. They were familiar to me—their dirty brass color, their fairly large size. Something about the links stayed with me. I gently pressed my fingers against my eyes for a moment and probed my thoughts for more memories.

I snapped my fingers and pushed up from the couch. I had to find Brandon.

Thirty-Eight

If nothing else, Cristina was good for one thing. She made me think before I made certain decisions. Decisions that, before I'd met Cristina at a women's self-defense class almost a year earlier, I would have easily considered not to be worth my time pondering. I would have taken the risks, hands down.

In this instance, I considered jumping into Black Beauty and driving myself across town. I knew better, though. My reflexes and vision weren't up to snuff. Cristina, who'd turned out to be a treasure as both a streetwise PI and a friend, would definitely be pissed if I tried it and probably lose all respect for me.

So, I took an Uber back over to Lee High School. I used my free time wisely and exchanged a few text messages with Cristina explaining my plan to confront Brandon. She first asked if she could come watch—she claimed it might be better than a UFC match. *Very funny, Cristina.* Then, she got serious and insisted that I pick her up so she could be my wingwoman. Not necessary, I told her. Once she knew that pressing me further was a lost cause, she said she was headed to the MACC to see if she could find any of the staffers who might have more information on Jasmine and why she was so skittish. She also said the social media search for Mia's alt ego had gone nowhere. She asked if she could somehow recoup those wasted hours. I told her to stop the drama and move on. Which she did.

I then called Stan. He said they'd learned a bit more about the arrow used to kill Benito Alvarez.

"It's actually not called an arrow." He had a lot of energy in his voice, which was rather surprising since he'd been working before the sun came up.

"So the long, thin rod with the deadly sharp edge at the end is not an arrow? I'm either confused or my brain was really scrambled by that punch."

"Yeah, this isn't one of those bow-and-arrow type of arrows. We're not talking Robin Hood here. The killer used a crossbow."

A crossbow. Well, I wasn't expecting that. "So were you able to figure out who sells crossbows, get a suspect list together?"

"We're looking at both crossbows and bolts."

"Bolts? Are there screws too?"

He clapped out a quick laugh. "No, no. Arrows fired from crossbows are actually called bolts."

"Since when did you become such the expert?"

"In the last two hours. We have two uniforms still pulling together data from retailers and manufacturers. Unfortunately, we can't really get a bead on the exact type of crossbow, since there are so many different types of bolts that can be used. For now, they're focusing on the bolts."

"Any luck? I mean, don't retailers have to keep records of sales of these bolts? Aren't they basically ammunition?"

"In some respects, yes. But since a crossbow is fired mechanically without the aid of burning, expanding gases, it's not considered a firearm. Retailers aren't required to record owner information. For the officers, it's been a very manual effort. They're on the phone, using all sorts of spreadsheets and pivot tables. It's kind of amazing what the younger generation knows."

Again, I thought of Cristina's exceptional skills. "I get it. Have they been able to put together a suspect list?"

"Very sketchy right now, just because it depends on each retailer, what data they recorded, whether the buyer used a credit card, check, or paid cash. So, maybe another day or so might turn up something. Hard to say at this point."

A day at best. I'm not sure I wanted to hold my breath for another night to pass. And lately, everywhere I turned, I seemed to run into a thug, or a thug wannabe. We were about to end the call when I thought of something. "Stan, if a crossbow is not considered a firearm, anyone can purchase one, right?"

"I guess so, why?"

"Well, aren't felons restricted from owning firearms?"

"You're sure as hell right," he said, catching on to where I was headed.

"Which means that a felon could easily buy one of these crossbows and all the bolts they could afford."

He said he'd share that thought with Brook and the two data monkeys and get back to me if they found anything. Feeling like I made a small contribution to the effort, I relaxed in the back seat of what was a reasonably clean Passat. I stared out the window for a couple of miles. My vision had just begun to glaze over when yellow and black ribbons snagged my gaze. I sat up and spotted dozens of ribbons tied to light poles, trees, school signs in front of Lee High School. I wondered if they were the school colors. The Uber driver let me off in the back parking lot.

I stepped out of the car and took in a full breath. The storms had cleared, and the cool air felt good to my lungs. Knowing most teens were creatures of habit, I walked toward the area where I'd last seen Brandon's pickup. With every step, though, there was a reverberation in my head, as though my ears were clogged with water. I found myself reaching my hand out to the nearest car to make sure I maintained my balance. It wasn't so much that I sensed I was going to fall as it was I just didn't trust my balance.

The parking lot seemed less full, but there was no sign of Brandon's pickup. Maybe he was driving a different vehicle. I wandered around as students began to filter out of the school. A few kids looked my way, and I looked back, hoping to spot the cocky teen. Dozens of students passed by me, but Brandon wasn't one of them.

Had he skipped school? Maybe he knew I'd be looking for him. I looked up and saw a kid wearing a letterman's jacket with a football on the sleeve; he was pulling out his keys as he cut between two sports cars. I quickly moved in that direction—that was a mistake. My head started spinning, and everything tilted to the left. I tilted too, my elbow banging against the hood of a car.

"What the hell, lady?"

It was the football player, but I was too busy trying to keep myself from tumbling to the ground to say anything. I twisted my torso, placed both hands on the hood, and let out a breath.

"Are you going to keel over and die or something?"

"Sorry," I said, glancing up.

His eyes got wide. "Whoa, what happened to you?"

I planted my butt against the side of the car, then touched the bandage on my face. "I was mugged." My ability to be subtle had left me. "Can you tell me if you've seen Brandon McCarthy at school today?"

"Oh, Little Bitch?" he said with a smirk.

What was it with everyone at this high school having "bitch" as a nickname? "So, have you seen him?"

"Not sure. Coach called off football practice today. We had a teammate, uh…"

"I heard. It's really sad."

"Yeah, I guess he was pretty cool and all. I didn't know him that well." He looked off for a moment.

"But he was your teammate, so it's okay to be upset."

"I'm not upset." He bowed out his chest.

I assumed he felt his reputation as a tough football player would be ruined if he showed any emotion. "No worries. I'm sure Benito had some close friends on the team."

"Eh." He rocked back and forth on his feet a bit.

How could I not inquire further after that response? "Was Benito disliked?"

He picked a nail for a few seconds, then said, "Some guys thought he was a little...you know."

"I don't know."

"They were thinking he might be a little light on his feet, if you know what I'm saying."

He was gay. In the regular world, that mattered very little to people, for the most part. On a high school football team, however, even in the twenty-first century, they probably weren't as open-minded. "Has anyone talked about why he was at the mission?"

"Huh? Nah. No clue. Wasn't he Catholic, though? Confession of sins and all that, maybe? Listen, I need to get going and everything."

"What about Brandon?"

"Some seniors left early since athletics is the last period of the day. What do you want with him anyway?"

I remembered he was the kid and I was the adult, so I ignored his question. "Any idea on where he might have gone?"

Another smirk. "What do I look like, his mother? Damn." He twirled his key chain around his fingers a couple of times. "You're asking a lot of questions about Little Bitch. You a cop? You don't look like a cop."

"I guess you answered your own question. By the way, why do you call Brandon 'Little Bitch'?"

"Oh, well, it's really something we picked up from Coach Rossi. He started calling Brandon his Little Bitch. He teased him a lot. Made him run a lot of gassers for mouthing off. Pretty much treated him like—"

"His little bitch."

A quick chuckle. "Yeah, that."

"Does Coach Rossi ride anyone else like that?"

His face went blank, and he didn't respond. I must have crossed some imaginary line, and he now saw me as the enemy.

I quickly said, "You don't have to tell me. I was just wondering, that's all. I mean, my basketball coach in high school was a tyrant. She'd push us around, throw balls at us, make us run until we puked our guts out. That woman was the most hated person in the school." I was a little surprised with my mental agility to create a complete fabrication on the fly. I was hoping he'd open up, give me the scoop on this coach-hating vibe we'd seen out of Jasmine's friends and Brandon.

He crossed his arms and nodded. "I need to get going. I've got a lot of homework."

I pushed off the car to a standing position. Hello, blood rush. I got lightheaded and reached for the car in the adjacent space. Was someone yelling my name? When I was able to focus, I saw the ugly scowl of Principal Peterson closing in fast from about ten feet away. "Ivy Nash, you have no right being on this campus, harassing my students. You are trespassing, do you hear me?"

Damn, this guy was a nag. "Do you even know what's going on in your school?"

His feet pounded the ground as he entered my personal space. "What are you talking about? I get the most out of my staff, and our students have higher test scores than any other high school in the district."

A waft of warm tuna fish blew right into my face. I tried covering my nose.

"Are you drunk too? Good Lord, you can't keep your balance. Is that booze I smell on you?"

Before I could respond, he had a phone to his ear. "I'd like to report a trespasser on our school property. Okay, yes I'll hold." He gave me another one of his smug looks.

I thought he was going to stick his tongue out at me. I wanted to slap him. I heard a chirp, and through the mental fog and the tuna-fish haze, I plucked my phone from my pocket. It was a text from Cristina.

Get ur ass over to the MACC. Brandon just showed up.

I tapped my Uber app and happily left Peterson in the parking lot.

Thirty-Nine

Cristina handed me a power bar, then she tore the wrapper on hers and took a bite. She noticed I was looking at her. "Go ahead, eat the damn thing. I'm telling you, it will help with all your…issues."

"I don't have issues. I'm just a little lightheaded, that's all." Still, though, all I'd had to eat was soup. So, I followed her lead and tried the power bar. "Mmm. Pretty good." I then noticed how many grams of sugar were on the wrapper. "Not sure this is going to help me."

"It's not Stan-approved, if that's what you mean."

It was amazing that Stan's approach to health and diet was the new standard.

"You lost Brandon how soon after he arrived?" We were standing in the large, open area downstairs at the MACC, as kids milled about in their various cliques.

"Five minutes, max. I texted you that I wanted to grab his ass, get Dr. Amaya to help me detain him, but you said to hold off."

"We're not the cops," I reminded her. My eyes were diverted to Dr. Amaya. He had a group of people in his office. He was standing at a whiteboard that had a bunch of numbers on it. "Wonder how long this budget meeting will take place," I said.

Cristina looked over her shoulder at the girl who logged in everyone who entered the MACC. "Why don't we just make her show us the logs so we can see if he snuck out when I wasn't looking? What she going to do, sue us?"

"And exactly how do you think we should go about that?"

"There's two of us…" She paused, gave me the once-over. "Well, right now, we're about at a one point five."

"Funny." I bit off another piece of the candy bar disguised as a power bar. "We're not bullying that girl into giving us the logs." I let out a frustrated breath and watched a group of teenage girls walk by. They were all on their phones, taking selfies and smacking on gum.

Cristina leaned closer to me. "I never knew cheerleaders could be so talented. Taking selfies, chewing gum at the same time." She brought a hand to her face, then mockingly said, "Can I be one of them?"

"You cheering for anyone would be a positive." I saw the same pack of girls ignore another girl who'd appeared to have asked one of them a question. She had a book and wore thick-rimmed glasses. "It's amazing how mean kids can be," I said, shifting my sights around the facility, looking for any sign of Brandon. "Are you sure you checked all those side rooms when you searched for Brandon?"

"Everywhere except the boys' bathroom."

"Maybe he was in there."

"I waited outside for five minutes."

"How about the ping-pong room?"

"That too."

"Did he see you when he came in?"

"Don't think so, but he doesn't really know me."

Just then, the door to Dr. Amaya's office opened, and a bunch of folks walked out. They either had gray hair or wrinkles, or both.

As I approached them, I could hear a number of them blowing out breaths, like they were exhausted after a torturous, long meeting.

"Were you holding them hostage in there, Doctor?" I joked as we met just outside his office.

He gave me a funny look. Actually, it wasn't funny. It was more like instantly pissed. "Uh, no, Ivy," he said with a serious tone.

"Dr. Amaya is way too kind to hold anyone hostage," Clifton said with a hearty smack on the doctor's back.

The doctor cracked the tiniest of smiles and explained Clifton's comment. "We went on a wild boar hunting trip in Louisiana a few weeks back. They wanted to trap the animals and hold them in the cage until we could get to them and kill them. Seemed inhumane to me. But hey, I guess I should have thought about that before signing up for a hunting trip."

I tried to get past the doctor's odd response and all of their testosterone-fueled games and asked if we could check the logs.

"Why would you want the logs, Ivy?" He tilted his head, acting as if he were holding back a more visceral reaction.

Clifton apparently felt the tension in our space. "I'll let the two of you continue your discussion without me prying into your business."

"I didn't mean to interrupt anything," I said. "But I do have some urgency with my request." I glanced upstairs and saw one of the doors open.

Clifton smiled. "No worries, Ivy." Then he turned and looked at the doctor, whose face was etched with disgust. "Lighten up, Doc. We'll figure out this budget issue."

Dr. Amaya shuffled his feet, nodding at Clifton. "I'm good. Think I might head out early today. Maybe I can go to that new target-practice place you told me about to try out the crossbow I picked up since our hunting trip."

I felt a prick at the base of my skull. *Crossbow?*

Clifton said he had some work to do on his family farm, waved goodbye, and headed toward the exit.

For a moment, that left Dr. Amaya and me alone in our space. It was like the great stare-off. I hadn't felt this way about him since I first met him, when his seemingly hateful glare had felt like a violation to my womanhood. Of course, it had turned out to be nothing. Apparently, he thought I looked like his daughter and couldn't stop staring at me. Now, though, I had a different vibe. Irritation bordering on outright anger.

"Did I upset you, Doctor?"

He looked off for a moment, releasing a breath. "It's nothing. Why did you need to see the logs? We have our policies for a reason, you know."

He was still being short with me. And it was starting to piss me off.

Cristina suddenly hopped next to me and smacked my shoulder. "Ivy, we've got a Brandon sighting." She took off for the front door.

I started following her, but my fragile state wouldn't allow anything more than a fast walk. I then spotted Jasmine and, about twenty feet behind her, Brandon. I couldn't see their faces, so I wasn't sure if they were running together or if he was chasing her.

My body wanted to break into a sprint, but I couldn't. As it was, I felt like I was driving forty miles an hour on a solid sheet of ice. Cristina was up ahead of me, but Jasmine had just run out the door, followed quickly by Brandon. "Dammit," I said, pumping my arms. Just then, a little kid holding a drink cut right in front of Cristina. She tried to jump over him and fell to the ground.

"You okay?" I asked, walking past her as she rolled to her side. I felt like I was moving at the pace of a tortoise.

She moaned, "I'm fine." She got to her feet, and we reached the door at the same time. We slammed the door open.

"I always thought you were a worthless slut." Brandon had Jasmine by her hair. She tried pulling away, whimpering. I bolted out of my stance, but before I took two steps, he threw her to the ground. She tumbled toward me and Cristina.

"Brandon!" I yelled.

But he paid me no attention. He ran off like the chickenshit he was.

Forty

Cristina sprinted down the sidewalk after Brandon.

"What are you doing?" I yelled, as I dropped to my knees. "Are you okay, Jasmine?"

Gasping out breaths, she tried to push herself off the sidewalk, but as she put pressure on her arm, she dropped back.

"Let me see your arm."

She raised her elbow to show a contusion. A large bruise had already formed around a bloody scrape. "Can you move it?"

She moved it about six inches but moaned in the process.

"You need to get to the emergency room. It might be broken." I helped her to a sitting position.

"I'm fine." A single tear rolled down her cheek, but she quickly wiped it away.

I heard the quick shuffle of shoes, and I lifted my sights to see Cristina pulling up next to us. "That motherfucker…" She put her hands on her knees, panting. "He's…he's frickin' quick. He hauled ass around the corner, then cut in front of this truck. Almost got hit, but somehow dodged it, then disappeared down an alley. I lost him."

"We'll get him." I pulled out my phone.

"Who are you calling?" Jasmine asked.

"Who else? The cops," Cristina said. "They better catch Brandon before I do. I'm going to beat his ass."

I glared at Cristina, hoping she'd see my signal to dial back the violent response.

"Are you? Are you calling the cops?" Jasmine asked.

I punched Stan's number and put the phone to my ear. "No need to worry, Jasmine. I'm calling a friend of mine, a detective. He'll know how to handle this. He'll make sure you're protected, and he'll pick up Brandon. We saw everything. He'll be arrested, and he'll go to jail for assault."

Before I knew what had happened, she snatched the phone out of my hand, hung up the call, and tossed the phone toward the building. She then got to her feet and backed away a few steps. "I don't need the help. I don't want the help."

"What the hell are you saying, Jasmine? He threw you to the ground."

"I'm fine. It's no big deal. We just had a disagreement."

"Jasmine." I took a step forward. She took two steps back, so I stopped. "Jasmine. Are you two a couple?"

"Kind of, yes."

"This has happened before, hasn't it?"

"I don't know. Maybe once, twice. Look, Brandon's got issues, but so do I. Hell, who doesn't these days?"

"He's an abusive boyfriend, Jasmine. He won't stop. It will only get worse. You need to stay away from him. And we need to call the cops and have him arrested."

"No, dammit! You're just going to make it worse."

Cristina moved next to me "How? He's got you scared. He's probably threatened you if you tell anyone, hasn't he?"

Before she could answer, the door to the MACC opened, and the throng of snobby girls came out. Jasmine glared at me and Cristina. "Just chill," she whispered.

"Hey, Jas," the lead girl said, swaying her hips from side to side as if it somehow designated her as the queen of the group.

"Hey," Jasmine, said, running her fingers through her hair.

They sauntered past us. Two of the girls in the rear of the pack looked over their shoulders at Jasmine and giggled. A few seconds later, Cristina said, "Who are those snobby bitches?"

"Oh, they're with the Highsteppers, our drill team. They're full of themselves, but they can make or break your rep if you don't watch your step around them."

"Your reputation," I said, still trying to wrap my mind around the social pressure I'd just witnessed. "You were just assaulted, and it wasn't the first time. You don't need to put up a façade for them."

"Dammit, you're just so naïve. If I say or do the wrong thing to the wrong person, then they'll trash me on Snapchat, Instagram, Reddit, you name it. And then what do I have?"

"Is Brandon one of those wrong people?" Cristina asked.

She tried stretching out her arm and winced. "Maybe, but it doesn't matter now. I just need to suck it up and I'll be fine."

"Is he the guy you had this so-called sexting scandal with?" I asked.

She opened her lips, but closed them just as fast. "It's complicated."

"Why?" Cristina said. "I'm in high school too. I know about all of the crazy shit that goes on in the popular crowd, and those who are trying to claw their way into that group. But you don't have to take part in that. You can break away."

Tears bubbled in Jasmine's eyes, and then she looked off for brief second. "I—" She stopped short.

Then she toyed with something through her T-shirt. It had to be a necklace. I wanted to ask her about it, but she was already on edge. I tried to bring down the intensity a bit. "Jasmine, it's okay. We're not going to do anything you don't want us to."

"Thank you." Her shoulders dropped an inch. "It's just that…there's so much going on. Benito died, and it really hit me hard. I was trying to talk to Brandon about it, but he's too wrapped up in his own drama to care."

I glanced at Cristina, then flipped back to Jasmine. "That police detective friend I told you about? He has a whole team of folks working Benito's murder case around the clock."

She nodded, but her gaze was still distant. "I've been one of those snobby bitches before. I was a Highstepper as a freshman. I've been mean, vindictive." Her chin quivered. "I'm not proud of it. We all need to be cleansed. None of us are perfect."

I wondered if this had anything to do with her sexting scandal, or for that matter, Mia. She was the one who had no voice. Everyone else was just surviving in this malicious madness.

Cristina opened her arms. "Life sucks, Jasmine. I get it. I've been there. But you know what? Life goes on. High school will be over before you know it, and maybe then you can realize how insignificant these people really are. But between now and graduation, you need to break free from these fucking losers."

"I don't know." She moved her arm, then flinched from the pain. "I just think it's best that I not rock the boat. Yeah, that's what I need to do. I know both of you are trying to help, but I gotta go."

She flipped around and walked off, cradling her injured arm.

Forty-One

With her knees clutched to her chest, Mia hummed a song that her mom used to sing to her at bedtime. It was bright and cheerful, and talked about little bunnies hopping through the grass on their way to play with friends before finally returning to home, where, without an ounce of energy left, they fell asleep as their mom sang to them.

She must have been five years old when she first remembered her mother singing "Little Bunny Foo-Foo," and it happened every night even as she advanced through elementary school. Mia had loved it. When she'd turned ten years old, things changed for Mia. The girls at school became catty, and everything she wore, said, or did was judged in some form or fashion. She started internalizing a lot of her thoughts, and became more covert in how and when she showed love to her parents. The best of times, though, were those nights when her mom would sing her that goodnight tune not just once, but three or four times if she was good. That went on until she was in the seventh grade. Eventually, she became too mature for such childish antics. Her family became less and less important in her life.

She'd give anything to be back in her parents' home, eating the same old food every night, sleeping on her sagging mattress, and yes, despite all that had occurred, lying in bed as her mom once again sang the tune of the little bunny who ran home to go to sleep.

Swaying back and forth on her bed in the mansion, the happy sounds of her mother's voice dissipated, despite her internal pleas for them to continue. She needed something to drown out the lecherous grunts that echoed in her mind. Sal had returned twice that day, as he'd promised. The first time he was good-natured, chatty even. Yet she knew what he wanted. He threatened her, but his voice was calm, his mannerisms gentle, as if he didn't really want to follow through if she didn't comply with his wishes.

On his first visit to her room, she had spent time talking to him about his farm, the horse she'd seen, what he did for a living—he was some type of financial advisor—everything and anything to make him feel important. Ultimately, wasn't that what guys wanted? Yes, they had a primal desire to have sex, to dominate another person. But it seemed to her like they also craved validation of who they were as men, their masculinity. It was all about their conquests. And to play this game, she had to make him feel like he was the most idolized man in the world.

The ego-building game had gone on for a good hour, and initially he seemed delighted in her interest, her engagement. But she knew it was only delaying the inevitable. With the grace of a three-legged buffalo, Sal finally made his move on her. It was wet and disgusting. She hadn't seen a male that awkward since she was a freshman. The difference, however, was quite evident: his strength. If he wanted her to move in a certain direction, it happened, whether she wanted it to or not.

She realized it was in her best interest to not fight his advances—to save her energy for a time when she thought she could escape. When Sal was ready, he removed all of his clothes and stood at the foot of the bed. Light sliced through a crack in the curtains onto a silver cross attached to a necklace around his neck.

He then kneeled, bowed his head, and mumbled a prayer. She couldn't hear the words, but her eyes had been drawn to his pants, which were draped over the chair.

She'd recalled him placing the key to her door in the right front pocket of his chinos. Did she have time to race over to the chair, pull out the key, and unlock the door before he could act?

No way in hell. Not unless he was incapacitated. Like a good swift kick to his balls. But she didn't have the right angle. Just then, he finished his prayer or chant or whatever, then crossed himself. He was Catholic. Like she was. Not that she'd received an A-plus for her worshipping efforts, but her mom and dad had taken her to mass at least once a week ever since she could recall.

He didn't speak again until he finally put his clothes back on, and then he said, "May God have mercy on my soul. I shall return later."

And he did.

The second time was nothing like the first. It was as if he were on drugs…or maybe had forgotten to take his medication. He was riding high one moment, then bitterly angry the next. He paced the room, smacking one hand into the other, initially talking about nuclear bombs and spies and assassinations. Then, somewhere in his speech, he mumbled about someone not doing what they promised.

Every time he reached one end of the room and flipped to turn the other direction, he grew more agitated, his movements more pronounced. Mia became scared, wondering how he'd ultimately unleash his fury, so she tried talking to him. At first, she attempted to change the topic, to get back to stroking his ego. But he hardly paid her any attention. She then tried to console him, saying she would gladly help ease his anxiety.

Without warning, he stopped on a dime and stared at her. "Do you think I'm a fucking lunatic, someone who belongs in one of those asylums?"

Thrown by his question, she paused an extra second. Then she said, "No, no. You're obviously under a lot of stress. You just need me to help—"

Before she uttered the last word, he'd backhanded her across the face. It stunned her, dropped her to the floor. She pushed herself up, wiped blood from her lips, and again attempted to console him. He swatted her face with his opposite hand. That one had cut her cheek, and she shrieked. He then rushed at her, grabbed her from behind, putting her head in some type of vice grip that choked off her oxygen. She became lightheaded, thought she might pass out, or worse.

"No matter what I do to you today, tomorrow, next year, or five years from now, you will not scream out. Do you hear me, young lady?"

She tried to push out a reply, but all that came out was a squeak. He let her go, and she gasped for air. But he wasn't done. He slapped her, threw her across the room. Then, after a couple of minutes he apologized, which somehow led to rants about world politics and some delivery that had been messed up. And then the cycle began again. Over time, she tried to separate her conscious self away from the beating she was taking. But she couldn't escape her memories. She had watched her father beat her mother. It didn't happen often, and she didn't think he'd seen her watching from the crack in her bedroom door. But it was unmistakable and broke her little seven-year-old heart. Flash forward ten years, to when Brandon had been physical with her. He'd shoved her to the floor, rammed an elbow in the small of her back...all because she hadn't kissed him right.

She hadn't even liked Brandon that much, and yet it destroyed her. Yes, she got over it. Still, she knew he was a punk and that she deserved better, someone more mature. Someone with a purpose in life.

And today that someone had assaulted her, raped her twice, and then locked her in her room.

She tried to bring back that tune her mom used to sing to her. Something to hold her thoughts, to cling to a bit of sanity. But it was as elusive as a greased pig.

Could she actually survive in this state for months or years, waiting for Sal to die?

It wasn't possible. Death would have to come soon. For him. Or maybe for her. But this couldn't go on much longer. That much she knew for certain.

She took in a single breath. In a slight pause, she heard a distant ding. Then, another noise. It was closer to a clank. Metal on metal. She looked toward the bathroom. Rushing in, she opened the cabinet and put her hand on the pipe leading to the wall. She felt a reverberation on the pipe; at the same time, there was another clank. And then two more.

Someone was trying to communicate with her.

Forty-Two

I was thankful for at least one thing: Saul's couch was first rate.

Beyond that, I was irritated, annoyed, frustrated. Night had again fallen upon San Antonio, and we were no closer to finding Mia. As was my typical MO, I tried to put myself in Mia's shoes. If she were alive—and dammit, I had to believe it was true—what was she thinking and feeling right now, at this very moment? Her existence, in my mind, was separated into two distinct and very different options. The first was that she had her freedom. She might be with someone or she might be alone. Was she walking around the city, camouflaged within the mass of humanity going about daily routines? If so, why hadn't she reached out to let people know she was okay? She might have issues, maybe some hidden ones at that, but it was hard to imagine her purposely wanting her parents to suffer.

I touched the bandage on my head, then sipped the smoothie that I'd picked up on my way back to Saul's. He'd intended on meeting me back here, but said he had to work late. He'd secured his first client—something about a family inheritance lawsuit. I told him we needed to celebrate, and he said we could do that after my meeting with the person who had information about my parents. I'd temporarily put the parent hunt out of my mind, probably just to keep my expectations in check. I did my best to not grill him about Kyra, and he said when he got home he'd wake me up in that *special way*. I reminded him of my weakened condition, and he said I could have a rain check.

Actually, I was feeling surprisingly strong. The smoothie helped; so did the couch.

My thoughts went back to Mia and the second option: she was being held against her will. Was she hurt? Was she afraid she might die? Where was she? Did she have access to food and water? And, more than anything, did she still have hope she would escape or be rescued and find her way back home?

More times than I could count, I'd been in that position of believing there was no way out, where despair wasn't just a feeling—it was a noose around your neck that got tighter and tighter with each passing day. I hated to think that Mia was being held captive. But I couldn't ignore the possibility.

While clues to her disappearance were minimal and the Romeros were still balking at filing a formal report with the SAPD, I'd done a lot of reading in the last couple of hours. Well, reading articles and watching brief videos on YouTube, all documenting the type of person who might kidnap a teenage girl. More often than not, the girl would know her kidnapper. The kidnapper was usually but not always male, and older by ten to fifteen years. The kidnapper and victim weren't good friends, but they typically had a casual, if not cordial, relationship. It could be the guy at the corner convenience store, the janitor at the school, a teacher, a person working retail at the mall, or someone else she might have crossed paths with. The list of possibilities was endless.

My phone rattled across the wooden coffee table. I picked it up to see a text from Stan.

Dropped by Brandon's house. No sign of him. Parents are worried.

I typed a quick response, told him to keep me in the loop. I'd shared my suspicion with Stan earlier in the day—that Brandon might have been the boy who punched me when I snuck up on the robe-clad kids defacing the field house. Of course, we had no real evidence. I hadn't been able to see the face of the boy who'd hit me. I based most of my suspicion on the links in his chain. They resembled the links of the chain I'd seen in his truck. Stan was less than convinced, but he didn't blow me off. And he was quite disturbed with Brandon's abuse of Jasmine. And just as pissed that she'd taken off, not wanting to "rock the boat." I was right there with him.

What was it with this generation? They had all of this access to reach out to authorities, yet they did nothing. They played politics like they were forty years old, working as a congressional staffer in DC.

I found myself studying the pictures of the graffiti on my phone. While the evidence from the recent mission murder seemed to be no more than an arrow, or a bolt as Stan had pointed out, the people involved in the animal sacrifices at the high school were trying to communicate something with their artwork. Again, they could be the same perpetrators as the ones who'd committed the brutal murders, but right now I leaned toward no.

A flash of Dr. Amaya's expression came to mind. It was like he'd flipped a switch and turned from a nice, gentle man into a creepy... What exactly? I'd learned he'd been hunting and had a crossbow. So what was I telling myself? That the man who'd put all of his heart and money into creating a community center to honor his dead daughter was behind the murders at the missions? I took another leap. Given the fact he'd lost a daughter, could he have kidnapped Mia, attempting to find a way to replace Mandy?

It sounded ludicrous in my mind, which was why I hadn't shared this latest theory with Cristina. For now, my instinct said to follow the path of Brandon. Find out where he was last night when the crime was committed at the high school. Find out more about his problem with the football coach. It appeared there might be a deeper issue with coaches in general at the school. Could one of them have kidnapped Mia? My eyes went back to the graffiti images on my phone. I focused on the first blob or letter or sign. I'd already ruled out any Satanic symbol. So, what did all of this mean?

Maybe nothing. Maybe it was just a couple of kids spraying gibberish just to get their jollies by defacing the side of the building. My eyes blinked, and the gibberish suddenly looked like a word, one that was similar to what I'd seen etched on one of the many signs in the neighboring yards around the high school the night before.

My phone buzzed, and I switched to my text app and found one from Cristina. I threw the blanket off and sat up. She'd spotted Brandon at Lee High School. I called for my chariot—my Uber ride—and headed back to the high school, hoping we could finally get some answers from a troubled teen.

Forty-Three

Walking around in the dark near Lee High School didn't exactly give me the warm fuzzies. Not even twenty-four hours earlier, I'd done something similar and found myself laid out by a guy with a killer punch.

I tiptoed up next to Cristina at the northeast corner of the main building, next to a metal door. After walking three blocks from where the Uber driver had dropped me off, my dizziness, thankfully, hadn't returned. "Where is he?" I asked in a hushed tone.

"Inside. Roaming around the school."

"Isn't it kind of hard to see people through the windows? How do you know it's him?"

"You want the long story? Okay, I decided to ride my skateboard by the school, you know, just to check out the scene where all this crazy shit has been going down, and—"

I put my hand on her arm. "By yourself in the middle of the night?"

She tilted her head. "You mean, like you? Anyway, I saw a figure looking through the front door, so I hopped off my skateboard and jumped behind the school sign by the road."

I started shaking my head. "You're making me nervous just listening to this story."

"I've been on the other side of this type of discussion, you know."

"Don't bog down. Keep going," I said, motioning with my arm.

"Well, this dude was trying all the doors in the front. Then he started walking by the building, trying each of the windows he could reach." She paused a second. "No color commentary on my story?"

Now I tilted my head. "Now you're definitely bogging."

"So, he got to the end of the front of the building, and he went around back." She smiled a wee smile.

"You followed him."

She nodded.

"You frickin' followed this guy? He could have been waiting on the other side of the wall with a knife!"

"But he wasn't. And I'm not that stupid. I took a different angle, hanging back about fifty yards. Hello...it's pretty obvious he didn't see me. Otherwise—" She stopped short and cocked an eyebrow.

"I get it. So, did you see him go inside this door?" I noticed she'd grabbed the door handle.

"Yep. But before you got here, I saw a light flashing through a window." She started opening the door.

"And if you were so far away, how do you know it's Brandon?"

She twisted her lips. "I was scooting on the other side of this wall here," she said, looking over her shoulder to the corner of the building. "And when I peeked around the corner, he was just opening the door. I saw his face for a split second. It was him."

I shook my head again. "Damn, you were lucky."

"What? If he'd seen me and started coming at me, I would have—"

"I know, I know. Beat his ass. I shouldn't have to remind you how strong he is, how volatile he is. But it doesn't matter. Let's go."

She opened the door halfway, then looked at me. "So, you're just going to go in with me? No warnings about breaking and entering? No calling the cops?"

"I already texted Stan. At any moment there will be a lot of cars rolling into the parking lot. But I want a chance to talk to Brandon about—"

We both flinched after hearing an ear-splitting crash.

"Come on," I said, pushing my way through the door. Three steps into the hallway, there was another smash. It sounded like glass shattering. I waved Cristina onward, and she passed me like I was standing still.

"Wait up," I said in a loud whisper.

She said something over her shoulder, but I couldn't hear it. I tried to increase my speed without shaking my brain. I actually found myself holding my head.

Cristina stopped where the hallway ended in a T. Another series of crashes, one after the other. They were getting louder. She jabbed her hand toward the hallway to the right. I held up my hand and told her to wait up.

"What do you want?" she hissed, pacing back and forth like she had to pee.

"You don't get to run ahead. We both approach him at the same time. He sounds like he's destroying school property. He could be on something, or just losing it."

"Okay, okay." She hopped once then took off again.

"Cristina, stop."

She didn't stop, but she slowed down.

Two more crashes. We took a left, then I saw a sign for the gymnasium and an arrow indicating the direction.

Another smash, and this one I could feel in my gut. With Cristina now at my side, we moved slowly down the hall, where it cut left about ten feet, then continued onward. I pulled up next to the edge of the wall. Another smash, and then I saw shards of glass sliding across the floor right in front of us.

He shouted, and then another smash. I peeked around the corner—he was mid-swing with a baseball bat, but he still saw me out of the corner of his eye. He finished his swing, connected with what was left of a trophy case.

"I don't care if you see me," he shouted.

I moved from around the corner, Cristina next to me. "Brandon, why are you so upset?" I asked.

"Because!" Spit flew out of his mouth, as he adjusted his grip on the bat. I noticed a trail of blood snaking down his forehead. "Everything is fucked up. That's why." He lifted the bat high above his head and screamed as he thrust it downward, blowing up a shelf of glass and trophies.

Cristina and I jumped back a step to avoid the glass. He turned and wiped sweat off his brow, but he smeared blood all over his face. Maybe he'd scraped a shard of glass into his skin.

"Brandon, you're scaring us."

"I apparently scare a lot of people." He noticed the top of a broken trophy on the floor, and he put the bat up against it, then swung the bat like a golf club, propelling the broken trophy against the wall. "Dude, just chill and we can talk it out," Cristina said.

He didn't lift his head, but I could see his eyes shift in our direction again. He didn't have a good history with girls her age. I nudged her with my elbow, hoping she'd get the hint to be quiet.

"Brandon, just put the bat—"

"She won't call me back."

"Who?"

He kicked a piece of a trophy, then took a swing at a wooden board that dangled by a nail. When he connected, the sound was like a solid hit at a baseball game.

"Who, Brandon? Who won't call you back?"

He finally glanced in my direction. "Jasmine, of course. We texted, but I wanted to apologize in person. To make things right. I know it's probably too late for that." He lifted the bat above his head, shouting to the point of his face turning red. He swung the bat with everything he had, but he missed his target, slipped on broken glass and fell onto his hands and knees. "Fuck it all to hell." He picked up each hand. Blood dripped to the floor. "Oh well, I guess I won't be able to throw a football the rest of the season." He chuckled, used the bat to push himself to a standing position.

My eyes, however, focused on one thing, my heartbeat rising rapidly. His necklace was now on the outside of his T-shirt. On the pendant, two letters were prominently displayed within a circle.

Forty-Four

I had to move closer to see. I shuffled a couple of steps, but Cristina grabbed my arm.

I ignored her and spoke to Brandon. "I hear the coaches here really suck."

He chuckled. "You have no idea."

"Why don't you fill me in?"

"They're just pricks, that's all. All they care about is winning a state championship. Meanwhile, they cut us down, throw shit at us, threaten us…well, some of us." He turned, extended the arm that held the bat as if he were pointing at something. "Hell, my teammate Benito was gay, and the coach encouraged some of the brainless losers on the team to harass him, make him feel like shit."

Could one of the coaches be involved in these killings? I wanted to ask his opinion, but he whirled around and took out another glass shelf. He spotted something on the floor, and he picked up a piece of a trophy. "And here it is. Last year when I was a junior, we made it all the way to the state semis. That was supposed to serve as motivation for us to work even harder to make it all the way to the championship. But dammit, they treated us like animals. Worse than animals. There was too much pressure."

"Is that when you started being physical with girls?"

He brought the bat to his head. For a second, I thought he might ram it into his skull. Then he turned and looked at me for a quick second. "How did you find out about Mia?"

"I told you I'm a PI. But it doesn't matter how. Do you know where she is?"

"I told you the other day I don't know anything."

"And nothing has changed?"

"I'm not a liar."

I wanted to challenge him on that one.

"I hope she's okay and everything. It's kind of weird how she just disappeared off the planet."

His rage had dissipated, and he sounded sincere. And since he was unloading everything else about how he felt, I was inclined to believe him. I took advantage of what seemed like a truth-telling trend.

"Do you mind if you tell me what's on your chain?"

He looked at the necklace with a blank face, grabbed it in his fist. "I don't care anymore. It has two letters, N-S."

"Does it stand for Nightsteppers?"

He cocked his head. "You're pretty frickin' smart. Wait, don't tell me. Did Jasmine tell you?"

"Nightsteppers, as in Highsteppers?" Cristina said with astonishment in her voice.

"That's right. Ivy just figured it out. Then again, we didn't exactly hide it. We painted it on the side of the fieldhouse. Then the rain came, and we figured it was fate. No one was supposed to find out. And we'd just continue doing our thing."

I heard footsteps behind me. I glanced over my shoulder to see Stan, Brook, and a horde of uniforms moving toward us.

"So you admit to killing those animals?" Cristina asked.

Brandon set his jaw, then looked at the mess surrounding him. After a few seconds, he said, "We had to. We had to make a statement. What we did to those animals…that's how they were treating us. All the coaches."

He put his hands to his eyes.

"Was Jasmine part of this little team of Nightsteppers?" I asked.

I heard people approaching and looked over my shoulder. Stan was in the lead, and I waved at him and his team to stop. We were getting so much out of Brandon I couldn't afford for him to clam up.

"Jasmine. She was supposed to be the one," he said as if he were only talking to himself.

I wasn't sure I understood. "The one what?"

"The one for me, dammit."

I could see tears well in his eyes. His breathing picked up.

"Were you aware of her sexting scandal and what that was doing to her?" Cristina asked.

"Yeah…no. I mean, I don't know. It was crazy. This other chick, Ashley, kind of threw herself at me at a party, and then next thing I know, I'm getting all these crazy text messages with her in handcuffs. Jasmine found them and went ape-shit, thinking I was sleeping with Ashley." He shook his head and gasped out a breath.

"Were you?" Cristina asked.

I nudged her again.

He looked up and nodded. "But I didn't mean to. It just happened."

I could feel my heart thumping in my chest. It was difficult to listen to Brandon's confessions. On top of being mentally unstable, he and his friends were swimming in shark-infested waters.

"The crazy thing is," he continued, "that's kind of how Jasmine stole me away from Mia."

I gasped. I couldn't help it. "You sure you don't know anything about Mia disappearing?"

Cristina leaned forward, her hands balling into fists. "If you're holding out on us and she's being held captive, I'm going to…"

I waited to see how he'd respond.

"Are you crazy or something? I may not be the best boyfriend, or ex-boyfriend, but kidnapping? That's not my style."

"That's true, you just kill animals and use Satanic symbols."

"Don't you get it? It was just to fuck with the minds of the coaches. They fucked with us, so we fucked with them."

I knew Stan and Brook could hear all of this. Brandon would be arrested and might serve time. But there was more going on at this school than a bunch of hoodlum kids crossing the line. The coaches were doing some bad shit. Hopefully, the SAPD could put a stop to it.

He held up his bat, then threw it to the floor. Stan and Brook appeared on either side of me. Brandon just nodded. "I get it. I'm guilty. But can you do me a favor?" he asked as the cops ran up to cuff him.

"What?" I said at the same time as Stan.

"Check on Jasmine."

"She's better off without you," Cristina said.

He rolled his eyes. "Seriously. She and I texted earlier. I told her I was sorry and I wanted to tell her in person. She invited me over, said I could sneak in through her window. I got there, did my three knocks, but she wasn't there."

"Don't you think she was just blowing you off? You did hurt her earlier," I said.

"Nah, man. I mean, at first I thought she might be. I called her about a dozen times. But I even called her parents, acted all coy and shit. They don't know where she is."

Brook read him his rights as Stan came over and talked to me and Cristina. But I was lost in my own thoughts, trying to reconcile everything I'd heard.

"Nice work, even if it was a little unconventional," I finally heard Stan say.

"It was all Cristina," I said, looking beyond Stan to Brandon. He was staring at me.

"You're going to check on Jasmine, right?" Brandon asked.

"Ignore him," Stan said, putting his back to the boy.

"I'm not joking. Too much crazy shit is going on with kids in our school. I know I hurt her, but I want to make sure she's okay."

I replayed the last several hours. We wouldn't have learned any of this had we not been in the MACC at the time Brandon had chased down Jasmine.

"Please. I'm serious," Brandon yelled.

I tried not to look at him.

"Are you hearing me? Do you want something to happen to Jasmine? Yes, she was a fellow Nightstepper, but she's not like me. She doesn't deserve to have anything happen to her. She's a good person. She even goes to church."

I heard shoes crunching on broken glass as they walked Brandon past us. He continued his plea. "So you're really going to turn your back on Jasmine? Damn. And here I thought you cared."

A snapshot of the first time I saw Jasmine at the MACC flew into my mind. I flipped around. "Is she Catholic?"

"Hell yes. Her parents make her go to Mass twice a week."

"Has she ever used the confessional at the MACC?"

"Earlier today, why?"

I grabbed Stan and walked as fast I could out of the high school.

Forty-Five

I made Stan pull out of the parking lot before I shared with him where my thoughts had gone—that someone from the MACC staff was the teen killer and, very likely, Mia's kidnapper.

"Are you losing it?" he practically yelled, putting on his blinker, about to do a U-turn to head back to the school.

I grabbed the steering wheel. "Hold on."

He punched the brake, and I lunged forward, his eyes moving from the steering wheel to me. "I may not have two good arms, Ivy, but I can drive just fine, thank you."

"Sorry. Look, I know this might be a long shot, especially since we can't verify my theory."

"Call Dr. Amaya. You have his number, right?"

I opened my lips, but all that came out was a pained grunt.

"What is it, Ivy?"

"Things just don't appear to be right with him. He seems off." That wasn't what I meant to say. "No, he's more than off. He's… I don't know."

"I can't read your mind. What are you thinking?"

"I'm concerned that Dr. Amaya has gone off the deep end and that maybe he's the actual killer." I released a long sigh. "There, I said it."

Stan groaned while shaking his head.

"Or maybe he's part of something bigger. I'm not sure. Something is going on, and if I call him, I might be alerting the very person who's in the middle of this. And then we might never catch him."

Now it was his turn to release a long sigh. "I should be home in bed, getting my sleep. That's as important as eating healthy and exercising."

I gave him a strange look.

"I'm only saying that because this, what you're saying, is a shot in the dark."

"I could debate you on that, but we're wasting time. Will you drive?"

He turned his palm upward and shrugged. "Where?"

"South on La Pressa." That was the general direction of the two missions where murders had not occurred, not including the Alamo. But I knew the Alamo was guarded like it was the US Treasury.

The government-issued vehicle rumbled down the mostly empty road as I thought about our ultimate destination. "You had guards placed at each of the missions, right?"

"Sure did." Stan pulled to a stop at red light.

"What are you doing?"

"The light is red."

"Someone…Jasmine, at this very moment, could be on the verge of being killed. Of having a stake driven through her heart."

"They did that to Dracula."

"Whatever. Just drive."

He punched the gas, ran the light—there wasn't another pair of car headlights within a hundred yards—and picked up speed. "So, what's your guess on where I should go?"

He was doubting my instinct. And the more I thought about it, I was too. "Look, we know the killer will strike again, right?"

"I'm hoping we can catch him, or them, first."

I nodded. "The first two killings came at the two most northerly missions, Concepcion and San Jose. We're leaving the Alamo out of this discussion, since it's guarded so well and it's right in the middle of the city."

Stan scratched his stubble. "But the Alamo property is huge. Plus it's all enclosed by a wall. Maybe they want us to think that they'd never try anything at the Alamo. Should I head back north?" He put his hand on his blinker, then checked his rearview.

"I'm certain about nothing. But I'm thinking there are just too many people around the Alamo for the killer to do what he wants. Remember, he plans all of this out; he typically lures his victim to the location. Your ME said the killings took place right there in the churches."

"I'm following you." He removed his hand from the blinker.

"Logic would say that if you look at a map, the killer would target the mission just south of San Jose."

He inched up in his seat. "So you think this is all going down at Mission San Juan?"

I rubbed the back of my neck, looking out the window into the starry nighttime sky, searching for some signal to tell me how this killer thought, where he set up. I knew I could be wrong about the whole thing, including Dr. Amaya. From my peripheral vision, I saw Stan playing with his phone. "What are you doing?" I asked, moving my hand toward the steering wheel.

"Don't you dare," he said, with his fake hand clamped on the steering wheel. "I'm going to put in a call to the station and have them connect me with the guard at Mission San Juan."

"Hold it."

"What now?"

For a moment, the only sound came from the tires crossing seams in the road.

He said, "Are you thinking he might skip one, just to throw us off? So I should contact the guard at Mission Espada?"

He went back to his phone.

I started shaking my head.

"What? You still don't think that's the right guess?"

"The two girls were killed at the most northerly location, Mission Concepcion; Benito at Mission San Jose. For some reason, my mind is thinking his habits have been established. He will kill all female victims at the original location, Mission Concepcion."

"I'll go with it, but it's just a WAG." He shot me a glance. "You know what that is, don't you?"

"Wild-ass guess. And I agree with you."

After a quick exchange with the station operator, he gave me a quick look and nodded. We turned west on Mitchell, but he wasn't talking.

I pointed at the turn into the parking lot. "Don't miss the—"

The car cut left, bouncing into the lot. He quickly shut off his lights and glided to a stop at the far end.

Forty-Six

Stan dropped his phone in his pocket.

"No answer?"

"It rolled to voicemail. Maybe the officer fell asleep. It's awful dark out here."

With our heads on swivels, we walked across the grass to the front door of Mission Concepcion. An empty chair sat off to the side. It was dark, but I could see the white in Stan's eyes as he looked my way. He punched something on his phone, then put it away and removed his pistol from his shoulder holster. He motioned for me to move behind him.

I complied, then he leaned his ear to the door.

"Hear anything?" I whispered.

"Nothing. I don't want to go in there blind. I need a…" He took a step back, then walked to the right. I followed closely behind. He stopped at a window, stood on his tiptoes.

"See anything?"

"It's dark. I think it's a side room next to the sanctuary."

"We going around back?" The complex was actually rather large. A stone-covered outdoor hallway was attached to the side of the sanctuary, and a low wall jutted out from the end. The main building of the church was rather deep and had several offshoots behind it.

"It's really dark back there with the trees behind it. If we turn on our flashlights, we'll be targets. I'm wondering if we should wait for backup."

"Stan, a girl could be getting mutilated right now. And the missing officer?"

He held up his gun hand and motioned for me to follow him back to the double front door. "You open it, stay low, and I'll go in with my pistol ready to fire, or at least ready to scare someone."

I reached for the handle and paused. He nodded, and I slowly depressed the lever trying to remain as stealthy as possible. There was only a slight click. I cracked the door enough to see a soft glow against the side wall. And then I saw a moving shadow, and my heart skipped a beat. But I couldn't panic. I held my breath, stayed low, and pushed the door open another two feet. The door knocked into something, and then I heard a clap of metal bounce off the stone floor. I nearly jumped out of my shoes as Stan slipped into the sanctuary. I put my head in, saw a metal chair on the floor, then looked up toward the altar. My eyes went straight to the back of a man's head. The hair was dark.

Dr. Amaya?

"Get down." No sooner had Stan lifted his pistol than I heard a pop, and then a swooshing noise coming right at us.

I dropped behind the last pew and looked up to see a bolt had punctured Stan's arm.

"Stan!" I lunged for him, but he waved me off. "Get my gun," he grunted, looking to the floor.

My eyes shot left and right, but I didn't find a gun. I looked up and saw a naked man with a knife above his head, a crossbow off to the side.

"Stop!" I yelled.

He thrust his arms downward, but before he connected, his head snapped back. Someone had hit him or kicked him from behind. He dropped the knife, or at least I thought so. I ran up the center aisle, but the floor started tilting—I was having another dizzy spell. I reached for the top of the next pew but tried to push through. I had to keep moving

The man turned and eyed me. It wasn't Dr. Amaya, but he looked familiar. He scanned the floor, then went to his crossbow, tried to quickly load another bolt. From the floor, a shoe swung in front of him and connected with his groin. He released the crossbow, stumbling forward. But he didn't drop to the floor, not like I thought he would. Maybe the person had just grazed him.

With Stan yelling something I couldn't decipher, I could now see Jasmine on the ground, blood coating her torso. She kept trying to kick at the guy. Now less than ten feet away, I saw the crossbow and dove for the handle. Just as I had it in my hand, I looked up to see the man disappear through a back door.

I crawled over to Jasmine, quickly assessing her wounds. "Are you going to be okay?"

"Father Abel carved me up pretty good, but I'll live."

Abel? As in Cain and Abel?

"He killed the others. He's crazy. Get him. Go get that motherfucker."

I saw her shirt off to the side and tossed it at her. "Press this against your open wound." Then I got to my feet and scrambled to the door.

Forty-Seven

On the other side of the door, it was so dark I didn't see the flight of steps going upward directly in front me. I tripped on the first stair and dropped like I was being yanked down by some invisible force, cracking my forearms on the unforgiving stone. I paused a second, took a breath, then heard a door shut above me.

This Abel person must have planned his escape. Sure he was naked, but he could find clothes. Probably had them hidden in the woods behind the church. This second floor might take him to another location in the back of the building where he could slip out into the thick of darkness. On top of being a Satanist, for him to carry out these acts, he had to be methodical, patient, and yes, a planner.

I groaned as I pushed off the step, the stabs of pain in my arms temporarily helping me forget about my headache. I reached for a handrail—there was none. With my balance limited at best, I bear-crawled up two flights of steps, banging my head against the dark wood door at the top. I paused a moment, wondering if Abel might be on the other side, holding another knife that he'd stashed in some cubby. I had no weapon. Maybe I should have grabbed one of those bolts. But if I'd done that, I might have skewered myself when I fell on the steps.

Without further analysis of my odds, I readied myself for the worst, slammed the door open, and took a single step.

I stopped. A chilled wind whipped loose strands of hair against my face. I was in one of the church's two bell towers. Abel was also in the small space, on the other side of the bell, his bare backside to me, standing on the wall looking down.

A few seconds passed, then he said, "There are sinners everywhere in this world. We all need to be cleansed. None of us are perfect."

I put a quick hand to my mouth, holding back a whimper. I remembered Jasmine uttering those same words.

I didn't respond. I didn't move. I wasn't sure what I should do.

"No one understands the root of our problems, though." His hands were at his side. He had no weapon. I heard sirens in the distance. I figured I should keep him talking until someone with experience in negotiations arrived and took over for me.

He looked like he was going to jump right off the tower. He might survive it; he might not. We were only two stories high, but he would at the very least sprain an ankle or break a bone or two.

Maybe making an escape wasn't in his plans at all. Maybe he didn't want to live.

Shit. I couldn't help but engage with him. "But you know the root of our problems?"

"I've worked with the youth for some time. In this day and age, they are enticed by so many things."

"You mean sick perverts like you?" My eyes went wide when I realized my thoughts had become actual words. I hadn't intended on baiting him into an argument. I froze.

He slowly turned around, his hands by his side. He looked down—at the floor, at his body?—and I followed his eyes.

"I was castrated," he said, now looking straight at me.

Okay. Wow.

I couldn't imagine why that had happened. Had he allowed it? Was it forced upon him? There had been instances where convicted rapists were given the option of being castrated for reduced time in prison.

I swallowed hard before saying, "Are you trying to prove how tough you are?"

"Before I started killing kids, I thought it was me. I thought I had the issue, so I tried to correct it."

I could hear car doors slamming shut, the din of voices.

"That still didn't work, so I castrated myself."

Okay. Holy—

I blinked hard. "Why didn't you get help from a psychiatrist?"

He lifted his arms to the sky. "Because I realized there was only one way to save our world, and that was to sacrifice the people who were sent to me."

Coming out of my shock from the unbelievable confession, I was now in full-blown anger mode. I tried to control it, but it was nearly impossible. "Sent to you? What are you talking about?"

"We all have a preordained destiny. Those kids were meant to come to confessional at the community center. To sit and share their sins with me. They were chosen. And I have been as well."

"Kids make mistakes. That's part of being a kid. They shouldn't be put to death because you have some kind of wet-dream fantasy of killing people." I spat out the last few words.

"You don't get it."

"No one gets it, Abel. You are fucked up. Royally."

He shook his head, then looked off. "I have evolved. Most people never get the chance, never seize the opportunity that I have. Hopefully, people will continue our work…my work. To take it to another scale we can't even conceive of."

"You can think whatever you want, but you killed someone's child, someone's brother or sister, someone's friend. That isn't right or justified. How can you even think otherwise?" My face was screwed up tightly in a grimace. I was thoroughly disgusted.

He stood there for a moment and didn't say a word. He had this weird peace about him, as if he were still lost in his own crazed world and would be protected. Then he looked at me and released a full breath.

"That was their fate." He looked down a second, and then lifted his gaze. "And this is mine."

With his eyes still on me, he dropped backward. I ran to the side of the wall and saw him hit the ground with the crown of his head.

He was dead. But Jasmine was alive.

Forty-Eight

Over the next few hours, I watched one body carried off in a body bag and another on a gurney. Paramedics ensured us that Jasmine's wounds weren't life-threatening. I told her how proud I was of her for fighting back.

"When I thought I was going to die," she said, choking on tears as the gurney sat on the edge of the ambulance, "I told myself if there was any way that God could get me out of this, I would change. I wouldn't care what other people thought all the time; I'd be a good person, treat other people how I wanted to be treated. And, more than anything, I'd make sure that every girl knew…" She paused a second, grabbed my hand as she took in a jittery breath. "I will tell every girl that they don't have to allow their boyfriend or some other mean girl to beat the crap out of them or treat them like shit."

She quickly covered her mouth.

"What is it, Jasmine?"

"Well, I also told myself I'd stop cussing so much. And I already screwed that up."

I told her again how proud I was of her, told her not to be so hard on herself. She thanked me for not giving up on her.

Just then Cristina ran up. "Brook got the scoop from Stan on our drive over here. Jasmine's going to be okay?"

I nodded.

"That's cool," she said, trading a quick smile with Jasmine.

A paramedic was about to shut the door, when I said, "Did Abel ever mention anyone else besides the others that we know he has killed?" I recalled Abel using the term "our" before he'd jumped off the ledge.

She thought for a moment. "No. no one else."

"Not even Mia?"

"Unfortunately no. Look, since I'm confessing all of my sins here, I need to—"

"No need, Jasmine. Brandon told us everything."

"I'm embarrassed by what I did. It just shows how desperate I was to be accepted. How I thought having the starting quarterback as my boyfriend made me better than everyone else."

"Live and learn, right?"

She tried to crack a smile, then winced from the pain of the carvings in her stomach. "I really have no idea what happened to Mia. She hasn't really been part of our clique for a long time."

A flash of the video I'd seen when Mia exited the high school zapped to the top of my mind. "So was Mia part of this Nightsteppers group?"

"She loved animals way too much." She coughed out a single chuckle, putting a hand to her side. "Mia wasn't into the group retribution thing. Actually, I think she kind of moved on after I came between her and Brandon. Didn't seem like she cared very much."

Cristina jumped in. "Hey, you want me to hang with you on the ride to the hospital?"

"That would be cool."

It warmed my heart to see Cristina reaching out to care for someone else. She reminded me that Leo was coming in town over the weekend just before the doors shut. I didn't have a chance to say another word. No doubt, that had been her plan.

I heard my name being called and flipped around to see Stan walking up with the end of his arm stump covered in bandages. Dr. Amaya was two steps behind him. I wasn't sure what he was doing here.

"Is your arm okay?" I asked.

Brook approached and asked the same question.

He held his arm up. "It's about ten inches long. I still have the wingspan of a three-year-old."

The bolt had actually punctured Stan's prosthesis while grazing his stub. But it had also severed a cable in his fake arm, making it clamp down so hard on his stub, it began to cut off blood circulation. It had taken firemen almost an hour to remove the damaged prosthesis.

"It could be worse. It could have hit your other arm."

"Or my leg, right? Then I'd be totally screwed for the Dallas Marathon next month."

I was glad someone was able to see beyond the here and now, and with a little humor to boot. While I was relieved that Jasmine's life had been spared—either by destiny or just dumb luck—we were no closer to learning where Mia was.

Dr. Amaya moved closer, touched my elbow. "I don't know what to say about Father Abel. He, uh…"

"It's not your fault, Doctor. One crazy guy, you know?"

I was actually relieved that Dr. Amaya wasn't the killer. He'd done so much good in our community that it would have been hard to reconcile the good with this killing insanity.

"Ivy, before I forget, I wanted to apologize for my behavior at the community center earlier. It was rude and it just wasn't me."

"Thank you for saying that."

For some reason, my mind replayed the last words from Abel. *Hopefully, people will continue our work...my work.*

Our work. It felt like a steel pole had been inserted against my spinal column. Was Abel working with someone? For someone? *Our work.* There was someone else. Maybe...

"Ivy, did you hear the doctor?" Brook asked.

"Oh, sorry. I missed that. Say it again?"

"I just said that today—well, since it's after midnight, I guess it was yesterday—marked the three-year anniversary of the death of my wife and Mandy. I think that brought out a side of me that was bitter. Resentful even."

I wasn't sure I followed his last comment.

"You know how I said you remind me of my daughter? Well, I look at you and sometimes wonder, what if? What if Mandy were alive? What would she be doing right now? Would she be married? Have kids? Work for the Peace Corps? And I see all the great work you do, and I think I'm jealous in a way. That maybe Mandy should be doing these great things. I know that's unfair and ridiculous. I'm just...sorry."

He wiped the corner of his eye.

"It's okay, really. I just wasn't sure what had gotten you so upset."

Brook and Stan waited a few seconds, then began to grill the doctor about Abel, if the MACC had done a background check on him to make sure he wasn't a felon, to ensure he didn't have previous issues in working with kids.

"We saw no signs of this," he said, folding his arms across his chest. "The board has strict guidelines to ensure everyone goes through a rigorous background check. Anything more than a speeding ticket, and they're not even considered."

"So, do you recall his background?" Brook asked.

He pursed his lips. "I'm sorry, no. The board handles most of that, just to make sure there is transparency with such an important task. I just recall him talking about growing up in El Paso, serving in a church there."

"What church does he serve here in San Antonio?"

"I don't think he's affiliated with one."

"Don't you find that strange?"

"Actually no. We have so many good-hearted people who do this just to give back to the community, to help kids who might go in the wrong direction."

"*He* was the wrong direction," Stan said.

"I know that now." He wiped his face, shook his head. "Maybe in your investigation, you'll learn where things went wrong for Abel. He seemed like a good guy when we were on that hunting trip a few weeks ago."

I grabbed his arm and squeezed. "The crossbow."

"Right. I wasn't very good at using it."

I let go of his arm, my mind cranking.

"It was just you, Clifton, and Abel on a hunting trip together?" Stan asked.

He nodded. "It was a little strange at the time to think about a priest wanting to kill things. But, you know, it's a different world. I've never been hunting before."

Another thought from my conversation with Dr. Amaya and Clifton stuck in my mind. Clifton had said, "*Dr. Amaya is way too kind to hold anyone hostage.*" I'd overlooked that comment earlier because the doctor had been so off. But the hostage remark seemed out of place.

"Doctor, if you're not a big hunter, then why did you buy yourself a crossbow?"

"I'd given the same one to Clifton, so I thought I'd pick one up and try to get better at it. He's been an enormous help to me over the last few months. Really has gone above and beyond his duties as a board member."

I could see Brook about to jump in with a question, but I beat her to it. "How?"

"How what?"

"How has he helped you?"

"Well, he's a former financial advisor, so he's great at balancing budgets. Anything to do with numbers. Plus, he handles most of the legwork on the background checks. Because of all his old clients, he has contacts everywhere."

Stan, Brook, and I all traded glances.

"Did I miss out on the joke?" the doctor asked.

Brook pulled out her phone. In looking over her shoulder, I could see her open an app and type in Abel's name in the search bar. Before she finished she asked Dr. Amaya for Abel's last name.

"Railey. You guys aren't wasting any time, are you?"

I reminded him that Mia was still missing. He said he'd forgotten about it, frankly, with the death anniversary of his wife and daughter.

A moment later, Brook said, "Headline from a year ago in the local El Paso paper, Metro section. Local priest quits after minor retracts allegations of sexual relationship."

"Does it mention his name?" Stan asked.

"Yep," she said, flipping the phone around. "And that's his picture right there."

"Dear God," the doctor said, running his fingers through his hair. "I didn't know."

Our work. "Doctor. Where does Clifton live?"

"He, uh.... Wait, what are you thinking?"

I didn't have time to explain. "Where does he live?"

He gave us the name of a farm, and I grabbed Brook and power-walked to her car.

Forty-Nine

The girl's skin that brushed against Mia's arm felt like that from a shriveled grape. Her eyes were hollow, her glassy gaze so distant it seemed like her brain had been scooped out. She swayed back and forth like a Weeble. But Mia couldn't help her. She couldn't help herself or the two others that stood in the dusty living room, all wearing skimpy nightwear.

Sal had just walked in with two large briefcases, set them on a table, and opened them, facing him. He pulled a pistol from the case, checked it for ammunition. A collective gasp from the girls—everyone except the girl next to Mia. He used the barrel of the gun to scratch his messy hair and began to pace, like he had done in her room the prior day. Since then, he'd been back to her room twice more, taking blue pills before each session.

In the last visit, he had been erratic, more violent than ever. He had slapped her around. At one point, he put both hands around her throat and squeezed. Her head had felt like it would pop like a balloon. She'd thought she was going to die—she knew she was going to die. And all she could think about was that no one would know what had happened to her. She would be one of those missing girls who are never found. Her parents would have no closure; they would slowly crumble. His phone had rung from his pants over on the chair—he leaped from the bed to answer the call. That call had saved her life. At least temporarily.

He continued pacing, his loafers clipping the hardwood at an uneven cadence. Everything about him was off. His shirt hung out from his pants, which appeared as though they'd been wadded up in a corner. He mumbled incoherent statements, but it was his fiery eyes that she couldn't turn away from. Radiating a fury she'd not witnessed in her seventeen years, his eyes had a crazed look. Like he was possessed.

Something had changed. She'd been communicating with two other girls, one through the pipe in the bathroom, another through the wall behind her bed. He must have learned that they'd been communicating. He'd brought them all into the living room and told them they would have some type of ceremony. She felt less alone by being around the other girls. There was power in numbers, right? But in looking at the others, a mutiny was out of the question. It would probably only get them killed even more quickly.

Sal stopped pacing, turned, and aimed his gun at a bookshelf. He slowly panned left until he had it aimed directly at the girl on the far end.

"Bang," he said, pretending to fire the gun. He moved to the next girl and repeated the same exercise. When he reached Mia, he paused and smiled at her. His expression looked as if he wanted to eat her limb by limb. "You are the youngest, Mia. The most pure. I hope you will survive. But we shall see how you hold up. If you are victorious, then it will be my honor to have you by my side from now until my last days."

She tried to breathe, but her throat had clamped shut. *Victorious at what?*

He finished his mock-shooting escapade with the girl to her right, the one who mentally was out to lunch.

"Okay," he said. "It's about time for the games to begin."

The girls, minus the emaciated one, traded glances, but he didn't notice. He was too much into his ritual. He pulled a knife from his briefcase, walked to the center of one of those fancy Persian rugs. He stood in the middle, where a circle had been woven into its design. "You have all broken the rules of the house. Therefore, we must hold a tournament to determine the strongest. It saddens me really, but there is no other way," he said, looking off for a moment.

He set the knife in the circle and walked back to his briefcases. "When I call out your names, you will each get on opposite sides of the rug. When I say go, you will then race to get the knife. The winner will be determined by who inflicts the most damage on the other in two minutes."

Mia tried to swallow, but couldn't. She needed water.

"First up we have…" He paused as he scanned each of the girls. "Fay and Carolee." The two girls to her left both cursed, then began to whimper. That didn't stop the proceedings. He guided each of them to their starting spots and returned to his station. "Are we ready, ladies?"

"Yes sir." Carolee, an Asian girl with hair down to the small of her back, released a deep breath. While staring straight at Fay, she tied her hair in a series of knots until it was a taut ponytail.

"Finally, someone who wants to be alive…who wants to be with me," the man said. "Fay, are you ready?"

Fay's cracked lips moved, but she didn't speak. She had to be in shock, Mia thought.

"We can't wait all night." He checked his watch, raised his arm, then lowered it at the same moment he said, "Go!"

Carolee burst out of her stance and got to the knife before Fay had taken one step. Then, in one fluid motion, Carolee bounced across the rug and swung the knife across Fay's arm. Fay screamed, grabbed her shoulder, and fell to her knees. Before Mia could take a breath, Carolee jumped on top of Fay, straddling her, and using two hands, plunged the blade into Fay's torso.

"Very nice work, Carolee." The man began to clap as Carolee hopped to her feet and raised her arms to the ceiling. Then she looked down at Fay, who was writhing in pain, her moans muted as if her oxygen supply was almost empty.

Mia's legs felt like rubber. She put a hand to her mouth and tried not to hurl. She wanted to run over to Fay, to help stop the bleeding. But all she could think about was how she would be punished. And that made her ashamed of herself.

"Mia, Lexie, you're up next. Please assume your positions," he said. "Carolee, you can stand over here next to me."

Mia walked over to the spot about five feet from where Fay was curled into a ball, blood gushing from her multiple wounds. She was quivering. Mia couldn't help but look down. Fay glanced up for a second, and their eyes locked. She mouthed, "Help me." Mia couldn't just stand there and fight. Not with the wounded girl dying at her feet.

The man snapped his fingers, and Mia's heart skipped a beat. She lifted her head.

"If I were you," he said, "I'd pay more attention to your present situation, rather than something you have no control over." After taking the bloody knife from Carolee, the man pulled a clean knife from his bag of weapons and placed it in the circle.

Mia looked across the rug. Lexie seemed as dazed as ever. She had to be on heroin or coke.

"Ladies, are we ready?" Sal seemed enamored with his own little survivor games.

Mia hopped up on her toes, trying to wake up her muscles.

"There we go," he said with a wicked chuckle. "Mia, my young fawn, your lithe body looks like it's ready for the fight of your life."

She didn't respond. She didn't trust herself to speak. She'd quickly developed a strategy—or was it more like false hope? She would do everything in her power to be the first to the knife. She would circle Lexie as if she were looking for the right opportunity to attack her. Then, once she got close enough to Sal, she would try to slit his throat. Hell, she'd settle for just giving him a hangnail. Anything to divert his attention. Then, she'd go in for the kill.

And yes, she knew she could kill him if given the chance.

As Sal checked his watch and raised his hand, Mia could feel her pulse double.

"Go!" he yelled.

Lexie shot out of her stance. With twig-like limbs flying everywhere, she dove for the knife. Mia could hear herself yell out of shock that this emaciated girl, who had appeared to be in a drug-induced state, had even known what was about to happen. While drained from the last three days, Mia's athletic body was better tuned for this type of event. She quickly lowered her center of gravity and leaped for the knife as well. She actually reached the target first—her fingertips nudged the knife's grip. But she wasn't able to grasp it. And that was a big mistake.

Lexie hit the rug, scooped up the knife, and rolled back to a standing position. Her body was now lower, in an attack position, as if some type of ninja survival instinct had kicked in.

"Mia, I forgot to remind you. Lexie here…she was the gold medal winner at the Kni-Com competition in Southern California."

Mia glanced at Sal as the two girls circled each other.

"Ah, I see that got your attention. Kni-Com is a special kind of knife-fighting expertise developed for the US Marine Corps. Her dad is a Marine. Not that he was able to help her when I convinced her to walk away from her mundane life as a secretary at a local junior college in San Diego." He laughed, as if this were nothing more than a big joke.

From the floor, Fay gurgled up blood. Mia then looked beyond the circling Lexie to see Carolee standing next to Sal, wiping tears from her face. Mia felt badly for every girl in that room and how this so-called charming man was pitting them against each other. But she wanted to live. And to do that, she might have to hurt another person. So be it.

Lexie had the knife and the experience on how to use it. True, Mia was in better shape, but she had no weapon. Using her peripheral vision, she quickly scanned every inch of the room looking for something she could use as a weapon.

She saw it. A brass candleholder on the buffet against the wall. She could use it like a billy club. She'd lunge for it on their next rotation.

"If I were a betting man, I'd have to put my money on Lexie," the man said. "I'm sorry, Mia. Lexie might look like she just walked out of a concentration camp, but she's a determined little hussy."

Mia was now as close as she would get to the buffet—and she didn't waste another second. She jumped off to the side. The moment she left her position, though, Lexie also made a leap…in the opposite direction. Mia's hand grabbed the candleholder just as Lexie crashed through the briefcases and swung the knife at Sal. He simply dodged out of her way and fired a bullet right into her face.

Lexie's body landed on the hardwoods with a strum of thuds.

Mia's legs gave out as her mind spun with what she'd just witnessed. He must have had a gun by his side behind the cover of the cases.

"Anyone else want to challenge me?" he barked.

A second later, the room went pitch black.

Fifty

We'd been too late.

That was my first thought after I'd heard the gunshot. I rushed the living room, right behind Brook, Stan, and a uniformed officer. After the fiasco at the mission, Stan had insisted on having a solid backup. He brought along two of SAPD's best. One had cut the direct line of power going into the house, while the other rushed the house with us, giving us a police unit of three people, five arms, and me.

I could hardly see two feet in front of me, but my sense of smell was on high alert. The aroma of blood was nearly enough to make me gag. Brook and Stan yelled for everyone to get down. A shot fired into the ceiling above me.

"Mia?" I called out amidst the chorus of screams and furniture tumbling to the floor.

I heard voices, more than one girl. Lots of grunting. Someone was struggling. I ran into a person on the floor, tripped, and skidded my elbows across the rug. I pushed up, but my hands slipped. I brought them to my nose. It was more blood. I could see the outline of a girl in a ball on the floor. I touched her arm. She twitched.

"Mia? Is that you?"

More yelling from across the room, but I focused on the girl right next to me. "Mia? Your parents miss you. They want to see you. Are you—"

Before I finished, lights popped on. Stan was using his one arm to push up from the floor—he must have tripped over the edge of the rug. Brook, though, was in her cop stance, her gun trained on Clifton, who had Mia pulled to his chest, his pistol at the side of her head.

"Why did you people have to ruin our fun little party?" Clifton asked.

The girl next to me was lying in a pool of blood. I saw another one on the floor near Clifton, motionless, half of her face blown away. The fourth girl, with black hair, hovered behind the cop, who also had his gun drawn. Clifton had nowhere to run, but he had the ace—Mia's life—in his hands.

I looked at Mia, her face painted with a raw fear. I'd never met her before, but after reading her Big Rules, seeing her on the video, hearing so much about her perfection from her parents, and her desire to be perfect through her Big Rules, I felt like I'd known her for years. Or maybe I just wished I could say that because I wanted to believe she was more than just another name, another missing girl that no one would find. But we had found her, dammit! She was one itchy trigger finger away from being the second child her parents would have to bury.

"Clifton, let her go," I said, moving to my feet.

He snickered. "Always trying to save the souls who shouldn't be saved, right, Ivy?"

Stan was now on his feet, his gun firmly in his left hand. "Clifton, just let her go, put down your gun, and you'll be able to live."

"Live? Where, in the Texas prison system? Ha! I'd be someone's bitch within a day of showing up."

"Put the gun down. Now," Brook said with precision.

I could hear an engine rumbling from another room. "Those are my generators," Clifton said, disregarding the warnings from Brook and Stan. "The end is very near for most of us. So many crazy people running the world now. I'm not naïve. I know that a couple of generators, some extra rations, and weapons won't prepare us for the last world war. But it might buy us a few days, maybe a week or two."

I had no idea why he was bringing up his post-apocalyptic plans right now.

Stan moved a step closer. "Clifton, you need to put the weapon on the floor and release Mia. Do you hear me?"

Clifton retreated three feet. "Mia and I have always dreamed of visiting Europe together, taking a ride along the canals of Venice, touring the Louvre, swimming in the ocean off the coast of Spain." He paused, looked down at Mia. "We have been dreaming about that, right, Mia?"

She nodded, but her lips were quivering uncontrollably.

Keep it together, Mia. Just a little longer.

"Take me instead." I walked past Stan toward Clifton and Mia.

"Stop! Stop or I'll kill the girl."

I did as he said. "Mia's got her whole life ahead of her. If you care about her at all, you'll let her live her life the way she wants to live it."

He blinked, but didn't respond.

"She's right, Clifton," Stan said. "Be the nice guy here. You can still do the right thing."

The right thing. I knew Stan was saying anything to get him to let her go. There were two dead girls in this room, maybe others.

"She just wants to return to her parents like any other normal kid," I said. "Don't you understand that?"

He looked across the room. "These girls were my family. It may not have been a regular family, but we were close, you know?"

I nodded and stayed silent.

He released a tired breath. "I suppose you'll know the truth soon enough. Abel and I had a deal. He would try to save the souls of a generation by sacrificing those who he deemed expendable, or those who needed to learn the greatest lesson. I knew his methods were out of the norm, but I also knew the younger generation needed to be saved. The older generation... Look at what we've created across this globe." He looked away for a second. "He would recommend the cream of the crop to me. To join my family, here. All I wanted was a few special friends to share my life with."

His gaze dropped to the girl whose face was destroyed. "In some respects, I guess I failed them. It's really quite sad, now that I see what has happened, what I did to them."

Did he just wipe a tear from the corner of his eye?

"You're right. Mia should go back to her family. I... I will now meet my maker and pay for the sins I have committed."

He pushed Mia aside, then put the gun in his mouth and pulled the trigger.

Fifty One

Brook and I drove Mia back to her parents' house. Actually, Brook drove, and I sat in the back seat as Mia leaned against my shoulder and unloaded everything she'd experienced. And it wasn't just the last three days.

She started with her captivity, what oddly had begun as an adventure. She was to meet Clifton in a parking lot, and then they would drive to a place where he would procure her a new passport. From there, they'd jump on the next flight from San Antonio to London. And then they would begin the trip of their lives.

Instead, he had taken her to his family farm, using his natural charm to convince her that they could relax, plan out the details of their trip. Initially, even despite numerous warning signs, she said she fooled herself into thinking there were no red flags, nothing to worry about at all. He'd locked her in her room "for her protection."

His control, his obsession with how the world would soon end quickly broke through her fantasy-like daze. She went on to describe the assaults, sexual and otherwise, and how he'd promised to keep her there until the end of his life or the world, whichever came first.

Looking back, she said she couldn't believe how gullible she had been. She said she wasn't even attracted to the older Clifton, but only his ideas of freeing oneself from the daily pressures and responsibilities, and experiencing new things, new cultures.

Brook and I locked eyes after Mia's comment. We knew there was a sad irony in what Clifton had promised Mia versus what he had given her—tortured imprisonment. But I didn't respond. I didn't say much at all.

When Mia finished discussing her captivity, there was a moment of silence. She sat up, used a tissue to wipe tears from her face. Then she talked about the cycle of abuse in her family, how she'd watched her dad abuse her mom when she was young. And then how Brandon had done the same to her. From there, she chose to bare her soul, discussing her obsession with perfection and how she had been so wrapped up in how she was perceived.

"Everyone knew my family had little money, but they saw so much in me. They thought, *If she can be all of this, then why can't I?*"

"You were…are a role model for kids your age."

She scrunched the tissue in her hand. "But I only felt pressure from having to live up to this persona I created. It felt like the weight of the world was on me."

She cried more, yet it seemed like her stress level had been reduced.

I asked about her necklace. She showed the pendant to me. It was half of a heart.

"Clifton gave it to me. He had the other half on a chain. But I learned that the other girls being held captive also had the same pendant." She paused, took a heavy breath. "Those poor girls. Who knows how long they'd been held captive? Who knows if there were other girls?"

"It's good to be compassionate, but don't put the burden of what one man did to others on your shoulders. It will only make you question everything you've done in your life. We can't relive the past, only learn from it. And really, the biggest thing I've learned in my life is that I have to believe in myself, accept the fact that I'm not perfect."

She stared at me. "It sounds like you've gone through something similar."

"Yeah."

"And you're doing pretty good?"

"Real good." A tear bubbled in my eye, but I was able to suppress further emotion.

Given Clifton's explanation for how he and Abel worked together, I decided to let her know what had happened with her classmates. The people that Abel had killed, and then the unrelated but disturbing animal sacrifices by the group known as the Nightsteppers. She said she was aware of the group, but wanted nothing to do with them and their revenge against the high school coaches. She knew Brandon was the leader of it, and while he'd been abused by the football coach, she said he took it too far, as always.

"He has no self-control. If he wants something, he takes it or makes it happen. He could do great things, but it seems like he uses his skills to do things that hurt people."

While all the Big Rules made sense, I was still curious about the Bible verse we'd found in her dresser.

"Brandon gave it to me. He's so extreme at everything he does, he just couldn't help himself. He found that Bible verse to give him justification for controlling a girl…me. After we broke up, I kept it as a reminder to never let someone control me again." She twisted her lips. "I guess it didn't work."

We entered her neighborhood, but instead of getting excited, she started to tear apart her tissue. I asked if there was anything else she wanted to share.

"It's like you're my shrink or something."

"Whatever works, right?" I gave her a tight-lipped smile. "You've experienced a hell few people can relate to. I'm here for you if you want to tell me something."

And she told me something that made me speechless. I hugged her, catching Brook's gaze in the rearview. Her eyes couldn't get any bigger. I was just glad she didn't hit one of the many cars lining the neighborhood streets.

Mia said I was the first person she'd shared that with, and would probably be the last.

She added, "In recalling all of this crap I've experienced or seen, it would be easy for me to be depressed, or to hold grudges against all these people. But when I sat in that room at Clifton's mansion, locked up, just wondering when he'd show up and assault me again, I told myself that keeping all this anger and resentment inside would just make me feel worse. It could tear me apart for years. I don't want to be dealing with this shit when I'm old, you know, like thirty-something."

I smiled, not just at her belief of what constitutes "old," but at how this tragedy had brought out the very best of Mia.

"You've learned a valuable lesson, Mia. Something most people never learn, regardless of their age." I patted my chest, swallowed back some emotion. "Redemption isn't something that comes from the approval of others. It's all inside. If you feel redeemed, then you are."

She hugged me with everything she had. And when we arrived at her house, she chose to look beyond the transgressions of her parents and hug them with every ounce of her being.

Fifty-Two

Saul opened the passenger door on his antiquated Mazda RX-7 and then kissed my cheek.

"What's that for?" I asked.

"Because I'm proud of what you're about to do. It takes a lot of courage."

I wondered if it was more foolhardy than courageous, but I didn't say anything. He started the car and we began to drive to… Uh, I wasn't sure where.

"Where are we meeting this phantom person who supposedly knows something about my parents?"

"We're meeting Sally the PI at the coffee shop over on La Pressa. Then, she's supposed to get final confirmation from her source on where to meet. She's hoping this person will just meet us there at the coffee shop."

"Any clue why there's all this secrecy? What does this person have to hide?"

"Sally couldn't say."

"Couldn't or wouldn't? I mean, I'm the one who's been paying her fees."

"I think you know that some investigations aren't black and white."

"Gray. Right."

We motored along another few minutes, and Saul asked more about how the reunion had gone with Mia and her parents. I'd given him only the basic info the prior day, so I spent the next few minutes reviewing all the details, finishing with the whopper that Mia had shared with me just before reaching her house.

"Wait," he said, shifting in his seat, turning his head toward me a couple of quick times. "I'm not sure I heard you correctly."

"Keep your eyes on the road please." I pointed straight ahead. "So you're saying you don't listen to me?"

He grinned until I could see his teeth. "Okay, I admit I was thinking about my first client. This family inheritance thing is a real hairball. But enough about me. Can you repeat what you said?"

"Mia's mom slept with Brandon."

His eyes got wide as he slowly turned to me. I saw headlights and said, "Brakes!"

He slammed his foot on the brake, and the little Mazda stopped on a dime. I released a breath. "I don't need any more excitement."

"Sorry. So, what the hell kind of family is this?"

"Sounds messed up, I know. Mia said her mom told her that she thinks she was getting back at her husband for hurting her all those years ago."

"But what about Mia?"

"I know, right? Well, she saw Mia getting older, not having time for her. She just felt alone, like no one cared. So, it just happened."

"And Mia's able to move on?"

I nodded. "She's an amazing girl."

"Just like you," he said, taking a right onto La Pressa.

"All of this flattery. I'm not sure—"

Just then I noticed a plume of smoke and fire engines at the intersection in front of us. Saul drove past the coffee shop, but a cop in the middle of the street held up a hand. I could see two mangled cars, and a small fire from one of the cars.

A sinking feeling washed over me.

Saul found a parking space on the side of the road. With our eyes still on the crash, we walked across the street and into the coffee house. We got our drinks and sat at the bar that faced the window and watched the first responders do their work. Neither of us said a word for fifteen minutes.

"It's ten after. She's late," I said.

Saul looked at me, then over toward the crash. We saw a body being lifted from the crash and then put into a bag.

Saul put the phone to his ear. "Let me see if I can find her." After three attempts, he said, "She's not answering."

We both looked out the window. I couldn't help but wonder if this attempt at feeling normal, at trying to fit in with the majority of people who knew their parents, would play out like so many other situations in my life: in crushing disappointment.

Saul put his phone away and scanned the shop behind me. Perhaps he was hoping that she'd snuck in without us noticing, or maybe that she'd been in the restroom when we had arrived.

He pursed his lips. "I'll see what I can find out." He walked out of the shop, moving toward the crash. As he got closer to the police cars that barricaded the road, he shook hands with one of the four cops standing guard, ensuring that onlookers stayed back. Maybe he knew the guy. A moment later, he walked back into the coffee house.

"What did he say?" I asked before he had a chance to sit down.

He shook his head.

"What does that mean?"

"I know the cop from a case I worked for Ross. He's a good guy. I gave him the lowdown, and asked if he'd break protocol and tell me the name of the deceased." He paused, looking into my eyes. "I'm sorry, Ivy. It was Sally."

"And we have no other name or number to find out who her mystery source is?"

He shook his head, then put his hand on my arm.

But I didn't feel it. I didn't feel anything. My body had gone numb, inside and out.

We went back to Saul's and turned on a mindless football game. And during those three hours, I told myself that I couldn't continue to search for parents who didn't give a damn about me. I had to let it go.

Fifty-Three

Looking up from the patio at the Belmont in Austin, beyond the white lights swooping from the second floor railing on one side to the ivy-covered brick wall on the other side, brush strokes of orange and purple cut across a darkening blue sky. There was a chill in the air, but the buzz at this legendary indoor-outdoor music venue made the temperature feel ten degrees warmer.

Our very own Cristina was about to walk on the outdoor stage and perform with the Batastics, who, I was told, were a hot new indie band right out of Austin—probably the most eclectic music scene outside of San Francisco. How had she landed such a prized gig?

I wish I could say I'd set it all up. But I had nothing to do with it. It was Leo, with whom she'd bonded over the tragic drug addiction of his sister, Nikki, a few months back. A lot had changed since then. Nikki was actually sitting at our table sipping on a Coke, smiling, having a good time, alongside her brother. Leo had known the lead singer of the Batastics for a couple of years and sent him a recording of Cristina performing a song. He'd flown in last week to personally deliver the news that Cristina would be performing with this band. If it was what she wanted. And she did. It was a kind and thoughtful gesture.

Yet as I sat there, it was still difficult for me to see them as a couple. It wasn't just the four-year difference in age—which at this juncture for Cristina was enormous. And I couldn't say he was out of her league. Once Cristina grew up, matured a little, maybe it would seem more natural. And I knew Cristina. For others witnessing this romance, it probably seemed nonsensical. I was trying to prepare myself for the inevitable questions from our group: *Our seventeen-year-old former street kid is dating a twenty-one-year-old Hollywood stud, someone who probably has to fight off girls constantly, hot, willing, whatever. How is this possible?*

"Can I get anyone else a refill?" Saul stood next to my chair, his hip against my shoulder. He had on tight jeans and a casual pullover, and wore a subtle cologne that had me clawing at his jeans under the table.

"I'm good," Nikki said on the other side of our eight-seater table.

Leo, who was talking to his friend with the Batastics, held up a hand and shook his head. Brook raised her glass. "I'm not driving, so bring it on. And make it a double."

"Gin and tonic, right?" Saul said.

Brook had already turned around to the stage as some band members, including Cristina, began setting up. The restaurant/club was piping out old rock music and Brook was into it, swaying one arm back and forth to the rhythm. Off to our right, Stan and Bev were in a conversation with another couple. Finally, Stan noticed we were all looking at him. "Sorry," he said, grinning. "Just found someone who's going to be competing in the same Dallas Marathon here in three weeks. Just more water with lime for me. Gotta keep training, you know." He patted his stomach, which had shrunk significantly, at least by fifty percent, in the last few months.

Saul ran off to fill our drink order, and I searched the scene for one more person of interest. There must have been three hundred people packed into the venue, even some loitering on the outdoor stairs. A number of folks wore colorful T-shirts with the familiar phrase on them, "Keep Austin Weird." That was a staple for this part of the state.

A howling laugh brought my eyes to the second floor, where I could see Zahera, my best friend, talking to a couple. She leaned over and gave them air kisses, then paraded down the stairs in an outfit that only Zahera could get away with. Lots of purple leather and lace and a fair amount of skin. She'd just returned to Texas after a two-week trip to "find herself." Turns out she found herself in French Polynesia.

"The emerald water was magical, but the general manager of the resort performed a magic on me that left me speechless," she'd said when she returned. Leave it to Zahera to "find herself" by finding a new hunk to rock her world. I told her she could have stayed in San Antonio, if that was what she was looking for. She replied with, "But have you ever done it on a beach before, with sea turtles meandering out from the ocean? It was a very organic experience."

She'd probably meant orgasmic, but I didn't correct her.

She came over and sat next to me as Saul returned with our drinks. Soon thereafter, Cristina walked up to our table.

"You nervous?" Zahera blurted.

"Not until you asked," Cristina said with a wink. She whispered something in Leo's ear, then made her way to our side of the table. "Thank you all for driving up to Austin to support me." Leo had actually paid for all of us to ride a luxury bus, so none of us were complaining. And Zahera had said she'd pick up the bill for hotel rooms at the W.

Cristina rested her hand on my shoulder. I placed my hand on top of hers and motioned her down. "You're going to kill it tonight. I just know it."

"Maybe. I only had two practices with the band for my three songs. But I'm feeling pretty good about them."

"Leo is something else," I said, looking across the table.

"Yeah."

I heard some hesitation, and I turned to look up at her. "You and Leo okay?"

"I think so."

"What is it?"

"He put me in the friend zone." Surprisingly, I didn't see sadness. "He didn't...?"

"He's cool. He's a great guy. He just said he knows we're in two different worlds. But he wants to keep in touch. Even invited me out to LA."

"Sounds like you're handling it really well."

"Better than I thought, actually. It kind of makes me wonder—" She stopped as her eyes were drawn to the stage, someone calling for her.

"Wonder what?"

"I don't know. Maybe I like girls more than guys."

She shrugged then walked up on the stage.

"Everything good?" Saul asked, then sipped his whiskey.

"Uh, I think so," I said, still processing what I'd just heard.

The crowd cheered as the lead singer rushed to the mic and welcomed everyone.

"I kind of wondered, to be honest with you." I turned to see Zahera an inch from my face. "Sorry, I was kind of eavesdropping."

"Kind of?"

"But seriously, more power to her. Cristina's just figuring out who she is in this world. We just need to support her. She's got no one else but us."

I patted her on the leg as Brook smacked her glass on the plastic table. "Did Stan ever tell you about Peterson?"

I looked at Stan, who caught my gaze. "Haven't had a chance," he said.

"Yeah, well, that asshat actually has a cousin working in our department, some kind of forensic fingerprint guy. Anyway, his boss caught him looking at our case file. He was Peterson's mole."

"He's a complete tool, I'll say that much."

"Yeah, well, he and his cousin might want to go job searching together," Stan said through a crunch of his ice. "Formal charges haven't been made against the coaches at his school, but four have been suspended without pay."

"Glad to hear someone is finally paying attention to the right stuff," I said. "He was so smug, acting like all that mattered were his school's stupid test scores."

Saul leaned toward Stan. "So the belief is that all the kids who were..." He paused a second, making sure no one else was listening at the table. "The kids who were killed all happened to go through Abel's confessional?"

"Yep," Stan said.

Saul nodded, sipped his beverage. "And so Clifton had just apparently lost it?"

"We found out that, in the last six months, he'd learned he had an inoperable brain tumor and wouldn't live another year."

"So, instead of making the best of his final days, he goes berserk and kidnaps these girls so he can abuse them whenever he feels like it." Saul shuddered. "Nasty."

Stan held up his prosthesis and then somehow used the muscles in his arm to shift a finger on the fake hand. "How about that? You like that?"

We all smiled.

"Anyway," he said. "Turns out we found his sister buried on the farm, behind the barn. We think Clifton killed her too. He quit his job a number of months ago and probably needed a place to pull off his crazy crimes."

The drummer started laying down a beat, and a minute later, the band kicked off its first song. Right away, the crowd was into it, although none more so than Brook, who whistled and hollered at every break. The Batastics played their first three songs minus Cristina.

"You're having fun," Saul whispered.

"Yeah, I am." I placed my hand on his knee.

"It's been a week since…you know."

"Since Sally died, as did my hopes of finding my parents."

He was about to say something else, and I put my finger to his lips. "It wasn't meant to be, Saul. It's okay. I just need to look forward, not backward."

I slid my hand up his thigh. He yelled out, "Check please," and everyone looked at him. I just laughed.

And then Cristina was announced. She hit the stage, thanked our table for supporting her, and then began to play her acoustic guitar and sing. By the time she reached the first chorus, she had the entire crowd in the palm of her hand. She looked and sounded like a natural.

"Frickin' amazing," Zahera said, as we all clapped after the first tune.

Cristina played two more songs, wrapping up her set with a ballad called, "Where Has My Mom Gone?" It literally brought a tear to my eye, for her and for me. We cheered and whistled when she finished.

I watched her soak up the crowd's appreciation. It was obvious that, as much as I'd connected with her, bonded with her through our journey to make kids' lives better, this was what she was meant to do. She had found her calling. And I wanted to help her pursue her passion.

She set her guitar in its stand, waved back to the adoring crowd. I stood up and clapped.

And then there was an explosion. For a split second, I wondered if it were some type of wild special effects from the band. But glass sprayed everywhere. People fell off the balcony.

Chaos erupted, and our space was engulfed in smoke and fire.

Fifty-Four

We'd been standing on the sidewalk across the street for at least twenty minutes. Fire, police, and ATF units were already on the scene. I heard people coughing behind me from smoke inhalation. A few had some scrapes that were being attended to by paramedics. I couldn't have cared less. My eyes were peeled to the entrance of the Belmont.

"I'm sure Cristina is okay, Ivy." Zahera put her arm around my shoulder.

Saul had ushered us to the sidewalk, then fought his way through the crowd back into the Belmont to find Cristina. Everyone else in our group had made it out safely. Stan had already spoken to an Austin police detective to try to locate Cristina. No luck. With his badge now attached to his belt buckle, he was prowling around the temporary support center. I saw a number of men and women wearing ATF jackets roaming around him.

I stepped off the curb, but was quickly told by a cop to stay on the sidewalk. Leo was pacing behind me; Brook was keeping Bev and Nikki company. A ripple of gasps turned my attention back to the Belmont. Two men carried a body bag to a nearby van. I grabbed Zahera's arm.

"You don't know it's her," she said.

My stomach twisted into a wicked knot. "You don't know it's *not* her."

A moment later, further up the block I heard a man yelling. Zahera quickly asked Bev and Brook to stand by me. "That's my friend, Ozzie. I need to go to him."

Ozzie. I'd met him a few months earlier. He was a lawyer and had been prepared to defend Cristina when she'd been falsely accused of manslaughter. He'd seemed like a nice guy, about to get married at the time, if I recalled correctly.

She ran off just as Stan walked up. "Any word on Cristina?" I asked, barely choking the words out.

He shook his head. "Too much confusion right now. There are pockets of people all over the place. We'll find her."

"How do you know, Stan?" I could feel a lump in my throat.

He opened his mouth, but nothing came out. Maybe he didn't know what to say.

"Have you heard what happened?" Brook asked.

Stan didn't respond. I looked right at him. "You can say it, Stan."

He moved in closer. "There are a lot of people around, so keep it to yourself, but ATF thinks a bomb was detonated."

"A—"

He raised his hand to Bev's lips before she could say it.

Brook spoke softly. "So they're suspecting this could be an act of terrorism?"

"Just an early theory right now. No need to alarm the public. The main thing is—"

Another scream from up the block. I leaned forward to see Zahera trying to console a man—Ozzie? He was tall, blond, and V-shaped. He was pointing a finger across the street and quite animated. I wondered if Zahera needed help.

A second later, more screams as another pair of men walked out with a second body bag. "I'm not sure I can take it," I said.

Leo and Nikki had pulled up next to me, both with hands to their faces. I looked at Bev, who said, "I'm saying a prayer, Ivy. That's all we can do right now."

I couldn't sit around and chant. Stan must have seen the look of desperation on my face.

"Let me go see if I can find out anything new," he said.

As he flipped around, I heard my name. I looked up and saw Saul and Cristina jogging out of the club. I jumped off the curb and ran to them. Cristina jumped into my arms.

"Thank God you're okay."

"It was horrible, Ivy. One of the band members died. A bunch more are injured." She started to sob. I rubbed the back of her head as Saul's arms embraced both of us.

I walked her back to the curb, and she was hugged by everyone, including Zahera, who had reappeared.

"Everything okay with Ozzie?" I asked her as my pulse finally dropped out of the red zone. I followed her gaze to see Ozzie bear-hugging a woman. "Is that his wife?"

"Nicole. Yep. She'd gone to the bathroom just before the explosion. He was thinking the same thing you were about Cristina."

I looked up again toward Ozzie. He was still holding his wife, but looking in our direction. We nodded at each other. Even though I barely knew him, the connection was there. Zero to sixty and back. And our loved ones were intact.

"Hey," Saul said, slipping his arm around my waist, "I think I might have another idea about your parents."

"Forget it, Saul. It's over. After going through this, I know more than ever that this is the family I was meant to have all along. It's my life. I will embrace it."

And no one could convince me otherwise.

John W. Mefford Bibliography

The Alex Troutt Thrillers (Redemption Thriller Collection)
AT BAY (Book 1)
AT LARGE (Book 2)
AT ONCE (Book 3)
AT DAWN (Book 4)
AT DUSK (Book 5)
AT LAST (Book 6)
AT STAKE (Book 7)
AT ANY COST (Book 8)
BACK AT YOU (Book 9)
AT EVERY TURN (Book 10)
AT DEATH'S DOOR (Book 11)
AT FULL TILT (Book 12)

The Ivy Nash Thrillers (Redemption Thriller Collection)
IN DEFIANCE (Book 1)
IN PURSUIT (Book 2)
IN DOUBT (Book 3)
BREAK IN (Book 4)
IN CONTROL (Book 5)
IN THE END (Book 6)

The Ozzie Novak Thrillers (Redemption Thriller Collection)
ON EDGE (Book 1)

John W. Mefford

GAME ON (Book 2)

ON THE ROCKS (Book 3)

SHAME ON YOU (Book 4)

ON FIRE (Book 5)

ON THE RUN (Book 6)

The Ball & Chain Thrillers

MERCY (Book 1)

FEAR (Book 2)

BURY (Book 3)

LURE (Book 4)

PREY (Book 5)

VANISH (Book 6)

ESCAPE (Book 7)

TRAP (Book 8)

The Booker Thrillers

BOOKER – Streets of Mayhem (Book 1)

BOOKER – Tap That (Book 2)

BOOKER – Hate City (Book 3)

BOOKER – Blood Ring (Book 4)

BOOKER – No Más (Book 5)

BOOKER – Dead Heat (Book 6)

The Greed Thrillers

FATAL GREED (Book 1)

LETHAL GREED (Book 2)

WICKED GREED (Book 3)

GREED MANIFESTO (Book 4)

To stay updated on John's latest releases, visit:
JohnWMefford.com

www.ingramcontent.com/pod-product-compliance
Lightning Source LLC
Chambersburg PA
CBHW021218250626
47155CB00008B/2852